# UNSEEN

# CATHY HIRD

This is a work of fiction. All of the characters, events, and organizations portrayed in this novel are either products of the author's imagination or are used fictitiously.

Brain Lag Publishing
Milton, Ontario
http://www.brain-lag.com/

Copyright © 2023 Cathy Hird. All rights reserved. This material may not be reproduced, displayed, modified or distributed without the express prior written permission of the copyright holder. For permission, contact publishing@brain-lag.com.

Library and Archives Canada Cataloguing in Publication

Title: Unseen / Cathy Hird.
Names: Hird, Cathy, author.
Identifiers: Canadiana (print) 20220451176 | Canadiana (ebook) 20220451206 | ISBN 9781928011903
    (softcover) | ISBN 9781928011910 (EPUB)
Classification: LCC PS8615.I73 U57 2023 | DDC C813/.6—dc23

*dedication*

# CHAPTER ONE

"Attention. Human intervention required," said Monitor in its hollow, non-gendered voice. An alarm blared. "Attention. Human intervention required."

Jen focused her dark brown eyes on the map of Toronto's core where a flashing red dot showed a traffic snarl. She stretched her long legs and stood to approach the map. The user interface glove on her left hand brought the location into view. "What kind of intervention, Monitor?" she asked, running her fingers through her short-cropped brown hair.

"Traffic halted," said Monitor. "Attention. Human intervention required."

"What do you think is the problem?" asked Raja, one of the other Traffic Department overseers on duty at Monitor Central.

"Attention. Human intervention required."

"We'll soon see." Jen moved her slender fingers to mute Monitor's voice. The system that oversaw traffic and so many other infrastructure processes in the city always sounded a little annoyed when it needed to demand a person step in and fix something. Most traffic problems Monitor could solve on its own with minor adjustments to stoplight timing or by instructing the AI pilots in the auto-cars to take an alternate route. In this case, the map showed that both lanes of west bound traffic on Dundas had stopped dead at Kensington, while east bound traffic moved just fine. Jen shifted to an access terminal and typed in the address to pull up the view from the overhead traffic cam.

Nothing seemed to be on the road in front of the first stopped cars. "Monitor, turn on the sound from this camera's microphone." Some traffic overseers never bothered with anything but the visual, but Jen often found a clue in the voices of observers, the sound of a dog barking, machines whirring in the background.

A car horn blared. The passenger seated in the third car back had reached over to hold the horn down. *Fool!* The auto-car ahead of him wasn't going to pay attention to a horn. Horns were such a redundancy in the city with AI piloted cars that five years earlier, manufacturers stopped putting them in the cars. People objected, and they were designed back in. And maybe in rural areas where people drove their own cars and animals ventured onto the road, the horn could be useful. But the sound would not convince an AI pilot to move if it decided it must stop.

Jen frowned at the screen. The stoppage made no sense. Zooming in the surveillance cam, she got the licence number from the plate attached to the roof of the first stopped car. She typed in the code that would query the car's AI pilot. A message came back instantly: "pedestrian crossing."

"Is someone standing in the road?" Raja got up and studied the map.

"Not that I can see." Was someone lying in the road? But the car claimed a person crossing. And if the bumper cam saw a person on the ground, the pilot would have summoned police and paramedics. Though it didn't make sense, she could not override the car's decision from a distance if a pedestrian was involved. "I'll go." She stripped off the user interface glove and grabbed her bike helmet and the backpack with her tool kit.

"One sec." Raja frowned at the map on the screen. "We had trouble at this same location last week."

"I remember that incident," said one of the other two overseers on duty. "Super weird."

Jen raised an eyebrow. "I read the report. A graffiti painting on the building wall. A person riding a bike. I didn't believe it."

"I swear that's all I found," said Raja.

"Well, it says pedestrian alert, so I expect to find an invisible person." She headed for the door. "Phone, summon an elevator," she said, hurrying down the hall. The doors opened as she arrived. The people inside looked annoyed. "Sorry if you aren't going to the ground floor and are in a hurry," Jen said. "Monitor called an emergency."

"In that case," one said, and the others shrugged.

Jamming her helmet on, Jen tapped her toe. At ground level, she ran out, not noticing if the others stayed or got out. At the bike rack outside, one touch of her thumb opened the lock. Traffic directors working in the core needed to be fit. Sure, you sat around a lot, but on the rare occasions that gridlock happened, the best way to get to the location was bicycle. There were personal helicopters on the roof landing pad for distant issues. At satellite offices in the suburbs, they used those helicopters more often as the distances were greater. Jen preferred working in the core and riding.

As she slipped between buildings and down a bike lane, she thought about the location where the traffic snarl awaited. It was an old part of the city with narrow streets where sidewalks on one side of the road had been removed to add a lane of traffic. Ten minutes, and she rode past the stopped cars. Some people on the sidewalk opposite hurried along, but a few stood and watched, fingers pointing at the traffic mess. Just in front of her a taxi door opened. She slammed on her brakes as a passenger got out. The car's pilot blared a warning, "Close door! Not in park!"

"I can walk faster than you drive." The passenger

slammed the door shut, glanced at the Monitor logo on Jen's shirt. "You took your time getting here. You're supposed to prevent this kind of snarl." The woman crossed the road and strode along the sidewalk on that side.

"Watch when you open doors!" Jen called after her. The taxi would be paid despite the sudden departure. The car scanned the passenger's phone at the beginning of every trip. But manufacturers had not solved the problem of car doors opening suddenly. Warning signals went off if a bike approached, but the public objected to allowing the car to force the door to stay closed.

"Get your car moving!" a voice shouted.

Jen looked ahead. A man was leaning into the window of the first car. "Sir!" she said. "It is not the passenger's fault."

Another car door flew open, and the passenger stepped out, arms folded. "Get this road moving, Monitor lackey."

A woman leaned out her car window. "Hey, give her a break. She's here now."

The man strode toward that speaker. "You are defending her?"

Jen slipped off her bike, raised her hands. "I'll have you going in a moment. Just let me do my job.

The man pushed her. "This is not supposed to happen with these smart cars." He spat on the ground. "Not so smart today."

"Sir," said Jen, "if you will step aside, I'll have you going in a moment. I just need to verify that no one is hurt."

"A car hit someone?" the woman leaning out her car window asked.

"No," said Jen. "There has been a mistake. Just let me check." She walked her bike toward the first stopped car. Just in front of it, a brick building jutted out right to the edge of the road. On it, the painted figure of a teenager seemed about to run across the street. *Graffiti again!* What was it about these pictures that made them life-like enough to fool a car's AI pilot?

The woman in the passenger seat of the first car opened

the window. "About time someone from Monitor got here."

"The man banging on the window didn't hurt you?"

"No. Such an idiot. As if I have any say in what this car does."

"Not to worry," said Jen. "I'll have you moving in a minute." She leaned her bike on the building. She looked in front of the car. Nothing there. Getting down on her knees, she checked under the car. Nothing there. Getting up, she stared at the painting of the youth. Touching the wall, she found that the paint on the face was still wet. Pointing the phone on her wrist at the wall, she told it to take a picture. Getting out the can of orange spray paint she used to mark significant potholes or other hazards, a colour the pilots were taught to recognize on the road, she gave the can a shake and painted over the face and the leg that reached toward the road.

The car beside her immediately started to move. Just after, the car in the second lane headed out, with the rest following.

Jen shook her head, studied the marred painting. A cyclist last week and a pedestrian this week. Who had painted this graffiti? And why did it confuse the car pilots? At least the answer to the question of who painted it would be on the recording from the traffic cam. Facial recognition would let them track the person down. *What ticket can we give? Faking a walker?* Jen frowned. Unauthorized graffiti carried a decent fine, so that would have to do. She sent a message to Metro's maintenance department to remove the graffiti immediately, then turned her bike up Kensington Avenue and rode north, back to the Monitor Central tower at Bloor and Devonshire Place.

\* \* \*

Finishing her online teaching, Amanda told the House to turn on the microwave for one minute and picked up the tablet that held the piano exercises for her afternoon students. She would eat the hand pie as she walked to the high-rise housing complex on the south edge of what was left of High Park. In the kitchen, she grabbed her lunch and headed for the front door. On the porch of the duplex next door, Brindle, the leader of the Houses, sat on the porch swing watching the street. A wave of dizziness hit Amanda. She grabbed the railing to steady herself when she saw Brindle with two different cups in their hand.

"Chai, Brindle," she said. "Choose Chai. This is not the right time of day for mint chamomile tea."

Brindle pushed back bangs with a slash of grey in hair otherwise a flaming red. "I'm sorry, Amanda. I did not realize you were still here. I would have flipped a coin rather than debating the options for tea. I don't like unsettling you."

Amanda forced a smile to her face, bringing gentler lines to a face that otherwise looked narrow and pinched. "My last student ran a bit late. I don't like hurrying. I lose focus. See all kinds of choices." *Not that I can ever avoid seeing the important ones.*

"Your Gift is not an easy one," said Brindle.

"Whose is? Your empathic ability picks up all our worries." Amanda sighed. "I'll be back about supper time."

Amanda walked carefully down the stairs and headed south, counting her footsteps. If she let her mind wander, she would see the possible choices that the people around her might make. When she kept herself grounded, she missed the little ones, like Brindle's choice of tea. When it was a big decision, a choice that would shape the future, she saw the options no matter how tightly focused she was. A Gifted physicist who lived at one of the other Houses theorized that her gift allowed her to perceive quantum divergence, the possible universes that existed for a short time at the moment of choice. His Gift enabled him to perceive shifts in gravity and magnetic fields, though it was his intellect that made him a successful theoretical physicist. Miles, a computer wiz, sensed electrical movements. Others in the Houses had different Gifts, different augmented senses and connections, an empathy that connected them to particular emotions.

*At least Brindle's Gift is useful.* The Houses' leader worked as a forensic accountant, and their empathic ability to sense worry gave them clues what to look for when asked to examine a company's books. Amanda's gift was simply disorienting. She never saw the possible consequences of her own actions, and with others, it was often too late to make a suggestion. She might keep a teenager from having her backpack stolen or stop an old man from placing his cane in an uneven spot if she was close enough, but usually there was not enough time between the sight and the choice. And she had to keep her mouth shut. The few times she explained to a stranger why the natural choice had been the wrong one, the person backed away, treating her like poison. With her colleagues in the Houses, she could describe precisely what would have gone better if the person made a different choice, but usually she did not bother. It felt too much like always saying, "I knew better." She only blurted out the possibilities with them when it cost her too much to keep it bottled up inside.

She crossed Bloor Street and headed into the housing complex that now stood where High Park had been. On this late June day, she appreciated the shade of the canyon-like streets. The hundred-storey buildings built on what had once been forest and gardens provided shade from the hot sun on this clear, blue-sky day. All that was left of that park was a small corner near Ellis Avenue.

It was warmer when she entered the park, though the air under the trees smelled fresh and clean. She walked this way whenever she could. Though privileged to have a house with a yard when most people in Metro lived in the high-rises that dominated the crowded city, this extended green space felt different. Birds chirped around her, and a squirrel scurried across in front of her. When the path branched, she turned right, toward the pond. Almost at the water, dizziness hit her again. A living green tree and one covered in brown leaves stood before her. Beside it was a sapling and a fresh stump.

Crouching over, closing her eyes, Amanda retched. *What is happening here?*

"Are you ill?"

Standing slowly, Amanda found a man in coveralls watching her. "Just a bit of dizziness. I'll be fine in a moment."

"There is a bench nearby. I can help you over."

Amanda stepped back. Was this man making a choice that affected the trees? "I'll be fine. The dizziness is gone now."

"If you are sure." The man looked her up and down, then walked by.

Amanda took a ragged breath, then headed slowly toward the pond and her waiting student, though she could not shake the memory.

\*   \*   \*

"If the paint was still wet, the cars stopped as soon as the graffiti was complete," said Raja as he backed up the footage again. The cam showed no sign of the artist. The traffic moved fine, then it didn't. "I'll slow it down." Eyes narrowed, Raja watched the screen.

"There. Did you see that?" asked Jen.

"See what?"

"That red car just disappears. Back it up and slow it down. Watch the red car."

Raja cut the playback speed to one quarter. A red car entered the view, moved to the centre and disappeared. "Where'd the car go? All I see is a panel van."

"Back up again and check the time stamp," said Jen.

"This is wrong. The feed with the red car is stamped yesterday! Then it switches right to today, with the cars stopped, the moment Monitor sounded the alarm." Raja leaned toward the screen. "It doesn't feel like a malfunction. It looks as if someone inserted false footage, but a hack is impossible. No one can breach Monitor's firewall."

"I don't see another explanation," said Jen. "Back up again. Zoom in on the wall." She studied the image, pointed at the picture. "Look. In the older footage, there is part of an image, but no head or leg. Go forward. See. When it goes back to real time, the figure is complete. And the cars stop as if a person is about to run onto the road."

"This is serious," said Raja. "Let's check the first incident. Monitor, show footage from this cam Tuesday, June eleventh, starting just before three p.m."

"Look at the wall." Jen pointed. "There is part of a bicycle but it's missing the front wheel, and there's no head on the rider."

"And here. The graffiti bike is complete, and the delivery truck disappears. In an instant, traffic stops. The pilot driving the first car thinks someone is about to ride right in front of them."

Jen bit her lip. "We'd better call our section manager. This is urgent. Monitor's surveillance has been hacked."

\* \* \*

The department head, Gerald, strode into the office. "Explain your claim that a traffic cam has been hacked."

Raja had the feed cued up. "See for yourself."

Gerald got him to play the footage twice. The scowl on his face deepened. "This was not the only one?"

"Here is the other." Raja called up the footage. "You can see the beginning of the graffiti figure but it isn't complete. Traffic runs normally. Now watch this red car. See, it's gone. The figure is complete. The traffic stops."

Gerald's fingers tapped the desktop. "Perhaps the camera is faulty."

Jen shook her head. "We can identify the origin of the

inserted footage in both cases. Someone did this intentionally."

"And there was nothing in the middle of the road, no sign of anything but this faked cyclist and the painting of a pedestrian?"

"That's all we found," said Jen. "Something about these pictures is able to fool the auto pilots into thinking a person is about to be hurt."

"When was the graffiti started?" Gerald asked.

"I'm still working to find out the start time for the cyclist, but the pedestrian was three days ago," said Raja. "First inserted video, and we have a torso. The second we have one leg and arm. Then, today's picture of a teen on the run."

"Why are they doing this?" Gerald asked.

Raja frowned at the screen. "Both times because a person might be injured, one of us needed to go."

Gerald turned to Jen. "How did you get the traffic going?"

Jen uncoiled her phone from her wrist, expanded the screen to its full size. "I spray painted over the face and leg." She showed him the before and after shots.

Gerald took the phone and flipped back and forth between the images. "The image quality of the cameras on these wrist phones is only adequate. I've never been tempted by them myself."

"I'm on a bike so much that it makes sense for me."

"I suppose." Gerald handed back the phone. "I can tell it's a painting. Why can't the cars' AI pilots?"

"A good question," said Jen. "No answers except that we have taught the AIs that people are unpredictable."

"The first incident seemed an anomaly," said Raja. "And a nuisance."

"Nuisance it is not." Gerald folded his arms. "We worked hard to get rid of the gridlock and traffic jams that plagued our city in the twenty-twenties. People can now predict how long it will take them to get where they are going. Can you imagine the uproar if people find that the travel time their phone gives them is not accurate! Our department will be inundated with complaints." Gerald took a deep breath, looked away into the distance. "Whoever did this succeeded twice. They may well do this again. How can we trace them?"

"We could set up a hidden camera," said Raja. "One not connected to the system."

"With just internal memory," said Gerald, "someone would have to manually download the information."

"I could do that on my way to work," said Raja.

"Do it. We need to stop these interferences." Gerald tapped his fingers on his wrist. "The hack into our system is significant. I'll report to Administration right now." He stalked out with a grim look on his face.

Jen ran the video again and again. She caught the moment when the hack started. One set of cars disappeared, and another took their place. A simple insert, but one that you wouldn't catch unless you were watching the footage of this particular camera at this particular moment.

The hacker must have known the department would catch on eventually. Two incidents in the same spot were impossible to ignore. She ran it one more time. Jen bit her lower lip. The painting had been completed over three days. If Raja stopped by this location every day, he'd see the start of another graffiti. They could clean off the graffiti before it took effect.

*What more can I do?* She asked her phone the time. Twelve twenty-three. The manager of the technology department would be in the cafeteria picking up a Mediterranean salad, an old-fashioned glazed doughnut, and two apple juices. He was precise in his routines. He was also the most skilled computer tech she had ever run across. He'd want to know about the hack, and maybe he could find a way to get a picture of the artist. She headed for the cafeteria and the rooftop garden.

# CHAPTER TWO

Slipping through the busy cafeteria, Jen took the escalator to the rooftop green space. Like the roofs of all new buildings, vegetables were grown here, but half of this roof was a garden where employees could relax. Miles sat, as she expected, beside the fountain, his hair in a complex set of extension braids. His vest looked like it belonged back in the sixties of the last century, but his white shirt was crisp, highlighting his ebony skin. Listening to the music of falling water, she understood why Miles came here for lunch. Sun warm, air fresh and moist, the sound soothing. She came to this spot herself when she could for a hint of the world outside the city. This day, her news would break the peaceful atmosphere.

"Jen," Miles said. "You are joining me today without your lunch?"

"Traffic's cams have been hacked. Twice."

With eyebrows lifted, his eyes narrowed. "We tell the people of Toronto that hacking Monitor's system is impossible."

"I know what we say, but I also know it happened."

"Be precise."

Jen sat down and described the incidents and what they found on the footage from the traffic cam.

Miles put the lid back on his salad and stood. "This is

significant. I will join you in the Traffic office in ten minutes."

"Do you think you can find the footage the hacker cut out? I'd like to identify the artist."

"And I need to find and stop the hacker." Miles rubbed the lines between his eyes with two fingers. "Can I find a picture of the artist? That depends. If they hacked the cam itself, then no. But, one of the redundancies built into our system is that the cam sends two signals, one to the appropriate office and one to storage. If the hacker intervened in the transmission, then the stored data feed will show us your artist." Miles headed for the escalator. "Based on another hack that happened last week, I suspect we will find this is the case."

"I didn't hear about another Traffic incident?" Jen had hurried to keep up with his long strides.

"Not Traffic. Remember that downpour that flooded the Don Valley Parkway last week?"

"Indeed. I was on duty that day," said Jen. "It was my job to stop traffic and get the cars rerouted. What a mess. What does it have to do with this hack?"

"That same rain storm caused a blocked storm drain to back up, threatening to pour water into a housing complex. If a friend of mine hadn't found it, it would have caused major damage." Miles stepped onto the escalator, looked away for a moment. "That friend is not the question here. The Water department missed it because someone hacked in and inserted a loop of green signals masking the build up of water pressure. Every other storm drain sensor showed yellow or orange. The supervisors only paid attention to those closest to red. They should have wondered why this section was green when everything else showed some level of threat."

Jen could understand making that mistake. When everything is blowing up, to have one place that is normal is a relief. "Why wouldn't Monitor catch an anomaly like that?"

Miles stopped at the bottom of the escalator. "AIs only

learn from the data we give. We have not taught Monitor to notice data that is inconsistent with the situation. We could and should." He moved toward the elevator.

"Miles, if someone has access to the system like this, do you think they work here?"

"Or used to and managed to keep their access codes active. That could be traced." An elevator arrived, and they stepped inside. "I will be in your office in twenty minutes."

"Not ten?"

"Thanks to you, there are two tasks I need to assign before I come and see if we can dig up a picture of your artistic traffic attacker."

\*   \*   \*

"Go back two minutes before the hack begins," said Miles as he pulled a chair with wheels in beside Raja. "Slow the playback speed by one third." Miles studied the screen. "Stop." He looked over to Raja and Jen. "I'm afraid the hacker knows our systems too well. Monitor has been taught to notice even a second with no signal. They ensured there was no gap in the video feed by starting the hacked loop two seconds before the real-time video ends. See the double image." Miles rolled his chair over to the second terminal, typed rapid fire commands on the keyboard. A blue circle spun in the centre of the screen. "Now, for the stored video feed."

Raja and Jen came over. A tall person in fashionable tight jeans and a bulky jacket stood face to the wall. A ball cap covered most of their straight, dark brown hair. Then, the artist looked up at the camera. A white face mask hid their mouth and nose. Miles froze the image.

"Damn," said Jen. "So much for facial recognition. Raja's idea for a second camera won't help either."

"They knew about the second data source," said Miles. "Covered their face so that when we pulled it up, they wouldn't be recognized. The bulky jacket also masks their body shape. Monitor, zoom in on the lower right, triple magnification. Long sleeves hide most of a tattoo on their wrist." Fingers on the screen, Miles moved the image up to the neck. "Looks like another here. From the eyes and skin colour, I would say Korean background or northern Chinese. Male?"

"Not sure," said Jen.

He tapped the screen to zoom out. "And that's why bystanders didn't interfere. They've got a Monitor logo on the jacket, front and back. They look legit."

"What legitimate reason would there be for someone from this office to paint graffiti?" Raja asked.

"None, but folks don't know that," said Jen. "They find us a bit of a mystery. Let's check the other event to make sure it is the same person."

Miles called up the saved feed from the first incident. Same lanky legs and bulky jacket. Same hat. Same fake logo. Same bits of tattoo. "I'll get a screen shot of the artist and the graffiti," said Miles. "I have a friend who is quite connected to the street art community."

When Miles zoomed in on the image of the cyclist, Jen frowned. "I have a question."

"You are full of them today."

"All good ones so far. The rider is bent over as if they're pedalling hard, and the wheel spokes are blurred as if they are gunning it. But I can tell it's graffiti. How come the car's pilot can't?"

Miles called up the two graffiti images, putting them side by side on the screen. "Twenty years ago, when the first auto pilot cars were being tested, programmers liked to joke that we could trick an AI into thinking an avocado was a cat. That's because with slower processors, the AIs could only make so many data comparisons. We speeded up the processing, learned to give more diverse data for the training algorithms, but still an AI has to compare images to what it knows. That is why we have rules about realistic 3D advertising photos in store windows. A specific clue must be inserted to tell the pilots that the image is a picture, not a person." Miles ran his fingers across the screen, zooming in tight to the faces of the images. "We also taught the pilots that humans and animals are unpredictable. This cyclist looks like they have no intention of stopping, so the car did. Monitor, send these images to miles dot franklin at monitor dot o n dot c a."

"Someone is going to a lot of effort to screw around with cars' AI pilots," said Raja.

"Who and why?" Jen asked.

"And why hack the system to hide the painter while at work." Miles chewed his lip and typed furiously. His frown deepened. Finally, he pushed his chair away from the computer keyboard and screen. "The hacker is good. They left no trace. I think I better go upstairs and see the administrator your manager reported to. Then, I meet with my computer team. We'll put an alarm on this camera to catch any overlap in the data stream." Miles rubbed his temples with his forefingers. "Then, we have to scale that program across Monitor's systems. We cannot miss these intrusions in our systems."

\*   \*   \*

Jen knew it would take time for Miles' team to accomplish the tasks he had listed. *And what if the artist doesn't use the same location?* On the elevator down to her office, Jen traced in her mind places in the core where buildings stood right at the side of the road, alternative locations that the artist could use. There were a few places, mostly where sidewalks had been removed to add a lane for cars or cyclists. Taking a different route to work and back home, she could easily scout the ones east of Monitor Central. For the ones west of the building, she could take a tour on Sunday. It would take just an hour if she caught green lights. Given that each time, the artist took a few days to complete the works, she might locate the start of a painting before their work caused a traffic snarl.

*What if they move out of the core?* Beyond the Don Valley to the east and Bathurst to the west Metro had left sidewalks in place as those roads weren't as narrow to start with. She couldn't think of a place like the spot at Dundas and Kensington except in the core. *What if they change tactics, do something like what they did with the storm drain?* If they did, Miles would have to worry about it. Her responsibility was Traffic.

\* \* \*

In the elevator, Miles pushed the button for the administration floor of Monitor Central, one level down from the cafeteria. As it rose, he pondered a way to get Monitor to recognize overlapping video images. Once he had that program, setting an alarm on the feed from the traffic cam aimed at the spot the artist had used before would be straightforward. The elevator opened. An elegant oak desk with a clear computer screen sat under a large abstract painting. Studying his screen, the receptionist spoke softly into an almost invisible microphone at his mouth. Thick carpet covered the floor. Miles strode up to the desk and waited until the receptionist ended the call, toes tapping impatiently.

"Who is your appointment with?" The receptionist looked at Miles with skepticism in his eyes.

"I'm Miles Franklin, Tech Support manager. I need to see the administrator who received the report about the hack into the Traffic cams." It looked like the receptionist would object, but Miles raised his hand to stop him. "There were two, plus a hack of the storm sewer system last week. This report is urgent."

"Take a seat," said the receptionist.

"No need," Miles said, "I don't expect to wait long." Still, he took three steps backwards to give the man space to make his call.

The receptionist spoke quietly into his microphone. A moment later he stood. "This way. Admin Chan will see you."

*Of course she will,* Miles thought. Opening a door that seemed to be made of real wood, the receptionist ushered Miles into a large office with a wall of windows. The administrator stood behind a desk with a glass top and a stainless-steel frame.

"I was informed of the hack into water monitoring. Two more intrusions are unacceptable. These took place today?"

"One today and one last week. Last week's hack was only found half an hour ago."

"Details."

Miles explained the issue that had caught Traffic's attention, then described the way Monitor's surveillance had been hacked to hide the artist at work. Describing the exact nature of the intrusion, he also informed the administrator of the plan to teach Monitor to recognize overlapping video feeds and the more complicated task of teaching the AI to recognize anomalies.

The administrator turned and walked over to the window, stared out at the Metro skyline. "This is a serious breach of our security. This is now your department's highest priority."

"Agreed."

"It is time," said Chan, in a quiet voice as if speaking to herself, "for a compliance blitz. We can circulate a memo saying that inspectors are ensuring that people have their eyes on their tasks. We can't put drivers in cars, but keeping those on Transit vehicles alert feels crucial. I can authorize overtime for the Inspection Department." The administrator turned from the window. "Pardon me for thinking out loud." Her face tensed and her eyes narrowed. Miles felt like an insect pinned to an examination board. "According to your personnel file, you are very good at your job. An unusual grasp of computer systems. But given the seriousness of these events, I am calling in a cyber security expert. We keep Ms. Tatiana Ricci on retainer so that we can make use of her expertise at times like these."

"As far as I know," said Miles, "there have never been events like these."

"Point taken. Nevertheless."

Miles thought about the name, realized he knew it. "I took the course she offers here every year. Four years ago. Bringing her in is a good call."

Admin Chan raised an eyebrow. "I am glad you think so."

"Sorry. I just mean my department and I can work with her." *Snap inspections also seems like a good idea, but I don't need to say that.* Miles turned to go.

"One more thing." The administrator waited until Miles turned back. "Speak of this to no one outside of your department."

Miles felt his jaw tense up. Trying to keep this a secret felt wrong. Monitor's administrators kept the public image of the super-AI and all the employees that worked with it as clean and dust free as the room that housed the main computer banks. It felt to him, however, that hiding these intrusions could be seen as a breach of trust. "Anyone whose department is affected is going to know."

"That is your last good point for this meeting. You have work to do."

\* \* \*

Back in the Tech Support office, Miles answered the questions of the team working on getting Monitor to recognize anomalies and handed a skilled programmer his thoughts on an alarm that would catch over-lapping data. Once the program was designed and installed on the traffic cam, he would find a way to scale it across Traffic and Water systems and beyond. That thought sent a shiver up his spine. What other systems might be hacked?

His stomach rumbled. He had barely started his lunch when Jen interrupted. As the team got to work, he picked up the salad where he left it on the corner of his desk and headed for the one enclosed cubicle in an otherwise open workspace.

Once settled in the quiet space, his mind raced. Monitor had been hacked three times. *That we know of. There could be others that have not been found.* Getting into the system at all was a serious challenge, suggesting that the hacker had access to Monitor credentials. But accessing memory data and inserting it in real time required getting through several firewalls. He tried to imagine how he would manage such an insertion.

And how did the hacker know when to return to the real time feed? Miles pushed himself off his chair and onto his feet. The hacker might have had cell phone contact with the artist, but may well have been watching the real-time, back-up feed. Focused on the artist, he had not looked for a trace of a ghost watching when he reviewed the real time footage. Time to go to the super AI's main banks. With direct access, he should find a trace if someone had accessed that feed.

When Miles stepped through the scanner at the door to the central processing rooms, the light blinked yellow, indicating his security clearance. With a wand, the guard checked that he brought nothing into the sensitive area. This space was the most protected in the building. Inside, the air vibrated and a soft whir indicated the operation of fans. A slight, metallic smell tickled Miles' nose as he moved to the area which distributed surveillance information to all appropriate stations. Calling up the record of the feed that had been hacked, he froze the image at the insertion point. He could see the overlapping images, then the smoothly running previously recorded images. He searched for any sign of the code that created the insertion. He rubbed the lines between his eyes. No sign of how the hack was accomplished, no way to track who did it.

Miles moved to the segregated area for backup data storage. Accessing the feed a minute before the hack, Miles slowed the images. There was not even a waver at the moment when the recorded images had been inserted in the feed that went to Traffic. As he watched the artist start to work, he studied every section of the image. The picture showed the street, the wall, cars and pedestrians passing by. As he got to the bottom, he caught a flicker in the lower left corner. A shape like a spider flashed into sight and disappeared. Slowing the feed further, he stopped the image when the spider appeared, made the cursor hover over it.

"Monitor, where did this image in the lower corner originate?"

"This feed comes from camera 2BB5X78."

"Did all information originate from that camera?"

"Unknown."

"How can that not be known?"

"Unknown."

Miles pushed his chair away from the console. If the system could not confirm that all the data originated from the camera, that hinted that the spider indicated some kind of spyware. The link between spy and spyware was not part of the record, but in real time, a program could tag and follow a spy like this. And even if the hacker hid their tracks, with his Gift, his special ability to sense electrical currents, even deep in a computer system like Monitor, he should be able to trace the spy back to its origin. Other Gifted people he knew had extra sharp hearing. Some were empaths, able to read emotions. A few could read details of a person's life from what they wore or the works they painted. Other Gifts gave connections to plants or water or a type of animal. His Gift, the ability to sense electrical patterns, made him adept with electronics. He had a feeling he would need every skill and Gift to catch this hacker.

The Tech team needed to get busy. It was essential to get a program that could catch overlapping data up and running. That alarm would alert the overseers to an emerging problem and give him the best opportunity to catch the hacker.

# CHAPTER THREE

As the program to catch overlapping data loaded, Miles felt exhaustion in his shoulders and back. Still, he decided that on the way home he needed to see for himself the wall where the graffiti artist had worked. When he got to the spot, he found only brick. The cleanup crew had scrubbed it clean. He had pictures of the work though, and he hoped that Darshani, his colleague at the Houses, the community of Gifted people he had joined, might recognize the style of the artist. She taught traditional art at the high school where she worked and her special Gift included the ability to read artists' personality and bits of their life story from their art. Her passion, however, was graffiti. He sent her a text, saying he would call after supper.

He walked toward the Queensway dedicated streetcar line, picking up Szechuan take-out on the way. With his brain still playing the options for tracing the hacker, he had no energy to cook a proper meal for himself. And taking the streetcar would give him a calming walk through High Park, at least the bit of High Park that had not been taken over with housing skyscrapers.

At Queen Street, he joined the line for the outside streetcar. The two inner lines stopped only at main intersections, so to get off in the middle of the park he needed to take the outer line. The rumble of a streetcar got his attention, but it drove up on the inner line. Not his. As it approached, the driver held his phone, stared at is as if reading. *Damn!* If it weren't for the fence that ensured people taking the inner lines used the overhead walkway, he'd go grab that distraction out of the driver's hands. The person's job was to stay alert, to catch unusual situations, and to assist the AI if it ran into an anomaly. Boring work, and he could understand why someone would crave distraction, but in the current situation, with a hacker interfering in Metro's systems, a distracted driver was dangerous. Admin Chan's decision to start random inspections to ensure drivers and supervisors were on the alert seemed crucial.

Another rumble. Miles looked down the track to see his car coming. This driver was awake and attentive. He breathed a sigh of relief. Climbing on, he found a seat and relaxed into the bench. His thoughts circled back to the questions that faced him: how to find a hacker who might be as Gifted as him, given how good they were at hiding, and how to locate a disguised graffiti artist. He could feel the muscles of his neck and face tense, rubbed the worry lines between his eyes. *The way I am radiating worry, I should probably let Brindle know before I get home.*

Brindle's empathic Gift was tuned to worry. Just over sixty years old, with decades of practice, Brindle coped better than many empaths with the psychic overload of living in the core. And as someone who identified as non-binary, Brindle understood how hard it could be to gain acceptance in the world. They were the most understanding and supportive person Miles knew, but strong emotions of anxiety and worry would affect them. Better to warn Brindle so they could prepare themselves for the uneasiness he could not shake.

The Houses were Brindle's way of supporting Gifted people. Inspired by the woman who helped him understand his Gift of empathy, Brindle found every way he could to help ground the Gifted—empaths like themselves, those who read weather patterns, the various Gifts of extreme sensory perception. Empaths new to their Gift needed help separating their thoughts and feelings from those of others, but all the Gifted appreciated those who understood what they could sense about the world that other people could not. *In another time, someone like Brindle might have been burned as a witch.* Even now, if they accidentally revealed that they read a stranger's private worries, they became the target of anger and suspicion.

When Brindle's partner, Giovanni, inherited a duplex on Gothic Avenue from a great-aunt, Brindle began their dream of a community of Gifted. When the attached house next door came up for sale, Giovanni mortgaged the first house to buy it. A few years later, the group bought a row of houses out in Scarborough, and more recently, a megahouse in a suburb of the ever-expanding city of Brampton. The three groups kept in close touch and had regular video chats that often included the Gifted they knew who lived in smaller centres. Miles loved living in the Houses. Even though the Gifts of each were different, it helped to be understood. *And believed,* he thought. Tell a non-Gifted person what he could sense about electron movements, and they would call him crazy. It only had to happen a couple times for Miles to learn to keep his mouth shut.

Gossip among neighbours who lived on Gothic Avenue suggested they were a commune with ties to some archaic religious group. Little did they know how unusual the co-operative of Gifted who shared these living accommodations were. *They'd call us magicians. Or witches. If they believed us.*

It was a privilege as well not to have to live in a high-rise. All Miles' siblings lived high up in one of the skyscraper housing complexes. Thanks to Brindle and Giovanni, Miles had a yard, a small space but green and growing. The front yard grew a hardy ground cover, with flowers and herbs along the path and front wall. The back boasted a large vegetable garden. These all flourished because Rickie, Gifted with a connection to plants, came by at least once a week to care for these gardens. The ones at the Scarborough Houses, where he lived, were spectacular.

Miles' phone chirped. "Phone, who is calling?"

"Brindle," said the quiet machine voice.

*Wants to know details of my worry before I get home, I guess.* He pulled out the phone and touched the screen with his baby finger to enable video. Brindle's face appeared on the screen. Deep lines marked their forehead, framed their eyes. "No need to be too concerned, Brindle. I'm getting control of my anxiety, shouldn't be in too bad a shape when I get home."

"Where are you?" Brindle asked.

"On the Queen streetcar five minutes from High Park."

"Perfect. Amanda thought you came that way. She's on a bench near the pond. Find her, and walk her home please."

"Of course. She had a difficult vision?"

"Two. In the same spot at different times. She's quite upset. I'll tell her you're on the way."

"I'll look after her." As well as seeing divergent timelines, Amanda's Gift sometimes generated a psychic connection. Today, it seemed, that connection allowed her to sense how close he was. Even at forty years old, with years of practice coping with her visions, Amanda was always mildly anxious. Her Gift showed her so many different possibilities she sometimes had a hard time keeping a grip on the choice a person actually made. If Brindle was this concerned, however, Amanda had a more difficult vision than usual.

Taking the streetcar one more stop than he'd planned, Miles got down in front of the high-rise on the corner of the Queensway and Ellis Avenue and walked toward the small pond at the edge of the park. For decades, right up to the late 2020s, High Park spread all the way up to Bloor Street and this pond covered acres of land. But the need for housing trumped the desire for green spaces, leaving just this five-acre patch of mature trees, trails and water. The memory of what the park had been—acres of trees and wild spaces, paths and gardens—was the reason Rickie chose to live in Scarborough. The contrast between past and present pained a man tied so deeply to things green and growing. For Miles, the green space that remained was a lovely change from the cubicles and computer terminals of Monitor Central.

Turning up the path beside the pond, he found Amanda seated, but leaning over with her head resting on her knees. "You okay?"

"Not really. I wish you hadn't stopped to get takeout. I had to wait ten minutes longer than necessary." Amanda managed a smile. "I shouldn't complain. At least you took the streetcar for a change. Why did you come this way?"

"Trouble. But let's get you home." Miles took her hand and slipped her arm through his. "I think we both have stories to tell."

As they crossed out of the park and into the shadow of the high-rise housing complex, Miles studied Amanda's profile. Her jaw was clenched. Two deep lines were drawn above eyes that stared straight ahead. "What did you see at the park?" he asked.

Amanda took in a ragged breath, and her shoulders shook. A tear ran down her cheek.

"It's okay if you want to wait until we get home."

Amanda put a shaky hand on his arm. "I think I need to be sitting when I try to remember the details. How did your day go?"

Miles put his other hand on hers and told her about the graffiti and the hack that hid the work, but in another part of his brain, he worried about Amanda sounding uncertain of her memory. She never had trouble describing the options she saw.

As they turned onto Gothic Avenue, he wished he could absorb the quiet of the neighbourhood the way he usually did. Today, Amanda's electric tension and his own concern kept his shoulders tight, his mind whirling. All he could do was force a light tone into his voice. Rounding the bend, their duplexes came into view. Brindle sat on the porch swing. Flaming red hair sculpted into a stylish cut with a slash of grey in their bangs, wearing their standard black shirt and black jeans, Brindle sat with elbows on their knees and chin on their hands watching him and Amanda approach. Brindle's partner Giovanni came out the door and leaned on back of the swing.

"I don't know which of you to ask to speak first," said Brindle. "Worry pours out of each of you like a river in spring flood."

"Because troubles are piling up like a stream behind an ice jam," said Miles.

Giovanni laughed in his bright tenor voice that always sounded cheerful. "Is this a writing workshop suddenly?"

Miles tried to smile and found he couldn't. "Let's be precise then: troubles are piling up just like the night rain water got dammed in an intentionally blocked storm sewer. And the same kind of hacker that hid that danger is at work."

"What happened?" asked Brindle.

"Someone has figured out how to paint graffiti that fools car pilots, and the artist's work is masked by a hack into Monitor's surveillance. It's happened twice."

"Good thing I made enough dinner so that both of you can eat here and tell your stories." Giovanni waved his hand at Miles. "The takeout you bought can be tomorrow's lunch. Maria and Juan are at their daughter's so it will be just the four of us."

"Our good fortune," said Miles. The two couples who lived in this house were older than the other Gifted. They routinely ate together, though the Guatemalans, Maria and Juan, had four children spread out around Metro and kept close touch with them all. In Miles' house, they were all in their thirties with jobs in the core, so that only on Sunday did they try to eat together.

Brindle gave a half smile. "My partner's Italian grandmother taught that a good meal will solve any problem. Come in, and we can take our time with these stories."

Amanda managed a weak smile. "What I saw..." A shiver ran through her body. "I'll be glad to have it said."

\*   \*   \*

"Vegetarian lasagna my grandmother would not approve of but you won't tell her," said Giovanni as he set plates in front of Miles and Amanda.

Amanda picked up her fork. Her hand shook.

"Tsk," said Giovanni. "You can't eat good food if you can't get the fork to your mouth." Coming behind the seer, he placed one hand on each shoulder, thumbs against the back of her neck. Closing his eyes, he breathed deeply.

Amanda's hand stopped shaking. Her breathing steadied. "Giovanni, what would I do without your Gift. Your ability to radiate calm is better than a large scotch."

Miles caught a glance between Giovanni and Brindle. When Brindle first arrived in the city for university, the psychic pressure of dorm life and the city overwhelmed them. Frosh week parties taught that alcohol would ease the pressure. Later that term, after a night of binge drinking had them sleep through a midterm, they went to Student Services for assistance to deal with the anxiety without alcohol. A counsellor, who happened to be Gilda, a Gifted empath, helped Brindle understand where the overwhelming pressure came from. Since that time, Brindle never drank. And since Giovanni, with his ability to calm anxiety, came into Brindle's life, the temptation had gone. Still, alcohol was not served in this house.

Giovanni slipped into his seat. "You can eat now?"

"Yes, thanks." Amanda breathed deep. "It smells wonderful." Still, rather than take a bite, she folded her hands together. "You know that Tuesday afternoons I teach in the apartment complex near the southwest corner of High Park."

"What is left of the once magnificent park," said Giovanni.

Amanda nodded. "Rather than walk up the busy Ellis Avenue, I walk through the park by the pond. On the way there, I saw dead and dying trees. On the way back, I was so dizzy I leaned on a tree, then it wasn't there."

"That's enough to throw anyone off balance." asked Miles.

"I almost fell, the sense of absence was so strong. In the here and now, the tree stood tall, but in some future, it was gone. I stood on a concrete pad surrounded by steel girders. At the same time, yellow tape marked off a grassy place with newly cut down trees. Insects crawled up my legs." Amanda shuddered and looked down. "My other hand touched a tender sapling supported by a stake. Then, I heard chainsaws and wood grinders all around me. That's when I fainted."

She looked at each in turn. "My Gift doesn't do this. Not normally. I see one person who has a choice to make and what each of their options looks like." Amanda rubbed her temples. "It was so confusing."

"Has this ever happened?" asked Miles.

Amanda shuddered. "A few times, multiple choices converge, and the vision is like this. Once, I watched normal traffic at Bathurst and St Clair, then a Buick Escalade slammed into the side of a taxi. At the same time, I saw a school bus, two cars and a garbage truck engulfed in flames. I closed my eyes to shut out the scene. A dog barked, and my eyes flew open. The Escalade's horn was stuck on with steam coming from under the hood of the taxi. A school bus drove by. The garbage truck pulled over, and the driver called 911 before making sure the people who actually ended up in the accident were okay. I just stood there shaking. When EMS got there, they were sure I must have been in the taxi, I was so dazed. I feigned flashbacks to a childhood accident and got myself pulled together to get home. I avoided that corner for weeks."

"Car pilots should be able to avoid an accident like that," said Miles.

"Maybe," said Amanda. "This happened a while ago. I still have nightmares about that moment. In the dreams, I see a rolling baby carriage in front of the school bus."

Miles cocked his head, thinking. "Something like that would be both important and unpredictable. Different pilots might make different decisions."

"I don't consciously remember seeing the baby carriage," said Amanda, "but everything happening distracted me. My guess is that someone let go of their carriage, then grabbed it again. But for that moment their hand was off, all kinds of accidents might have happened."

"Back to today," said Brindle. "Your Gift is triggered by a person with a choice to make. Who was in the park?"

"The first time, a man in coveralls offered to help me. The second, when I came to, a teenage boy leaned over me checking if I was okay. I thought maybe I still dreamed because he was dressed in purple, with hair bleached white and skin tinted violet, you know those kids who dress to look like the aliens in that new television series. But when he helped me up, all I saw was him choosing between focusing on his English or Chemistry homework." She turned to Brindle. "There probably were other people nearby. There are always people in that park, but I didn't notice anyone in particular. They could have been in a car driving by or on the other side of the trees." Amanda folded her hands together as if to stop the shaking. "When the boy helped me to my feet, the park looked totally normal."

"You saw concrete and iron," said Giovanni. "Sounds like a building project, something like a new high-rise. But the city has stayed solidly committed to keeping what is left of the park. On the other hand, a new sapling suggests renewal. Very strange."

"Don't forget the insects," said Amanda.

"Rickie could go check that," said Miles. "It is in his job description with Metro Green Spaces." Rickie's green thumb Gift would help him figure out if bugs were attacking the trees. If they were already in the park, not just something that might happen.

"I'll talk to Rickie after supper." Brindle turned to study Miles. "Amanda's story is disturbing. Her anxiety is unsettling. But you aren't an empath. What happened to upset you?"

Miles folded his fingers together and laid out the traffic incident and the hack into Monitor's system that he'd uncovered. "Stopping traffic is little more than a nuisance, but no one is supposed to be able to get into Monitor."

"If you weren't able to track the hacker, they must be good," said Giovanni.

"None of the normal tracking programs found a trace," said Miles. "My own sniffer program could not catch a breath of a trail. Nothing." Miles took a deep breath. "I suspect that the person who got in is Gifted."

"And using their ability to disrupt." Brindle stood up to put the kettle on. "The temptations that power presents."

"The scope of the actions don't make sense," said Giovanni. "Could the graffiti cause an accident?"

"The cars just stopped," said Miles. "It seems almost as if the artist wanted to show the car pilots making a mistake. But the hacker who covered for the artist is more than a nuisance," said Miles. "I have to find them and stop their interference." He turned to Amanda. "I plan to show Darshani pictures of the graffiti and the artist, disguised though they are. If she has time to visit the site, would you go with her, just to see if you sense anything?"

"I can, but it's likely too late." Amanda gave a small shrug with one shoulder.

"I'd appreciate it if you try," said Miles. "Unless Darshani can tell who the artist is from two corners of tattoos, I'm grasping for clues."

"I'll go with her."

A woman's voice with a Spanish accent called from the front door. "You are home?"

"In the kitchen, Maria," called Brindle.

A woman in her late fifties, still in her security guard's uniform, came into the kitchen. "I won't disturb your dinner," she said. "But I felt it again, Brindle, the anger. Twice today. *Tanta ira!* So much anger. First, on the subway platform when the voice explained the cause of the train delay. I couldn't tell who was so angry, but I felt fire running along the platform. You asked me to tell you if I came across this again."

"You said twice?"

"*Si. A mi trabajo.* At the office, many are angry when they come. Insurance claims take so long to process. I would be angry too. But today, *muy differente*. This young man harangued the receptionist claiming that Monitor caused the accident by shifting the traffic signals on a whim."

"Monitor shifts signals to get around accidents, construction delays and the like," said Miles.

"According to the picture he showed, the damage to his car is real. What caused it?" Maria threw up her hands. "*Yo no se.* But he blamed Monitor's interference for causing the accident. And his words. Dios mio. The things he said about computers and big brother surveillance and much more. Another guard and I had to escort him out the front door. I gave him a card with the direct line so he could call in his complaint. I thought he would hit me, but he argued for five more minutes with words I shall not repeat about getting stuck in telephone no man's land. I wanted to tell him what no man's land is like, describe the desolation that stands on the Mexican side of America's border fence." Maria shook her head. "I told him he is allowed to return in person a week from today. Because we gave him the direct number, he shouldn't need to come back. But that one is so angry about the systems that manage everything, I expect he will wait his week so that he can argue in person."

"Do you sense a lot of anger like that?" Miles asked.

Maria wrapped her arms around herself. "I am tuned in to anger at Monitor now. A couple weeks ago, a woman jumped out of a taxi, almost knocked me over when she threw open the door. She leaned back in and swore at the empty driver's seat, saying that the pilot was an abomination to be wiped off the planet. She brushed past my shoulder as she stalked away." Maria wrapped her arms more tightly. "Her touch was fire. So much anger in her! I stepped backward and almost fell. A young man caught me." Maria shook her head. "His genuine desire to help drove the anger away. But I cannot forget that woman's outrage. And she tuned me in to the frustration people have with Monitor's control."

Miles looked at Maria carefully. Born in Guatemala, she and her husband had slipped north and into Canada with their two children in the late 2020's when an H1N1 outbreak hit Central America hard. Maria's ability to sense anger helped them avoid police and border guards. When they got to Canada, they were placed in a refugee centre. Thanks to Maria's Gift, she was aware that fury was building against the refugees, blaming them for job loses and even for causing that pandemic. She moved her family out of the centre just before arsonists burned it to the ground, killing many. After that, the government offered amnesty to illegal immigrants and fast-tracked refugees. Juan and Maria and their children took the opportunity to gain proper papers. Their other two children were born in Metro as they settled into life in the city.

"Do people really want to go back to the time before cameras and AI's?" Miles asked, curious about the anger directed at Monitor. "The technology we have makes Metro run much more smoothly. Before, vehicles could hardly move at rush hour."

Maria put her hands on the back of Amanda's chair and met his gaze. "I know your arguments. But I understand these people who feel Monitor does too much. I want to make my own mistakes."

Amanda sat up on the edge of her chair, hands under her thighs to keep them from shaking. "For me, those days were horrific. Standing at a corner, I would see cars hitting and not hitting a pedestrian. A car would not stop at a red light and get slammed on the side, and it would stop suddenly and get hit from behind, and…" She closed her eyes. "Now, walking down the road is not nearly so hard. Most days."

"My dear." Maria wrapped her arms around the younger woman. "I am glad I do not have your Gift. Mine is enough trouble."

Miles folded his arms. "Monitor doesn't control our choices."

"Por supueso. Of course. But sometimes when people are feeling trapped by a go nowhere job or a dead dream, they put their anger on what does seem to control things," said Maria. "Enough. A long day. Juan has already gone upstairs, and I need to put my feet up."

"I better call Rickie," said Brindle. "The potential for destruction in High Park will upset him, but he's the best chance to understand what caused Amanda's vision and ease the worry that I know is going to keep her on edge."

"And Amanda needs to sleep." Giovanni helped her to her feet. "I'll take away more of that anxiety, dear, so that you get a good rest."

"I'll clear up here," said Miles. As he put the dishes in the dishwasher, Miles thought about what Maria sensed, wondering if the anger at technology hinted at the graffiti artist's motivation. When the table and counters were clean, he decided Darshani would be home. Time to give her a call.

# CHAPTER FOUR

Back in his room, Miles opened his laptop. "Video call to Darshani."

When the call connected, Darshani was seated cross-legged on the bed, her brown-black eyes focused on the screen of her computer. "Just one sec, Miles. I've finally got the right phrase." Darshani's fingers tapped the keyboard, then pushed back the glossy umber-brown hair that had slipped from her braid. "Report cards."

"But final assignments aren't in yet."

"No, but the comments are the hardest part and while the final project will affect their grade, it doesn't change their work habits, their skill, their willingness to co-operate with others. Once in a while I am stunned by what a mediocre student can do in a big project, but in that case, I can go back and change the comments. But you didn't call me to talk about report cards."

"No. Though it is interesting to see how precise you become with this."

"I'm always precise. Each pencil line, each brush stroke is exactly where it should be."

In the background of the video, a closet door stood open with clothes slung over the bar. Books and papers were piled on the desk, dresser and bed. An easel held the beginnings of a Toronto street scene. Paints with a water glass stood on the stool beside it. "How can you live in that disorder?"

"I can find everything I own. Just ask for something."

"It's okay, Dar. I have an important question." With a flick of his finger, he shared his screen and showed her the side-by-side images of the graffiti. "Do you recognize who might have painted these?"

"People get a licence to paint in a specific area. That should narrow down the choice."

"Richmond Street near Spadina. A week apart. But given the circumstances, they may be outside their licensed area."

Darshani raised one eyebrow. "That's a bit risky. Fines are hefty. Computer, focus on the left side of image one." She studied the front wheel of the bike. "Amazing the way the bicycle wheel seems to be in motion. A skillful artist. Why are you asking?"

"The pictures shut down traffic. Car pilots thought someone was heading onto the road. Computer, next picture. This is all we get of the artist."

"Weird body structure."

"Wearing something bulky on top to confuse physical recognition software. Legs suggest someone pretty lean. One point seven five metres tall. There is a hint of two tattoos if you look closely at the neck and wrist."

Darshani checked the wrist, then the neck tattoo. "This might be John-boy. He has a constellation tattooed on his back, a dragon on his arm. Lean and lanky describes him. Show me the graffiti again." Staring at the screen, she frowned intently. "This isn't the kind of image he usually paints, and that certainly isn't the area where he is licensed to work, but he is good at capturing movement."

"Do you know where we could find him?"

"Don't know where he lives, but he works in the west end. I can find out where his club hangs."

"Ask questions discreetly. If he hears he's being sought, he might disappear."

"I don't read him as skittish."

Miles exited the shared screen so he could see Darshani's face. "This isn't public, but someone hacked into Monitor's surveillance so that no one would see the artist at work. The artist is complicit in a major breach of Monitor's security. That's a pile of trouble."

"How did someone hack into our great Metro manager?"

"That is the question I have to answer. The artist is just one clue. Could you do me a favour tomorrow and meet up with Amanda to take a look at the location? You might figure out something seeing the location first hand, and Amanda may sense the intentions. She is a bit doubtful, but I'm grasping at electrons here."

"Sure. I'll connect with Amanda and plan a time. If your cleanup crew is sloppy, there might be a bit of paint left. Street artists are pretty particular about their materials."

"Thanks. Knowing you are checking out the site will help me focus on figuring out how this ghost got into Monitor's system."

\* \* \*

The news gnawed at Rickie's stomach. He rubbed his narrow, pointed nose, closed his deep-set eyes. Amanda saw potential destruction at High Park! Those trees must not die. The fragment that remained of the park, a tenth of what it had been twenty years earlier, was the last substantial stand of trees south of Highway 9 and east of the Niagara Escarpment. When Rickie was a young child, every chance he got, he dragged his parents from their apartment in Korea Town to wander the three-hundred-hectare forest. He loved the streams, ponds, and gardens. The wildness of those forests excited him even more than the trees and gardens of Christie Pits where he played every day. That green space had been buried beneath concrete and steel high-rise housing even before developers tore High Park apart.

As soon as Brindle had called, he texted Jainyu, another

Gifted man who lived in the Brampton Houses and also worked for Metro Green Spaces. The name of their department annoyed Rickie. In his own mind he called it, "Raccoon, Sapling, and Building Gardens duty." Hydroponic and rooftop gardens were highly controlled, not a wild sprout or creature allowed. The few trees left scattered around the core were a dot of green, not a space rich with plant and animal life. All the larger creatures—deer, foxes and coyotes—had been driven out when the large parks and then the green spaces in and around the Don Valley and Humber River were built on. For his friend and colleague Jainyu, the lack of wild creatures hurt like a chronic headache. His Gift connected him with birds and forest animals. Living in Brampton meant a longer commute, but from there, he could visit the escarpment and Rattlesnake Point Park every week to feed his spirit.

Running his fingers through his black bangs then pulling on a ball cap, Rickie headed out to the vegetable garden. Snow peas were ripe, and if he encouraged them just right, there would be another crop or two. Kneeling to pick the ripe pods, his thoughts were all on High Park. It hurt to think of those majestic trees attacked. His phone vibrated. A text from Jainyu: "meet you at 8am what did amanda see." Rickie told his phone to send a reply: "buildings no trees insects all i know."

In this moment, he could do nothing to protect the trees. To ease his mind, he concentrated on the plants he could touch. Raising one of the pea plants that had pulled away from the support, he wound the delicate tendrils back into the wire to hold it off the ground, whispering thanks for the substantial crop already produced.

A door slammed. He heard giggles and then silence. Bracing himself, he pulled his hands back from the snow peas. A moment later, two five-year-old girls squealed as they tackled him. He rolled onto his side and joined them in a good laugh.

Samantha, their mother, came out the door. "My bad,

Rickie. If I'd known you were out, I'd have reined them in tighter."

"Rickie didn't mind Mama," said Trinity. Her smile faded. "You didn't mind, did you?"

"Of course not."

"You knew we were coming." Trinity scrunched her small fists and put them on her hips. "You sure you're not an e'path?"

"Of course, he's not like Brindle and Giovanni and Geoff," said Gillian. "Do you ever see them in the garden?"

"Maria helps sometimes when she comes to visit," Trinity said. "And she's an anger e'path."

"Rickie has a green thumb. And so do I," claimed her sister.

Trinity dropped her eyes. "What Gift do I have?" A tear trickled down her cheek.

Gillian wrapped her in her arms. "Being the best sister ever!"

Rickie made it a group hug. He sympathized with little Trinity. Everyone in the Houses suspected she would grow to become an empath, but no one wanted to push a young child to use that Gift. For now, she needed to develop her sense of self. Her family, and by extension her extended family in the Houses, could help her gain a strong sense of her own thoughts and feelings. When her Gift developed, she would sense something—thoughts, a particular type of emotion—from other people. At that point, their job would be to help her distinguish what came from within and what she drew from others, a task that could be challenging if the Gift was strong.

Gillian's Gift was simpler and oh so clear. Like him, she nurtured plants. She spent every minute she could outside. If Rickie worked in the garden, that's where Gillian wanted to be. "Daddy needs time to think," she said, explaining why the females of the family had come outside. "He's working on some star problem."

"Missing your nanny, is he?" Rickie asked.

"You know it," said Samantha. "We were glad to free her up to go home to the Philippines for her grandmother's funeral, and the girls are loving building a Lego space-port while their dad putters in his workshop. But for his real work, when he wants to think about the nature of gravity waves or quantum entanglement, he needs peace. And of course, his current line of thought could not wait until they are in school tomorrow, so we've been sent out for backyard time. Croquet anyone?"

"Yeah!" said Trinity.

"Rickie needs my help." Gillian knelt beside a row of lettuce. "We've let the weeds get ahead here, Rickie." Her small fingers reached between the strong plants to pull a seedling. "Oh! Coriander!" She held a small plant with delicate, cut leaves between her fingers. "How did you get here?"

Rickie moved to the row of spinach beside her. "What do you think we planted in this part of the garden last year?"

Gillian pushed her lips together and folded her eyebrows, thinking hard. "I was a baby then. I don't remember."

"That's okay. A thing to know about coriander is that you want to pick all the seeds. Not only will we grind them to make yummy food, the seeds we miss will sprout the next spring."

"Ooooooh!" Gillian bent over and found four more coriander plants. These she gently removed with their roots, then dashed, carefully placing her feet in the rows and not on the plants, to the far end where herbs were planted this year. Carefully, she made a hole with her finger, placed the seedling in the ground and gently patted them into place.

Rickie knew the seedlings would thrive. Gillian skipped back along the row and chatted constantly while she worked beside him. He enjoyed teaching her, and her chatter distracted him from the deep shadow of worry cast by Amanda's sight of devastation in High Park.

\* \* \*

With her guide dog Juniper at her side, Julie rounded the bend on Jenkinson Way. "Almost home, Bub." Children laughed in the backyard of the house she walked past and footsteps on the other side of the road told her that Suzanne was out walking her two golden retrievers.

"Hi Julie," the woman called. "It's Suzanne. Just out for a walk with the dogs. You're getting home late."

Not bothering to say she already knew who was there, Julie stopped and turned toward her neighbour. "I ran a training session for new hires. It went late, and I grabbed supper in town with my co-worker to debrief."

"You'd be great at that. Such people skills. Just because you can't see doesn't mean you're blind. I mean..."

"Thanks Suzanne. I know what you're saying. And fortunately, the session went well. I think I'll get this kind of assignment again."

"I hope so. You deserve the recognition." One of the retrievers whined. "Gotta go," said Suzanne. "These guys have been crated all day. Juniper is so lucky that he gets to go with you everywhere. And you're lucky too, having him to see for you."

Julie laid a hand on Juniper's head, felt the dog look up. Juniper was the best, letting her know if she forgot something she'd brought with her. Until Juniper learned that, Julie lost more scarves and umbrellas than she could count. But guiding her movement was not Juniper's job. Her hearing Gift did that for her. The Gift gave her a way to sense location by listening to sounds like the echoes from her footfalls, but filtering out all the background noise had been a slow skill to learn. Fortunately, the Gift came slowly at puberty. Evolving when it did made her teenage self independent. If she'd been born with it, her blind, baby self could not have coped. She might have ended up deaf as a defence against it. As it was, her dad had the same Gift, though with less intensity, and he'd been able to help her come to terms with it. As an adult, the ability to sense echoes, along with her eidetic memory, meant she could map where she was and where she was going for herself. Juniper helped when there were potholes she might miss and retrieving her stuff. *And being good company.*

"Let's go, Juniper. Three more houses, and we're home to relax. And you get supper." Julie cocked her head. "I hear one of the twins, so they're both outside. But I think someone is sitting on the porch next to home. Shall we see who's there?" She walked past the sidewalk to her house. Juniper started to whine and pulled forward. "Geoff?"

"It's me."

"You sound upset."

"Of course, I'm upset. You can probably hear Rickie's racing heartbeat."

"I hear him chatting with Gillian, but he's too far to hear his heart. Outside at least."

"Lucky you. If you could, you wouldn't be able to hear anything else."

"I take it you can't sense anything but his worries."

"Not the way he's reacting." Geoff breathed in raggedly. "He told me why. It is awful. But he needs to control himself."

*Rickie* should *know better.* Everyone in the Houses knew how ultra-sensitive Geoff was, so something must be really wrong. Julie cocked her head. Geoff's pulse raced, his breath quick and shallow. He was not doing well. "Is there a chair for me?"

"I can feel that your day went well, so sure," Geoff said. Julie heard rubber scrape on concrete.

Julie climbed the steps and settled in the chair with Juniper beside her. "What set Rickie off?"

"Brindle called."

"That shouldn't upset anyone."

"He called with bad news. Something's wrong with some trees."

*That figures.* "Juniper needs his supper, so give me the compressed data version. It'll help for you to share it."

"I guess. Then I'll try my meditation chamber."

Julie squeezed his hand. What Geoff called his chamber was a modified closet, lined with insulation to make it sound proof, with a surround sound system that usually played ocean waves. He only used it when he could not distract himself from other people's psychic noise, when the build up got to him. He had been known to sleep curled up in the closet when overwhelmed. She hoped this was not going to be one of those nights.

\* \* \*

After releasing Amanda's pent up stress, Giovanni decided to check on Miles. Brindle sensed waves of complex concern in the Gifted man. *Concern that is completely justified by the events,* Giovanni thought. He could not change the shape of what had happened, but he could make sure that Miles' worry did not build in a way that upset his ability to sleep or to think straight. When Miles wasn't in his room, Giovanni tried the basement workshop.

At the bottom of the stairs was an almost life-sized poster of the actress Jeri Ryan in her reprise role as Seven of Nine in *Star Trek: Picard*. In the depicted scene, her hands reached into a holographic control panel on a Borg cube. Giovanni turned into Miles' workroom where overhead lights blazed. One wall had shelves with carefully laid out electronics and parts of computers. Against another were sets of drawers, all carefully labelled

Miles looked up from his worktable in the centre of the room. "Wondering what I am working on, Giovanni?"

In the middle of the workbench was a display of light lines, vibrating with different colours, looking very much like the holographic computer interface in the poster. "I came to see how you are, but yes, I am curious. Is it what it looks like?"

"It's a prototype."

"I think I heard that holographic interfaces are impossible."

"Which is why the lasers are in a closed glass cube filled with dust. The dust enables us to see the beams. The cube keeps it stable."

Giovanni approached gingerly. "A funny thing that we can't see light, just what it reflects off. But if the cube is a closed system, where is the interface?"

"This space in front of the case is monitored by cameras. Actions here are mirrored inside the case." Miles moved the index finger of his left hand. "There. I just turned on the oven."

"This is keyed to the house?"

"Right. We already have the house computer tied into lots of functions, so I built this to connect with that network."

"Can you turn on the porch light at my house?"

"Sure." Miles moved his right pinky finger. "House, is the porch light on at house A?"

"Affirmative," said the non-gendered, uninflected voice.

"Can I try to turn it off?" asked Giovanni.

"Sure."

"I don't need some kind of user interface glove or other hardware?" Giovanni asked.

"No, just exact placement. So come closer. Move your right hand so that your pinky goes right where mine was."

Giovanni looked at the beams of light, then at the space in front of the case. The table was marked with a grid and many small circles. Slowly, he reached his hand forward.

"Stop! You were about to turn on your coffee maker."

Giovanni moved his hand back. "You try."

"Just like this." Carefully, Miles moved his right hand with all but the pinky finger pulled into a fist. "House is the porch light at house A off?"

"Affirmative."

Miles moved his hand to the left, pushed it slightly forward. "Ruth and Deena have gone for a walk. I'll turn the light on here for them. House, is the porch light at house B on?"

"Affirmative."

"Let's see if I can turn that one on and off." This time, Giovanni imitated Miles' semi-fist, concentrated on exactly following where Miles had moved.

"Stop. You were going to turn the oven on again."

Giovanni could feel Miles' frustration. "Sorry I can't get the placement yet."

"Don't apologize. You are just proving the problem with my design. As I move my hand close to the right position, I can feel the electrons activate in the light columns. If it's the wrong signal, I can tell I need to move." Miles moved his left hand over the grid. "I can sense how close I am to activating a switch, here." He moved his hand left and forward. "Here." He pulled his hand back and down. "And here. I can operate this system because my Gift allows me to sense electron movements. That's the only reason."

"Another person would have to memorize the exact positions."

"Which is inefficient." Miles moved his right hand again. "Watch the laser as I turn the porch light on and off. Did you see the slight shift in the light?"

"I think so."

Miles rubbed his temples. "I think an ordinary person could be trained to notice the fluctuation when the laser array is activated. I might be able to increase the variation in the array to make that easier. But for now, user interface gloves make more sense for anyone without my Gift."

"And for a person with your Gift, this is a toy."

Miles nodded. "And a good place to practice. Because I can see the results, and check with the house monitoring system whether I succeed or not, it provides a way to hone my ability to sense electrical movements." Miles put his palms on the workbench. "And if I'm going to identify the hacker, given how well they hide, this is a skill I may have to put to use."

"Tomorrow," said Giovanni. "I came to ask if you could use a shoulder massage. To ease the tension and help you sleep."

"A shoulder massage with your Gift pulling tension out of the body." Miles rolled his neck. "I'd like to say I'm fine, that I don't need your help. And that would be half true. Working here changed my focus. But, without your help, as soon as I lie down in bed, worry would roll back in like air filling a vacuum. So sure. Use your Gift. I'll be much more ready for tomorrow."

# CHAPTER FIVE

Half asleep, Giovanni rolled over and reached out to Brindle. His hand touched the light cotton sheet. Eyes flying open, he saw Brindle standing in the open space of the room, moving into the last part of a Tai Chi set. Tai Chi was the practice his partner chose when other people's worries piled up inside them. Leaning on his elbow, he watched the smooth movements. By the slow tempo Brindle had chosen for this set of moves, he could tell the leader of the Houses had absorbed an ocean of worries.

The moves were graceful despite the tension. Hips and hands moved with precision. Arms created delicate circles, then lines, while Brindle shifted weight back and forth and legs reached out to move to the side, ahead, behind. Tai Chi had been a lifesaver for Brindle. After getting Brindle off alcohol, the university counsellor Gilda sought relaxation and meditation practices that would help separate their own thoughts and emotions from those pouring in from other people.

At first, none worked. Massage was worse than useless as with every touch, the therapist poured his or her worry into Brindle. Spas were good, but only if they were alone. Yoga was impossible as the aspirations of the students conflicted—some looking to get fit, some seeking calm, some wanting to ace the poses. Stepping in the door of a Tai Chi class with Gilda, Brindle almost turned and ran right out, whispering that the instructor had an ego the size of China with ambitions to match. Then, the instructor demonstrated the first seventeen moves of the set. As soon as the man began, all his other thoughts and worries disappeared. Brindle relaxed. When the instructor finished those moves and started to talk about teaching this part of the set, their tumultuous desires flooded back. But Brindle was caught. If this kind of moving meditation could get that driven man to settle, they were sure it would work for them.

At subsequent classes, they sometimes needed to leave when one of the other students broadcast too much anxiety, but overall, the classes gave Brindle a practice that worked. Brindle did Tai Chi at home every day and checked in with a class every week for three years. Classes did not always help. Sometimes a different teacher would perform a move slightly differently, projecting concern that the regular instructor was not teaching the set correctly. Those classes would so disturb their emotional balance that they would not return for a month. Then, one class, when the teacher's attention focused completely on the breakdown of his marriage, Brindle walked out and never went back. But the practice remained part of every day's routine.

Giovanni knew that Gilda had done more than just get Brindle sober and introduce this practice that helped keep them sane. Meeting other Gifted people gave a new sense of belonging to this young adult whose family rejected their claim to a non-binary identity. She also gave Brindle a dream to work toward. It had been Gilda's idea to create a network of Gifted so that people with these special perceptions and connections would not be so isolated. "We need to help each other understand that we are not strange or alone," she had said. She also thought that Brindle's Gift would locate many who were struggling to figure out why they knew what they knew, why they had a sympathetic tie to whatever their Gift was. "Find them, and we can help them," was her summons.

Giovanni smiled as Brindle bent to the floor in the second snake move at the end of the set. He had been one of the first Gifted that Brindle came across. The law firm where he worked as a bookkeeper sent him to meet a forensic accountant. A senior partner believed someone might be stealing from the firm. Brindle had been that accountant.

On the fifth intense day of combing through records, Brindle had suggested the two go out for lunch. Giovanni, already infatuated, readily agreed. It was nothing like a date, however. Brindle asked if he knew who stealing. Giovanni hesitated. He had no proof, just an instinct. When he said that, Brindle assured him that was correct, that the evidence was there. Giovanni had in part figured it out from the emotional disruption he sensed in the senior partners. Because his Gift included the ability to soothe worry, others had let their concern slide for a long time. Brindle argued that he should quit the firm before the difficult legal and criminal proceedings started. "Come work with me," Brindle said, "after you meet Gilda, and we convince you of your Gift."

Dinner with Gilda blew to pieces Giovanni's sense of natural reality. He clung to his job just to hold on to some sense of normalcy. But a week later, when he rode the elevator with the partner who had sent him to find the thief and sensed burning emotions so strong he could smell them, he resigned. He met Brindle for lunch the next day and every day for three weeks. He joined Brindle's nascent forensic accounting firm. A month later, they moved in together. Later, when he inherited this duplex from his great-aunt, they began to draw together a community of Gifted. They'd worked through the ups and downs of this work-life partnership for thirty years.

"I will always love you," Giovanni said as Brindle finished the Tai Chi set with a bow.

"We can never know what twists life will throw at us."

"Life's path can't be controlled, but I will always love you."

A small smile came to Brindle's lips. "Thank you."

"You still look worried."

"I am."

"If Tai Chi didn't clear your mind, the worry is powerful. Come sit on the bed, and I'll ease the rest away."

Brindle sighed. Once seated, Giovanni knelt behind them, knees touching their lower back, and placed his hands on his partner's shoulders, massaging gently. Running firm fingers across neck muscles, Giovanni released the tension he sensed there. "What part of yesterday upset you this deeply?"

"Amanda. She felt quite off balance at supper."

"Is that all?"

Brindle sighed. "She is already awake and still worried. And Maria's upset. Miles is cranked. And I know Rickie well enough to imagine how troubled he is."

Giovanni laid his palm in the centre of Brindle's back, closed his eyes, thought soothing warmth and sunshine.

"Thank you. I don't know how I would have held it together without you."

"You're strong, but I am glad you find me indispensable."

Brindle turned and kissed him. "We'd better get started on the day."

\*   \*   \*

Arriving at the forty storey Monitor Central building, Miles went directly to the Traffic Department. Jen looked relaxed at her desk. "No emergencies?" he asked.

"Not yet."

"Raja?"

"On his way. His text says there is no sign of graffiti at that spot, but he reset the camera just in case." Jen swivelled her chair around. "I'm concerned that they might not use the same location, that they'll guess we will add surveillance."

Miles rubbed his temples. "That would make them harder to find." If Jen was right, scaling up the program to recognize overlapping data streams just became a higher priority.

"Before I left yesterday, I mapped out some other possible locations, places where there is a wall right by the road just like that spot. Checked three last night and three this morning on my way in."

"Where are these places?"

Jen went to the map, touched fifteen places in the lit-up air, then zoomed in on one. "This is a really busy road. If I wanted to cause the most trouble, I'd choose this one."

Miles studied the location. "A snarl there would cause back ups on these feeder roads too."

"Blocks of traffic would be slowed to a crawl."

"Still just a nuisance. Why are they doing this?" Miles watched Jen shrug. She was right. They didn't need to know why. They just needed to stop the interventions. "The artist took three days to finish both times. You might find the location before we have a traffic incident. Email me the locations, and I'll set an alarm on each of the nearest cams." If he could get online while the hacker was active, he'd have a better chance of tracing them.

Jen smiled. "You've a real gift."

Miles' eyes went wide, then realized she meant gift as skill or talent, not the kind of special sense that he had. He cocked his head, studying her. "Have you ever been tested for eidetic memory?"

"No. Why?"

"The way you could, in a short time yesterday, identify that many locations. The way you carry maps in your head."

"It's easy. Locations just come clear to me."

"And you know the relationship between the locations without looking at a map." Miles paused. "I think you may have a spatial orientation Gift."

"I never get lost if that's what you mean."

"That, and more. Leave it for now. Just be sure to let me

know at the first sign this graffiti disrupter has acted again."

"Will do." Jen turned back to her terminal.

Miles studied her for a moment. Not the time for him to pose the question of Gift. Too much immediate concern. Maybe later, he would introduce her to Brindle and let them explore the nature of Gift with her and the possibility that her spatial sense went beyond the norm.

\*  \*  \*

A streetcar heading east raced by. Every three minutes, another passed the streetcar Rickie rode west. This was not a peaceful trip. When Metro removed car traffic from the Queensway and two more lines of streetcars going each way had been put in, transit on the southern edge of the core speeded up, but for someone like him who relished the peace of a garden, the noise and energy near the shore of the lake were hard to cope with. The Gardiner Expressway contributed to the roar. Traffic now raced along that route at one hundred and twenty kilometres per hour day and night, even at the busiest times. Severely limiting who could drive that route had sped up the highway. Only vehicles travelling at least twenty-five kilometres and a few cars with permits—emergency vehicles or Monitor employees on duty—were allowed to use the route.

As unsettling as the ride was, arriving at his destination would be worse. Rickie's gut twisted. Every time he went to what remained of High Park, he had to block memories of the expanse of forest and streams and wild things. Trees had been cut down, and meadows destroyed. Streams were redirected into underground conduits. Two ponds were drained and filled, killing the willow and honey locust trees even before they were cut down and hauled away. The third pond on the western edge of the park was cut back to a tenth its original size. That's where he was headed, to the one bit of forest that had not been turned into high-rise housing.

Approaching the Parkside Drive stop, Rickie closed his eyes so that he would not have to see the buildings that now covered land that had been forest. Getting off the streetcar at Ellis Avenue, he rode the metal escalator up to the rolling walkway over the outer eastbound tracks, then descended to street level. Stepping onto the sidewalk, a single dandelion with wilted leaves peeked through a crack in the concrete. Its sun-bright flower held him still. He crouched down and touched the yellow petals, which waved as if a breeze caressed it. He poured a little water from the bottle he carried, then stroked the leaves, which stretched out and up. He could feel the plant's gratitude.

He considered pulling it and replanting it in among the trees, but it took determination to grow in the bit of earth caught in the concrete. "Try to survive until your seeds ripen." He stood and walked on. It pleased him to think of seeds carried on the wind, flying to find more cracks, more tiny corners of earth, producing more bright flowers and wild green. He moved on, passing the tall building whose ground floor boasted a year-round skating rink with a wading pool on the second floor, both open to the public, replacements for the recreation facilities that had once been open to the sky. Beyond it, he breathed the scent of water and green. A complex filtration system kept the pond clean, and wild water plants flourished along its border. He turned in along the shore to the ancient willow that stood beside the pond. He touched its bark, felt life flowing inside it. The long wispy branches swayed like fingers, reaching toward him. Rickie rested, breathing air freshened by this ancient friend.

"Hey, Tree Man, good to see you."

Turning away from the tree, Rickie flashed a smile at Jainyu, clasped his colleague's raised hand and gave him a hard, one armed hug. "Bird Boy. You ready to check out these trees?"

"I have friends who are up to the task." Jainyu trilled a

high-pitched whistle, *tseee tseee tseee*. He repeated the call. Two cedar waxwings fluttered past Jainyu's head to land in a tree just in front of them. "You said Amanda saw insects." Jainyu whistled again. "Here come a couple hairy woodpeckers to help out."

"Too bad no one will pay for a bird whisperer. Connected to dogs or cats, you could have been a famous trainer."

"Do not mention cats." Jainyu made a warding sign that he must have learned from his Mandarin grandmother. "You should hear the noise when I walk into the bird section of a pet store." He shrugged. "You know I reach more than birds. I can usually get a squirrel's attention and summon raccoons. Some luck with porcupines."

"Your connection is all about creatures that hang out in trees."

Jainyu punched Rickie's shoulder. "Green and growing is all you think about."

Rickie's smile faded. "The place where Amanda sensed trouble is just along this path where the trees are thicker." Rickie reached into his backpack for the sample jars he had brought with him.

"What do you think we'll find?"

"Maybe insects. Maybe nothing. Amanda is never wrong about what might happen, but sometimes people come to their senses and don't choose what she saw they might." The slightly curled leaves of a maple caught Rickie's attention. He walked over and put his palm on the trunk. The branches above waved as if a gentle breeze ran through them, but he sensed stress. Behind it, a dogwood shrub was covered in wilted leaves. Other trees showed signs of trouble that shouldn't be there in a warm June with a reasonable amount of rain.

"Something's wrong," said Rickie. "This dogwood is almost dead. Ask your friends what they can find. I'll take samples of the earth here and a couple twigs. If there is a chemical poison, we might find residue."

A complex whistle from Jainyu sent the woodpeckers up

into the beech and maple trees, while one of the cedar waxwings combed the dog wood. The other flew deeper into the shade under the trees. Rickie heard the distant rumble of two streetcars and the tapping of the woodpeckers. Using his pocket knife, he peeled back the bark on a branch of the shrub. Not a sign of green. He worked back along the branch, but found no green until he got almost at the central trunk. "This shrub got sick suddenly. Really sick. Really fast."

One of the woodpeckers swooped down and landed on Jainyu's arm. In its beak hung a wriggling insect. "Hand me one of those jars." Opening it, he clucked and the woodpecker dropped the insect. He put the lid on, and the bird took off. "I don't recognize this. Do you?"

Rickie studied it. "It's like... but no. The colours aren't right." The head area was a bright orange, with purple in the body and a blood-red back end. Lifting the jar above his head, he saw the underbelly was pale blue with black stripes. "At least with colours like this, they should be easy to spot."

The cedar waxwing that had gone deeper into the trees swooped in. It dropped a bug that looked identical to the other into the jar in Rickie's hand.

"If there are two, there are many." Jainyu bit his lower lip. "Let me go to the northern edge of the park, see if birds find anything there."

"I'll look deeper among the trees here." As Rickie stepped off the path and into the woods, the birds kept a steady stream of insect deliveries. Several more trees looked stressed, but as he explored deeper among the trees, the signs of stress stopped. The rest seemed healthy. Rickie moved back to the stressed ones, thinking about the unusual insects. Jainyu waited for him.

"Trees north of here seem fine." Jainyu frowned up at the trees with narrowed eyes. "The birds didn't find any of these insects except right here."

"We still need to take those soil and wood samples," said

Rickie, "but given how many of these insects there are and how localized the infestation is I suspect they are the cause. And given the way this dogwood suffered, they are trouble. I think we'd better try to clear out the infestation and do a thorough check of a broader area." Rickie studied the wriggling bugs in the sample container, moving in all directions as if seeking a way out. "I'd like to know more about them. How fast they reproduce, for example."

"We need to find them all, given how destructive they are. We can come back mid-afternoon, bring a couple of the interns to check a wider area. Get all the bugs. As for learning about them, there's an entomologist I've worked with at the Royal Ontario Museum. I can go see him after my next appointments. Two hydroponic facilities are due for their regular inspections, and I have to check on the report of a fungal infection in a green roof that specializes in growing broccoli and cauliflower. That building's maintenance manager's concern got labelled as top priority by the office."

Rickie laid his palm on one of the stressed trees. Feeling a stab of pain, his worry increased. "I know somebody who knows as much about tree issues as any professional. Likely more. We'll hope one of these experts can tell us something about these things before we come back."

\*   \*   \*

"I am looking for Miles Franklin. Which of you is that?"

Looking up from his desk, he saw a tall, willowy woman with short-cropped black hair and a backpack slung over her shoulder. She looked vaguely familiar. "That would be me."

"You have a work station ready for me, I assume."

"Which means that you are...?"

The woman pulled out her phone and thrust it toward his nose. "Tatiana Ricci. You should remember. You took the course I offered here five years ago."

The memory of her voice and manner slipped into place, though he looked at the identification on her phone just to be sure. This was the cyber security expert that Admin Chan had called in. "You have a good memory."

"Not that good. I looked you up. You're skilled at your job and smart. But someone found a hole in Monitor's security, and so you get me."

"Glad to have you. How much do you know about the hacks?"

"Just the vague information that the administrator had absorbed. Fill me in."

Tatiana followed Miles' outline of the three incidents with a stream of detailed questions and an examination of both the hacked cam feed and the original. She froze the screen to study the little bug that might indicate someone was watching the artist. Her fingers raced over the keyboard, then she grunted. Typed again, then pushed her chair back from the desk.

"What a shy little ghost you are. And quite the skilled hacker. We should be able to trace it in real time, but from this recording, I get nothing. What prevention have you initiated?"

"We've a program that enables Monitor to notice overlapping video feed. It's already watching this cam, and the cams at a few other possible locations that the artist could use to the same effect. A plan to scale the program across the system is underway."

"Good. Lets us know when to look for our ghost. What about the problem with the sewer system warning signals?"

"That one is harder. The data stream works differently. We're working on it, but I've also got a team working on how to teach Monitor to recognize anomalies."

"How are they defining anomalous data?"

That was the problem. The programmer defined the parameters of what was normal for Monitor to learn to recognize what was not. And that meant that the assumptions of the programmer were at work. "I'll introduce you to that team now."

Tatiana grinned. "This is going to be fun."

"Glad you like a challenge."

"Don't you?"

Miles felt the tension in his body, the whirling of worry in his head. Knowing that Monitor's surveillance could be hacked was disturbing, but it seemed like a lot of work just to confuse the AIs in a few cars. The storm sewer blockage had been potentially destructive, but the motivation for that he could not imagine. "I don't like this challenge. It's too much of a mystery. And it feels reckless."

Tatiana nodded. "Hackers are inclined to recklessness. And a big ego. Among other things. So, let's get to work and find this ghost."

# CHAPTER SIX

"Emergency. Emergency," said the monotone voice of Monitor.

"Help!" yelled a woman, voice tight and high-pitched.

"What?" asked Raja.

Already accessing audio communication with the car where the 911 button had been pressed, Jen took a breath to calm her voice. "You have an emergency in the car?"

"What is it doing? It's going the wrong way. The speed is 140k. Help me!"

"That's impossible," said Raja.

"Is it your own car that you are in?" asked Jen.

"This taxi is going to kill me."

*Not her car.* "That is not going to happen," said Jen. "Can you read me the identification number in the taxi licence. It is on the headrest if you are in the back seat; on the visor if you are in the front."

"The frame is empty. I noticed that as soon as I got in, but the doors locked right away."

"And at 140k you don't want to release your seat belt to locate the other." *And if somebody managed to take one, they took both,* Jen thought. "Tell me where you are."

"Gardiner expressway. Just raced by Bathurst."

"Pressing the 911 button alerted the police. We will work

together to get you stopped." Jen muted her intercom. "Raja, check the traffic cams and get me the licence number from the car roof. Then get the police on line."

"Already on it."

Jen unmuted. "Using the traffic cam, we can identify the taxi, and I will override the pilot. Did you notice anything else unusual when you got in?"

"It's frightening to drive this fast!"

"I can imagine. I am working on the quickest way to stop you."

"Jen," said Raja. "I'm sending you the licence number. I have a sergeant on the line."

"Fill the police in." Jen typed in the number and then the override code, ordered the car to pull over to the shoulder.

"When are you going to stop this thing?"

*Damn.* "I take it the car is still moving?"

"It speeded up."

Jen called up surveillance video, instructed it which car to follow. The picture made her dizzy as the car raced into the field of one cam, out the other side, picked up by the next. "That's okay. We've got this. Plan number two is underway." Again, Jen muted her intercom. "Raja, link me to your open line to the police."

"Done."

"Sergeant." Jen waited for an acknowledgement. "The car in question is out of control. Our override signal is blocked. My colleague told you where the car is. You will have to physically stop it. Safely. There is a passenger."

"What do you mean you can't override it? That's what Monitor is for."

"Normally yes, but something is blocking our signal. I can't stop the car. Can you?"

"We still have spike belts but never use them. Given the speed the car is going, we'd have to set them out pretty well at the 427. What about the rest of the cars on the highway?"

"I can order the other vehicles to stop on the shoulder." Jen bit her lip. That action would make the problem public as drivers would demand an explanation.

"Officers are on the way. Are you sure you aren't blocked from stopping the other vehicles?"

*Good question.* Jen chose a delivery truck and a taxi from the video feed, ordered both to pull over to the nearest shoulder. Immediately, they slowed, one changing lanes to the right, the other to the left. "I can get the rest stopped."

"Do it," said the sergeant.

"Raja, call Admin Chan. A public statement is going to be needed." Jen heard the sergeant barking orders in the background and unmuted her intercom. "What's your name?"

"What does that matter!?" shouted the terrified woman in the taxi. "Stop this car." Her voice descended into a sob.

"We are working on that. I'm clearing the road for you so that you will not hit another vehicle, and the police will bring you to a stop shortly. I'll let you know when they confirm they are in position." Jen typed in a code that she had only used twice before, both instances on the Don Valley Expressway when sudden heavy rains flooded the highway. Signals would be sent from roadside stations along the Gardiner ordering all cars to pull over and come to a controlled stop.

Raja cleared his throat. "Admin says do what you have to do, but be prepared to explain. Sounds pissed."

Jen rolled her eyes. The vulnerability of the car pilots was about to become very public.

"How can you be so calm?" The woman in the car was silent a moment. "Other cars are stopping. Why am I still racing?"

"It seems that something is blocking our access to the auto pilot of the car you are in. The police have a physical, safe way to stop your car. Please, tell me your name."

"Barbara Ann. Stanford. Like the university, the one in California."

Jen heard an edge of hysteria in the woman's voice. "All right Barbara Ann, make sure your seat belt is secure. If you have any packages or a purse or backpack, put them on the floor, tucked under the seat. Now, I'm sure you have seen movies where in an airplane crash people are asked to bend over, hands over the head. I'm going to ask you to do this as an extra precaution."

Jen's computer indicated an incoming call. She forwarded the call to one of the other overseers so she and Raja could focus.

"Monitor," said the sergeant, "spike belts deployed in five minutes."

*That's going to be fairly tight timing.* Again she muted her connection to the car. "Tell them to hurry. The passenger is ready. And tell your officers to secure the car and everything in it. We need to find out what is jamming our connection to the AI pilot. Raja, call Miles and fill him in."

"Can we lay the belts across one lane, block the others with cruisers?" the sergeant asked.

Jen hesitated. Normally that would be fine. The AI was programmed not to hit anything. It should switch lanes to the open one. But normally, the car would have stopped when she told it to. "No. I don't trust the standard protocols to work properly. Lay the belts all the way across."

"I'm going to die," said Barbara Ann.

"No," said Jen. "We are going to get you out of this, and you will be fine."

"I'm never taking another taxi."

"I can imagine why you feel that. This has never happened before."

"It's happening to me!" A sob escaped from the woman. "The car will just stop, not skid into something?"

*I have no idea how those spike belts work,* thought Jen. "Just breathe slowly and quietly. I pulled the other cars out of the way to keep you safe."

"Or so this car won't kill someone else as well as me."

Jen took a deep breath. "I am right here and watching. I have a direct line to the police." *I need to keep her talking, try to calm her.* "Where did you get in the taxi?"

"I only care where it stops." The woman's voice sounded muted, as if she had tucked her head into her lap.

"True," said Jen. "But do you mind telling me?" The woman named an intersection in the core. "And the taxi seemed normal when you got in?"

"Yes, except the missing ID. And the doors locking so quickly. And the person getting out tried to tell me it was occupied. Even though it wasn't."

Jen muted her microphone. "Raja, see if you can get an image of her getting in the taxi."

"Spike belts are in place," said the sergeant. "How close is the car?"

"Two minutes, approx." Jen took a careful slow breath. "Barbara Ann, the police are in position. They are going to blow out your tires so that the car won't be able to go on."

"This car is insane. It will keep going."

Jen chewed her lip. Barbara Ann was right. Normally, as soon as tire pressure dropped to a critical level, the car would pull over and stop. But the jammer might interfere with that safety protocol as well. How far could a car physically drive on its rims before failing? What would such a catastrophic failure look like? *I sure hope we don't find out today.* Jen made a mental note to learn the answer to that question.

"Car sighted by officers," said the sergeant. "Spike belts stretch all the way across the road."

"Be ready, Barbara Ann." Jen watched the taxi speeding along the highway. *This better work.*

"I'm scared. Tell my kids I loved them so much."

Jen opened her mouth, then closed it. She had no more reassurance to offer. Her hands clenched.

"Tell the officers to secure everything in the car," said Tatiana.

Startled, Jen looked back. Miles and Tatiana hurried into the office. "Already done."

"Including everything the woman has on her and with her," said Miles. "We have to find the device."

"I'll do that," said Raja. "But take a look at when she gets in the car. A man is getting out, tries to close the door so she can't get in. He looks upset when she slips by him."

"Take a close-up screen shot of the man and forward me the photo. Then, find where he got into the taxi. And get his ID from the taxi company." Miles kept his eyes on Jen's screen.

Jen counted seconds. The cam showed three cruisers parked on the shoulders, and the taxi raced across the line between them. It skidded to a stop. An alarm sounded.

"Emergency. Total tire failure," said Monitor. "Human intervention required." The location followed, and Monitor repeated the message.

Jen muted Monitor with a sigh of relief. "Barbara Ann. You are okay."

"The door won't open! Tell the police to get me out of this death trap!"

"I will, but I want you to know that we have to find out what caused this. The police are going to take you in for a statement, and we'll have to go through everything in the car, including your things."

"Raja," said Tatiana, "tell the police Miles and I are on the way. Get them to tow the car to the same station they take the passenger. Nothing leaves the car." She hurried from the room with Miles at her side.

"On it," said Raja to her back.

"Can't the police just take me home?" asked Barbara Ann.

"I know you want to go home, but we have to ask you to help us. The two people who are on the way to investigate are the best there is. They will figure this out in a snap. We can't have this happen to anyone else."

"I know. I know. But I'm just so...." Barbara Ann gasped. "Oh! The police just broke one of the windows. I'm getting out. Thank you for saving my life."

"That is my job," said Jen. *Though I prefer less drama in my life.*

"Jen," said Raja. "I got the location where the man caught the taxi. You can see that he had a bag in his hand getting in. He carried nothing when he got out. Seems to have left something in the taxi."

"Message Miles and Tatiana and forward them the image. They can pass it on to the police." Curious, Jen ran the video where Barbara Ann got into the taxi. A man got out with his hand on the door as if ready to slam it shut. As Barbara Ann slipped by him and pulled the door closed, the man pulled off his hat and stood looking dazed, watching the taxi. He pulled out his phone, made a call, and walked away shaking his head.

Jen's computer indicated an incoming call from Admin Chan. She hesitated, needing a minute to process what had happened. "Raja, as soon as the police clear the belts, get the cars moving. Just keep them out of the lane where the taxi is."

"On it. Accident protocols should keep them away."

"Don't depend on normal." Jen took a deep breath. "Monitor, I accept the call." Admin Chan's angry face filled the screen. "Jen Sutherland here."

"Tell me when the Gardiner will start moving. Then, slowly and carefully explain why this major highway ground to a halt."

\*      \*      \*

"Phone," said Rickie, "tell callers I am away." It was quarter to twelve, and he was headed for the subway and Koreatown, a trip that would take him by what had been Christie Pits. He remembered rows of ash trees, one towering elm, lots of pine, gardens flaming with flowers, the real grass on the ball diamond and soccer field. When the area was given over to a developer, the city insisted that a public pool be included in one building, a shortened soccer field with artificial grass in another. Between the high-rises, five maples remained surrounded by concrete. *Twice in one day I have to deal with my memory of the green growing spaces that were.* His chest ached. He wished Jainyu could have sent him to the entomologist at the ROM so that his colleague made the trip to the former Christie Pits. But this was his task. Had to be. The old man he was going to see spoke Korean, only a little English. Although Rickie only spoke the language when he went home to see his parents and grandmother in Mississauga, he could still manage.

A subway train pulled into the platform. Rickie let a mom with two kids slip in ahead of him. Once the train started to move, he could see his reflection in the window. A Korean face with a modern Metro haircut and clothing, a man who looked like he belonged in the city. No lines beside his wide-set eyes showed his worry. His quirky mouth looked happy, but he could feel the pain in his gut as he anticipated getting off the train. If he closed his eyes, he could imagine Christie Pits as it had been. And Koreatown. Once, Korean grocers and restaurants abounded in the neighbourhood around the park thanks to a wave of immigrants and money from South Korea. But when the next generation moved west to Mississauga and Brampton, the grocers and the good restaurants—the ones his grandmother would deign to enter—had moved with their clientele. For someone who lived in the core, or in the east end like him, getting good Korean food required a long taxi ride or hours on public transit to travel west to a good restaurant or his mother's home cooking.

The train pulled into Christie Station. Steeling himself, he squeezed through the crowded car to the door. It opened, and he stepped onto the platform, headed for the stairs. At street level, he glared at the housing complex. The towering apartments hemmed him in. Pulling his eyes away, he walked east, dodging a dog walker and an old woman in a wheelchair. He passed a juice bar and a hole-in-the-wall pizza shop, a convenience store, a restaurant that claimed the best, authentic Korean food. A glance at the menu in the window, all in English, told him this was not a place his grandmother would approve of. So much for what was once Koreatown.

Waiting for a green light with his back to what had been

the park, Rickie stared straight ahead while traffic hurried past. The light turned, and he crossed the road, heading south to the storefront he knew well. When he opened the door, he breathed in the complicated smells of the herbs, spices, and traditional medicines sold here, one store that remained in this neighbourhood.

The woman behind the counter smiled at him. "Ryung. So seldom you visit. Busy, busy, I am sure. It is good to see you."

He slipped into Korean-culture mode with a jolt. This always happened when someone called him by his given name. "My mother, my eomma sends greetings. Auntie Chin-sun also."

"Carry my good wishes with you when you go to visit." The woman tapped the counter. "Now did your eomma send you for herbs? I can look up what she bought for your father on her last visit. Or is it Hal-abeoji, Grandfather, that you seek?"

"Father is well. I have a question for your Hal-abeoji."

"He's almost your grandfather too, the way he relishes your visits. He's in the back yard, of course."

"Thanks." Rickie knew that grandfather's garden was what kept this family from moving west with the rest of the community. The established shrubs and perennials would be hard to move. Rickie made his way down one of the narrow aisles of the store, past the row of drawers, counters with stacks of boxes and the centre rack loaded with packets of herbs. Opening the back door, he stepped into a yard with vines climbing up the fences and across the overhead trellis. Wisteria, begonia, wave petunias, and nasturtium flourished in the baskets that hung from the trellis, while roses grew along one fence and herbs beside the other. Irises and lilies provided a riot of colour against the back wall. An old man, almost bald with delicate tanned hands, skin like fine paper, knelt beside the herbs.

"Ryung," Grandfather said without looking up.

Rickie wondered again if the man was an empath or

Gifted with a special sense of hearing, but when he once hinted the question, the man looked so frightened, he never repeated the inquiry. And his skills in gardening were what mattered this day. Rickie knelt beside him, watching him carefully remove volunteer plants, untangling leaves and roots so that the herbs were not disturbed and the volunteer could be replanted in a more appropriate place. He rehearsed again the Korean words he had practised, let them spill into the space between them.

"Boweojwo. Show." The man held out his hand.

Gently removing the sealed jar from his pocket, Rickie laid it in the old man's hand. A frown creased the grandfather's forehead as he muttered words Rickie couldn't catch. Grandfather pulled a magnifying glass from his shirt pocket, studied the insects Rickie had collected.

The old man glared at him, fire in his eyes. He thrust the jar back into Rickie's hand, speaking with a rush of staccato Korean.

"I'm sorry. I don't understand." Rickie caught the word for death and tree, but no more. In halting Korean, he told the old man that the tree had not died, yet, but the leaves suddenly turned brown, the stems dying as well.

The old man stood, backed away, and spoke a rush of words.

"Wait!" Rickie ran inside to the old man's daughter. "Can you come, please. Grandfather has something to tell me, but I can't understand."

"Sure, Ryung, sure." She turned the lock in the front door and followed him to the garden. There, Grandfather paced, hands interlaced behind his back. "Sit Abeoji, sit." She led him to a metal arm chair, and pressed him to relax. "Now tell me."

The old man placed his hands on the arms of the chair and looked up at his daughter with his mouth set in a tense line. Again, words poured out like a rushing river. He closed his fist, raised it, and he spat out the last words.

His daughter's hand went to her mouth. "No," she

whispered.

"Yes." Grandfather turned to Rickie. "Tell him."

"My father says that these are not real. No such insect exists. He is furious that such a monster lives in this city. How did you get them?"

Rickie swallowed. *How do I explain that?* "We found them on some stressed trees in High Park."

The shopkeeper translated for her father, who nodded vigorously, pointing sharply with his forefinger at the jar in Rickie's hand.

"Father says they would make trees sick and any bird that tried to eat it. They are so foreign nothing can stop them."

"If they are a hybrid, they may not be able to reproduce," said Rickie. "Does he think they are an intentional cross or bio-synthetic?"

His daughter struggled to find the words to translate Rickie's question. When she did, the old man threw up his hands, declaring in words that Rickie understood all too well that he was not the one who could answer that question. The old man waved him away.

"Kill them." Then, with an angry scowl, the old man insisted Rickie never bring such an abomination to him again.

Rickie stood. "Gamsahabnida. Thank you. And I won't offend you by bringing such a thing again."

"Good." The old man muttered under his breath, wondered what the world was coming to, and told Rickie to make sure to capture all of the horrible creatures.

"That is the plan," said Rickie. As he left, he texted Jainyu about the grandfather's reaction. Then, as he headed for his next task, he decided to take this sample home to Samantha to see if she could sense something about the insects' biology. Her Gift connected her to the biochemical processes of animals. *Somebody better come up with an explanation for these destructive little things, something that will explain Grandfather's horror. And we better be able to remove them all when we get back to the park.*

# CHAPTER SEVEN

The desk phone rang again. Jen and Raja looked at each other. "It's your turn," said Raja.

"Phone, answer the call," Jen said and sighed. "Sutherland here."

"This is the switchboard. I have another call from a passenger who was on the Gardiner Expressway demanding an explanation."

"Give me a second. Raja, call admin and suggest they put public relations on this. Switchboard, put them through."

Jen hardly paid attention to the string of complaints, the meeting missed, the inconvenience, the fear at seeing a whole highway shut down. When the passenger took a breath, Jen jumped in with her now standard reply about an unexpected emergency, an apology for the delay, and an assurance that there would be a public report that would appear on the news sites—online journals, social media, video, however this person wished to access the official explanation. "Thank you for your call; I have another coming in," Jen concluded.

Hesitating before picking up the next call, aware that Raja was already answering one that appeared to come from a produce delivery company complaining about the cost of the delay. "Phone, take the call. Sutherland here."

"You should not sound as weary as me," said Admin

Chan.

"Perhaps, but I did have to manage the task of getting the taxi stopped before answering the slew of complaints."

"Public relations will handle the complaints now. A cyber crime officer is on the way in. Don't go home until you've been interviewed."

Jen nodded. "Agreed. I hope they get on this. We've gone from nuisance to dangerous."

"Has progress been made figuring out how this happened?"

"It would be better to ask Miles or Tatiana. I'm just Traffic."

"Tatiana said she did not have time to take my call."

"I am sure that means she is digging for the answer to your question as we speak."

"Your quick thinking today prevented the loss of an innocent life. Good work." Chan ended the call.

*What will be next?* Jen started to shake so hard she had to sit down. A woman could have died this afternoon. More than one person could have been involved in an accident fuelled by such speed that it would have been catastrophic. It had been years since a fatal collision in Metro. Still shaking, she folded her arms on her desk, put her forehead down on her arms, and wept.

\*　　\*　　\*

"Warning," said Monitor. Two orange lights blinked on the traffic board.

Both Jen and Raja jumped to their feet and approached the board. Jen felt her heart start to race.

"What can go wrong next?" Raja asked.

"At least, they're orange warning lights, not red." Jen zoomed in on the locations. "One is City Hall. The other is right here. Out front." She called up the video for the sidewalk in front of Monitor Central. A crowd on the sidewalk spilled onto the street. That slowed the movement of vehicles. Many carried placards. As she zoomed in to read them, she turned on the audio. The crowd chanted in rhythm: "No more hidden AI. Give us the wheel." Some of the placards declared the same message. Others read "Back off Monitor." Switching to the cams at City Hall, a crowd filled the square. People handed out leaflets to pedestrians and any car that slowed. Jen frowned.

"Protests?" Raja leaned in to examine the signs. "Against us? Didn't we just save somebody's life?" His personal phone rang, and he backed up to answer it.

Switching back to the crowd in front of Monitor Central, Jen zoomed in. They too were handing out leaflets. Printed leaflets. Well made signs. The taxi had been stopped barely an hour earlier. How did they pull together this much organization?

Raja came back up beside her. "That was my partner calling to warn me. News of the rogue taxi is out on social media. A blitz started calling on concerned citizens to protest the use of AIs."

"How did they get the news? And how did they get this organized?" Jen bit her lip. Whatever the answer to that question, she had better make sure that administration knew what was happening. Still watching the screen, she told her phone to call Admin Chan. She thought the administrator looked harried.

"This better be important," said Admin Chan.

"Protests. Here and at City Hall. They are so well organized that I suspect..." Jen hesitated. She had nothing but an instinct to go on. "They are protesting our use of AI."

"I did not need one more thing today."

"They may be connected. Social media called for the protest based on a rogue taxi."

"Why do I not know that?" The administrator looked away. "Because PR is fielding calls from drivers on the highway. They are not keeping track of the media the way they would on a normal day." The administrator turned back to Jen. "I'll get police over here, see if they can identify the organizers. You route traffic away from the slowdowns." The administrator broke the connection.

*Monitor is already making that correction,* thought Jen. Avoiding slowdowns was part of the AI manager's job. Rerouting cars would mean less people would see the protest. First hand at least. The protesters would likely share pictures on social media. She did a search for the anti-Monitor blitz. Found it immediately on five different platforms. These were shared posts, not original. *Better call Miles, although he'll also say he did not need one more thing.*

\* \* \*

Exiting the subway at Museum station, Jainyu's phone vibrated in his pocket. "Phone, read text." As he listened to Rickie's message, he swore in Mandarin. He took the stairs into the Royal Ontario Museum, affectionately known as the ROM, two at a time. The grandfather's reaction was disturbing. What made the insects unnatural in his eyes? Were they far from their home habitat? Surely, the museum expert would be able to answer that question. Then, he and Rickie needed to get back to the site and make sure they had captured all of the dangerous little creatures. Bypassing the ticket line, he showed the entry attendant his Monitor credentials and announced he had an appointment with the head of the Entomology department.

"Your name?"

"Zhang Jainyu."

"One moment." She touched a button and a paper thin, clear screen rose from the desk beside her. With deft movements of her user interface glove, the screen flickered, and she waited. "Yes, Doctor Pachenko, a man named Zhang Jainyu from Monitor Central is here to see you." She cocked her head, listening to the voice in her ear. "Yes Doctor. I will admit him." She held out her hand to Jainyu. "Your phone. Please."

When he handed it to her, she placed it against the

screen and moved her gloved hand again. "Doctor Pachenko is in the entomology cataloguing room. Your phone will direct you there. It will also unlock the appropriate doors for thirty minutes."

"I know my way, but thanks for the key." As Jainyu climbed up the stairs to the second floor, Rickie's message played in his head. What did the old man see in the insects? At the top of the stairs, he made his way past the crowds gazing at the dinosaurs to the quieter entomology section. He found the cataloguing room, rapped on the door just to let folks know someone entered, and reached for the handle. A slight vibration from his phone, and he heard a click as the door unlocked. Stepping inside the brightly lit room, Jainyu took a moment to let his eyes adjust.

A woman looked up from a crowded desk. "You are expected I take it?"

"Doctor Pachenko knows I'm coming."

"He working with the photographic microscope down that hall."

The door to the room was open. Inside, Timur Pachenko spoke soft commands to the microscope, adjusting the zoom and the focus. "Picture," he said, and a quiet click indicated the image had been recorded. "Zoom out." He touched the screen lightly, moving the image to the insect's head. "I'll be with you in a moment. Just a couple more shots of this interesting specimen. A student I worked with a couple years ago sent this sample from a tiny island near Tonga. Previously unknown, this insect has become quite prolific there. They want to know where it came from. Picture." Studying the screen, he nodded. "That's got it." With quick, precise movements, Timur removed the specimen from the microscope, carefully returning it to a labelled container. Facing Jainyu with an eager look, he put out his hand. "Now what have you found in our fair city that you cannot recognize."

"These were burrowing into the bark of some stressed

trees in High Park." Jainyu handed him the sample jar with the insects.

Lifting the jar to his face, Timur watched the insects squirm. "You found these in Metro? Well. Let me put you little ones to sleep." Lifting a pen-like tool from the desk near the microscope, he sent a sonic wave into the jar. The insects stopped moving. Working with tweezers, he moved them around the jar. "Very curious." Lifting one, he closed the container and placed the specimen inside the microscope. When the image came up on the screen, his eyes went wide. "Double magnification." Timur chewed his lower lip. "Four times magnification." Again touching the screen, he moved the image slowly along the length of the insect. He glanced back at Jainyu. "These are most strange."

"Why?"

"The head is like the emerald ash borer. The body resembles a bark beetle. The colour and legs are that of the long-horned beetle." He looked at Jainyu. "By appearance, it looks like someone cobbled together the worst pests this city has seen. That is not reasonable."

"It couldn't be a natural cross?"

"Impossible. The emerald ash borer is a weevil. The other two are beetles but belong on distant branches of that tree. But I must not jump to a conclusion based on appearance. I will have to do a DNA test."

"Timur. It's moving."

"Damnation." Moving quickly for the sedating tool, Timur gave it a jolt, then replaced it in the jar where the other insects were also beginning to move. "That should have held them for an hour at least." He rubbed his fist against his chin. "More and more unnatural."

"You think someone created them? Trans-genetic work usually just inserts a specific trait."

"Work is being done to create hybrids." Timur studied the now squirming insects. "If it is created, someone has broken the law and betrayed their scientific integrity. Hybrids must not be released freely into the environment."

His frown deepened. "If it is manufactured, it may be resistant to pesticides. Certainly, no predator will eat it."

"A bug can be squashed."

"Or burned. That would be more efficient. But they must be caught. I will keep these ones to study. If you bring a few more, I can test possible control measures, identify any vulnerability."

"That would help. Let me know what the DNA shows."

"You better check within a kilometre or more of the infestation. Our urban forest is so limited, we cannot afford to lose any trees." Again, Timur rubbed his chin with his fist. "I will have to check for reproductive capacity."

*What would their eggs look like?* Jainyu stared at the insects moving faster now in the jar. If these little monsters started to spread, there would be big trouble. "I will bring you what I can. Thanks for your help."

"I am glad to be of service. This kind of bug should not be free. But perhaps my guess is wrong. I must not jump to conclusions. I will get to the DNA analysis immediately." Timur opened a drawer filled with delicate instruments.

Jainyu shook his head. Two very different people with a great deal of knowledge agreed that these insects should not exist. But they did. "I'll aim to be back this afternoon with more samples." Timur nodded but did not turn around. Heading down the stairs, Jainyu texted two of the department interns to meet him and Rickie at the High Park site. Once they knew what signs of stress to look for and the shape of the insects, they could survey other trees in the area. Then, once they captured the creatures, an incinerator would be the end of them.

# CHAPTER EIGHT

After Rickie showed the interns what the bugs looked like and what kind of stress to watch for in the trees, Jainyu sent a map to their phones with directions to the trees they needed to check and sample containers in case they found any of the insects. Once the interns headed out, he whistled for woodpeckers. Two arrived and began inching up the trees. Another whistle drew a flock of quick moving nuthatches. While the birds worked at collecting the insects, Rickie laid his palms on the trunk of one of the stressed trees. The leaves rustled as if a gentle breeze wafted between the branches. Rickie sighed, and moved to the next.

One of the woodpeckers landed on Jainyu's shoulder and gently pecked his head behind his ear. "You want to eat one?" He put out his hand. "Bring one and sit here then so I can watch." The bird hopped back to the tree and returned quickly with one of the strange insects in its beak. Biting the thing in half, a squirt of orange burst from inside. The bird dropped it and lifted off from Jainyu's hand with a loud trill.

"Sorry it isn't food. Best let us deal with them." The liquid on Jainyu's hand felt slick and oily. The bird flew back to the tree while he picked up the pieces of the insect. Though it had to be dead, he'd rather everything got incinerated. He watched the steady movement of birds to container, worrying about this confirmation that no natural predator would help control the infestation.

One container was almost full of wriggling insects. Jainyu closed the lid and locked it. It would not do to have any of them escape during transport. While the birds kept at their task, he wandered farther into the park. These trees seemed healthy to his eye. A robin hopped across the grass, looked at him carefully, then pecked at the ground. Jainyu circled back.

Rickie stood with his back against a tree. "This one's healthy. It's just that group close to the corner."

"A highly visible infestation. With a strange new insect. Could have caused quite a panic."

"Indeed." Rickie stroked the bark of one of the affected trees. "Do we assume that the bugs can reproduce?"

"A horrible thought, but for now yes. Once Timur Pachenko does his DNA analysis, we'll know for sure. In the meantime, one of us better stop by here every couple of days." Jainyu ran his fingers through his short-cropped hair. "Look. The flock of nuthatches is leaving."

"And one of the woodpeckers."

Jainyu watched as the remaining bird hopped up to the top of one tree and slipped over to the next. It made a steady ratatat on this one and flew deeper into the park. "They think we're done. For now."

"I'll believe the birds that they got them all." Rickie closed the lid on the second container of squirming colour and legs. "Incinerator?"

Jainyu nodded. "Seems like the best idea. And no escapees."

"Tell your doc the same thing."

"He's the most careful man I know." Jainyu lifted the container. "I'll take these to him. A good thing you got opaque containers. I don't think ROM security would let me in if they could see what I brought."

\*   \*   \*

With the end of term approaching quickly, students needed time in the art room to work on their final projects. At this point as their projects reached completion, they did not really need Darshani's help. She begged a favour from the music teacher and had him cover the art room for the students who wanted to stay. Amanda had warned that checking the graffiti site needed to happen as soon as possible, and after being so unsettled by what she saw at the park, the seer did not want to go alone. Darshani wasn't sure what she could sense given that the graffiti had been cleaned away, but she would try. She and Miles had been friends since high school, and later, he was the one who introduced her to Brindle and thus helped her understand how she could read so much about an artist from their work.

With good connections on the light rail train, she got to Chinatown a little earlier than Amanda, enough time to do her errand for her housemate, a Gifted veterinarian. Finding a grocery store near the corner of Dundas and Spadina, complex scents filled her nose. People leaned over counters, pointing to drawers marked with Chinese letters she could not read. She loved tracing those graceful strokes, wondering if by feeling the shape she could figure out their meaning. Not understanding Cantonese or Mandarin, the voices in the shop sounded like music to her, giving her the sense that the meaning was just beyond her reach. She waited in a line with the carefully written out list, an order for oil and herbs not available outside Chinatown, some for the kitchen, some for the veterinarian's practice.

When the grocer motioned her forward, she handed the paper and her cotton net bag to the him. A quick nod, and he motioned her to wait while he hurried from one crowded counter to another, pulling open drawers and cabinets.

"Pay now." The grocer handed her the loaded bag, then turned to walked to the front of the store.

"Sure," said Darshani to his back. She smiled. He reminded her of the oldest shopkeepers in Little India. These still spoke little English, treated third and fourth generation South Asians as if they were naive and ignorant of proper cultural practice. "Foreigners" they treated with careful, distant respect.

At the check out, she touched the reader with her phone, heard the quiet bell that indicated the transaction was approved. "Thank you," she said, bowing her head. A beep from her phone, and the message it spoke told her that Amanda just gotten off the Spadina streetcar. Once outside, she waited for a green light, then joined Amanda on the walkway in the middle of the road. "How was today?"

"Not bad," said Amanda. "Did some virtual teaching from home."

"Any issues on the way?"

"A little boy might have been accidentally pushed down the streetcar steps. I moved him away, but the mom was furious. Started to yell at me, told me not to molest her child. I tried to explain that I thought he was off balance, but she accused me of being an ignorant busy body, said she had her eyes on the boy. Then, she dragged him to the front of the streetcar."

"Hardly fair when you saved him from what could have been a bad fall. Too bad she didn't believe you when you said you saw him off balance."

Amanda rolled her eyes. "When she was looking right at him and didn't see it?"

"Do you ever think about explaining that you anticipated an accident?"

"Who but another Gifted would believe me?"

Darshani nodded. People would be afraid of Amanda's ability to see the consequences of choice. Or if they believed her, would try to use her to win at the stock market or roulette table. Her own gift of reading information about the artist from their work did not have a monetary value, could pass as something like reading personality from handwriting.

Amanda shivered despite the warm, sunny day. "I'm so shaky since the vision at the park. All those time lines. I normally only see a couple possibilities. Like, I didn't see what would happen to the child if he fell. Would he be bruised, but okay? Would he break something? Would someone somehow lean on the button and open the door and..." She shivered again. "I just saw the moment of fall or no fall."

Darshani took Amanda's arm. "You've said before that human contact helps keep you grounded. So let me help keep the multiverse away until we get to this interesting graffiti location."

After a few steps, Amanda spoke up. "How was your day?"

"Typical end of term panic for those who took on a big project and postponed working on it. A couple were not impressed that I had a commitment and wouldn't stay to help them, assured them I would be in early tomorrow." Darshani shook her head. "For one student, I declared his multi-media piece finished and give an extra assignment. The piece is gorgeous. But like most of us, he keeps wanting to touch it up. Learning when to stop and leave a work is hard. Someday he'll figure out for himself when to step back and leave a piece as is, without someone else saying, 'You're done.'"

Amanda smiled. "Not something you've mastered."

"True enough," said Darshani, "but I make my living as a teacher. I don't create masterpieces, just stuff for friends and family to enjoy."

"I love your work."

"You're biased, but thank you." Darshani slowed. "That's the building." She pointed across the road. "The city cleaners did their job well. The picture is gone."

"There may be a few strokes they missed." Amanda gently pushed her arm aside. "Let me approach on my own. I need to be open to sense anything."

"Don't fall." Darshani stayed just two steps away. If her

companion was overwhelmed by the timelines, being close enough to catch Amanda seemed wise. She stopped at the edge of the sidewalk, watched Amanda run her hands along the wall from the height of a person downward. Crouching, feeling the wall at knee level, Amanda's body went stiff. She leaned her shoulder against the wall and groaned. Darshani hurried forward and wrapped Amanda in a hug and lifted her to her feet. "What did you see?"

"The city. As it is, almost. But car horns blared. Traffic drove at erratic speeds. I think drivers had their hands on the steering wheels."

"What?"

"I know. I don't get it." Amanda stared at the wall.

"It sounds like a flashback."

"My Gift does not work like that. It's always the near future."

Darshani ran her eyes over the brick. "You saw nothing as you approached, nothing as you touched the wall until you bent down?"

"Until I touched the wall, I saw you speaking in frustration and spouting off about the remarkable accomplishment of the graffiti artist."

Darshani blushed. She did think it amazing that this street artist created a picture that could fool the car pilots. Crouching to examine the spot where Amanda had been able to sense the possibilities, Darshani ran her fingers across the brick, found a smooth layer of red paint. "Gotcha Artist." She snapped a picture.

"People are looking at us funny," said Amanda.

"If anyone asks, I've a stomach bug that is really contagious, and they should stay away. I think I am going to be sick and can't move until the nausea clears."

"I didn't see you throwing up."

Darshani shook her head. Truthfulness was a consequence of Amanda's Gift. When she lied, she threw herself off balance. The timelines became tangled. "Tell them I said I am going to be sick, and I think it's very contagious."

Amanda sighed. "I can do that."

Darshani ran her finger across the paint. Digging in her backpack for pencil and sketch pad, she tore out a page and folded it into an envelope. Then, she used the back end of the pencil to scrape off a sample of the paint.

"You are the only person I know who carries stuff like that. The rest of us have phones, tablets, and electronic notepads."

"My grade nine students panic when I hand them a sketch pad and three pencils of different hardness and tell them to keep them in their backpack at all times. They can create three dimensional sculptures on the computer in no time. Manipulating a pencil takes all term. Some come to love them. Not many, but some. In this case, the pencil end got me a sample of the paint. I'm sure Samantha knows a chemist or two at University of Toronto who can analyze it for us."

"Why?"

"The composition might help explain how the image confused the auto pilots. And street artists are particular about their materials."

Amanda bit the corner of her lip. "Why did I see people driving their own cars? What do you think this is about?"

Darshani shook her heard. "No idea. You okay to get home?"

"I think I'm fine." Amanda straightened. "And we're together to the subway. If I need a hand when I get off, I'll call Brindle." She looked at the wall again. "Such a strange vision."

\*   \*   \*

Tatiana had her laptop hooked up to the taxi's AI pilot, leaving Miles to examine the box that hijacked the car. A forensic technician cleared everything the passenger had with her, and an officer took the exhausted woman home.

When he lifted the box in his hands, Miles could sense two electrical pulses, one as regular as a heart beat. Miles told his laptop to record the signals. "Tatiana, this box is emitting two sets of signals. One is on the same channel as Traffic would use to issue instructions. Because it is constant, there was no access for Monitor."

"One part of the explanation. The second set of signals must be the instructions."

"Analyzing those now."

"And how did those signals get through the AI's firewall," Tatiana muttered to herself.

*And now, box, let's see what makes your heart tick like this.* He found the tiny screws that held the frame together, and began to loosen them.

"Be careful," said Tatiana without looking away from the screen. "Could be booby trapped."

The forensic technician came to look over his shoulder. "The bomb squad sniffed it. The box is clean."

"I think she is more concerned that opening this contraption the wrong way might destroy the coding and our clues." Miles turned the box over, found screws on the opposite side as well. Closing his eyes, he sought to feel the direction of the pulse, decided it originated from the other end. *If there is a booby trap, it won't be in the area that generates the code.* He flipped the box over and removed the screws. Feeling his heart beat speed up, he thought a thank you to the technician that checked with the bomb squad. Holding his breath, he lifted the cover. Nothing happened.

Inside was a complex set of microchips. He identified the emitter, the circuitry that held the coding for the signals, and a receiver. "I think that this sequence might be triggered by a particular signal. The man left the device, sent a signal with his phone to begin operation, and left the taxi."

"And I have found the gap in the firewall that the manufacturers of this AI pilot should have caught. This is irresponsible computer work in our day and age." Tatiana closed her laptop gently and slammed her fist on the taxi. "They know better than this. How do I get their attention? The company needs to fix this now. And we have to make sure Monitor staff can counteract the interference."

"Admin Chan has a position in Monitor that opens doors."

"Call her. Now. And we head back to Monitor Central. We have work to do."

# CHAPTER NINE

Two blocks from Monitor Central, Tatiana's phone chirped. A message from Admin Chan told her that the video conference with the company that built the taxi's AI would be at seven p.m. local time. "What could possibly be more important than my information?" Tatiana asked aloud. "Three hours to pull together the people I need to talk to. Ridiculous."

"I hear voices," said Miles.

Turning the corner, he faced a crowd of people with placards chanting, "No more hidden AI. Give us the wheel." This was the protest Jen mentioned, organized immediately after the taxi take over through a social media blitz. As they approached, a woman thrust pamphlets at them. Tatiana brushed by her, but Miles took one. He looked it over as he made his way through the crowd.

"Tatiana, this is well put together. To produce this within hours of the taxi going rogue suggests they knew ahead. I think we'd better trace the social media blitz that called for this."

"Before the trail disappears. As if we did not already have enough to do. Who are the best two of your team for that task?"

Miles thought for a moment and named James and Liling, both curious digger types.

"Get them on it, and then join my briefing of the rest. We need a way to get through the kind of disruption that box created." In the elevator, Tatiana typed a long message into her phone. Entering the technology office, she clapped her hands together. "I need everybody's attention. We are here for the duration. Supper is on its way. Anybody allergic to Mexican food?"

"Not me," said Jerry, one of the programmers. "I mean, not me staying. I've got to pick up my daughter at daycare in an hour."

"Someone else can do that. I need all brains here."

Seeing the pained expression on Jerry's face, Miles intervened. "The rest of us can make arrangements, Tatiana. Jerry needs to go." His wife had died of cancer just four months before. Jerry balanced work and parenting, trudging forward but with little energy and a tight schedule.

Tatiana glared around the room. "Anyone else?"

"Take ten minutes to let folks know you are staying late," said Miles. He instructed his phone to text Brindle that he'd be staying at the office. Someone should know where he was. *In case.* In case of what, he refused to consider.

"Thought you were single," said Tatiana.

Miles looked up. "Housemates."

While Tatiana gathered the rest of the staff in a rough circle, Miles took James and Liling to a far corner and explained what they were looking for. "Dig deep into this social media frenzy. Someone knew the taxi hijacking was about to happen."

Miles joined the circle around Tatiana as she explained the cycle of code that overloaded the portal where Traffic overseers would normally access the pilot. Three suggestions were made, then one of the programmers suggested they access the pilot through the same gap in the firewall the override mechanism used. Each of the four options were assigned to a team.

"How will we test our program?" one person asked.

"The taxi and the device are at the police lab. Tomorrow,

you can start them up and see which of you solved the puzzle. And don't worry. The taxi isn't going anywhere. The transmission's disabled. Now to work." Tatiana waved the back of her hand at them. "Miles, what were we working on before that taxi went rogue?"

"Scaling the program to recognize overlapping video across Monitor's systems and training Monitor to recognize anomalies."

"Right. Anomalies is just my thing. We'll push those tasks along and keep an eye on how the rest of the team is getting along."

Miles's phone vibrated. A call from Admin Chan.

"You are not going home early today," said Chan. "A detective will arrive in your office with a warrant to run the image of the man who left the taxi through recognition software."

"We are all staying late. Taxi company didn't give a name?"

"Credit card was fake."

Miles whistled. These folks were good. There were three layers of protection to make sure cards presented for payment were valid. "That is a problem."

Chan looked away from the screen, frowned deeply. "And now I have to explain to the city's media hounds why the Gardiner shut down." Chan ended the call.

*And admit that our modern tech can be hacked. That will give the media even more to chew on.*

An hour after supper was delivered, a woman's voice spoke Miles' name as a question. He looked up to see a white woman flash her badge. A colleague directed the officer to him.

"Detective Carol Madison here. I have the warrant and a laptop with the recognition software. Can you call up the image we are comparing?"

"Take a seat." Miles made room for the officer's computer. "I'll show you the sequence where the woman got in the taxi."

The detective studied the images, backed it up and ran it slowly forward. "I can see why your administrator said that it appears the people planning this wanted the vehicle empty. The man we are looking for clearly tried to stop her from getting in. One point in his favour." She backed up the video. "Wearing a long coat on a hot day, masking body structure. But we get good views of his face and head." Taking a screen shot of the man looking almost directly at the camera, she zoomed in on his face, copied the image onto her cloud account, and opened her computer.

"Finding him will take a while."

The detective shook her head. "Not so long. Now days, the computer analyzes the facial structure and that directs the search. The database is much more organized."

Miles frowned. Part of that would be racial profiling. Kinky hair and eliminate all the white folks. An epicanthal fold of the eyelid and pull up the Asians. Uncomfortable, Miles studied the picture of the man's face. Something bothered him. He zoomed in tighter. "I'm not sure you're going to find him, Detective." When Carol looked over at him with raised eyebrows, he pointed to the nose and then the chin. "The colour is off."

"Stage makeup. These people are careful." She tapped her fingers on the keyboard, then hit pause on the program. "Where there's a will, the criminal finds a way. But so do we. We've an artist who specializes in undoing disguises. I'll send her a clip of the video. A couple angles will help her find the additions. Once she has an image of the real face, I'll run it." She waited while Miles copied a section of the video, then sent an email to the artist. "This kind of identification gets challenged in court, but it should be enough for a search warrant."

"The sooner the better," said Miles.

James called him over. "I found the threads calling for protests on Chit Chat and Galaxy. Some of the comments suggest that objecting to AIs is craziness. But there were lots of shares, lots of thumbs up. The shares do not say who originated the post. Kind of unusual."

Miles and the detective pulled up chairs. "Those who started this knew they needed to hide." He typed in a code, and waited. "Shared from Martha Hollingsworth. Check her Chit Chat account."

James called up her feed. "I don't see any posts today at all." He kept scrolling back.

Miles studied the posts. Family pictures, lakeshore sunsets, some good quotes on meditation. Nothing about technology. Nothing about a protest. "Try her deleted posts."

"How? Once they are deleted, they're gone."

Miles moved the keyboard. "Wrong. After the Chicago riots that were sparked by false claims on several platforms that went up and were deleted, the U.S. threatened to put in a law forcing social media to keep a record of all posts. To prevent that, they agreed to voluntarily shift the programming so that deleted posts are simply hidden."

"The icon says delete," said James.

"Indeed." Miles typed the code that would reveal any hidden posts. One appeared with a time stamp just after police stopped the taxi. A call to protest reliance on AI. He took a screen shot. "Check her other platforms. Use this code to reveal any hidden posts. Screen shot them and let me know what you find."

"And I'll do a little research on this Martha Hollingsworth," the detective said.

\* \* \*

Arriving back at the Scarborough Houses, Rickie continued past his duplex to the last in the row, the one where Samantha, Nathan and the twins lived. Samantha's Gift enabled her to sense biological processes. While it gave her unusual insight into living creatures, the Gift had a downside. Genetically modified grains, beans and other products made her sick. As a result, the family needed to be really careful with the food they purchased, and she seldom ate away from home. He knocked on the door and stepped inside, calling out his name to announce who had walked in.

"In the kitchen," called Samantha.

Rickie walked slowly, fingering the sealed sample container in his pocket. He remembered the horror on the grandfather's face as he touched the container, examined the insects. Knowing what he sensed when he touched the trees that hosted these bugs, the anguish and helplessness, he hated to think what Samantha would feel when she examined these creatures.

"Rickie, you look like someone just stuffed a rotten grape in your mouth," said Nathan as he slid roasted potatoes onto the children's plates. "What's wrong?"

As the children dug into their dinner, one murmuring with delight, the other complaining that the chicken felt sticky, Rickie told them that he and Jainyu found the cause of the distress to trees in the corner of the park where Amanda had her vision. Then, he took a deep breath and spoke of the grandfather's reaction to the insects they collected.

"I know you suspect the old man is Gifted," said Nathan, "but his reaction doesn't tell us much. What about Timur Pachenko? His interpretation will be shaped by science."

Rickie met Samantha's eyes. She smiled and shook her head. Nathan was a skilled theoretical physicist and Gifted with the ability to sense shifts in gravity and magnetic waves. Despite the Gift, he claimed to trust logical thinking more. Wanting to explain what the Gifted were able to do, he started to develop a theory of hyper-tuned senses as a type of neurodiversity. As well as the usual five, he included perception of spatial relationship, time, movement and velocity, magnetic fields, electricity, along with his own ability to sense minute shifts in gravitational fields and Amanda's way of sensing quantum shifts. As he could not share this work with scientific colleagues and had not uncovered any other work on the topic, he had not made much progress, in his own opinion. And he admitted his theory did not, yet, explain the connection Rickie had with plants or Jainyu with birds. Rickie turned back to Nathan. "Timur is running their DNA for us. He thought they did not look natural."

"Unnatural in that they don't belong in this ecosystem?" asked Nathan. "Or unnatural as in a miniature machine or unnatural meaning a hybrid that cannot occur without human intervention."

"Mom!" demanded Trinity. "Apple juice!"

"Yes dear," Samantha poured both girls a glass.

Rickie shrugged. "He's a scientist like you. He would not guess until he studied them. All I know is that when a woodpecker bit into one, it spurted a weird liquid, and the bird dropped it as if it hurt."

"Killed the insect?" asked Samantha. "Bird was fine?"

"Bird dropped it like it was on fire, but seemed fine. The insect looked dead, but Jainyu picked up the pieces just to be sure."

"More likely a hybrid, not a machine," said Nathan. "You gave some to the entomologist. The rest?"

"Incinerated. Made sure there was nothing left but ash."

"Then, why are you here?" Nathan asked.

"I saved a few. I want to see what Samantha senses."

Trinity glared at him. "Mama's busy."

Samantha put a hand on the girl's head. "Daddy will look after your dinner just fine. Come, Rickie. We'll go to the workshop."

The finished basement was lined with workbenches and cabinets. It was not hard to tell which belonged to whom. Samantha's had microscopes and petri dishes, tubes and a set of trays with plants growing under lights. Nathan's workbench displayed sky charts and astronomical instruments. In the corner near the door to the outside, an area rug was littered with Lego pieces around the beginnings of a complex construction. A stuffed two-seater couch faced a large 3D television screen.

Samantha led Rickie toward a table with a large microscope. "Let me see them." She held out her hand.

Rickie pulled the sealed jar from his pocket. He placed it on her palm.

Samantha gasped, wavered, put her hand on the bench to stay standing. "These are awful."

"Awful in what way?"

"They feel wrong." Samantha took a deep breath. "I need to touch one." She reached for a petri dish and tweezers. "Take out one, and put it in here with the lid closed. Then reseal the jar and put it on the bench."

"If these feel so wrong, will touching them make you sick?"

"Probably. I've been known to faint if the material is modified enough." Samantha pulled up a chair. "You keep your eye on the bug no matter what. We can't have it escape."

"No argument from me." Rickie took the lid off the dish while Samantha reached out a shaky hand. The insect scurried to the side of the dish as if trying to avoid her. With two fingers, she pinned it to the side.

Samantha screamed and pulled her hand back, turned aside, and vomited on the floor.

"Sam!" Nathan called.

"Watch the girls," Samantha whispered. "I'm okay."

Rickie thrust the lid back on the dish. "I've got her. She says to stay with the girls." Rickie put a hand on Samantha's shoulder. "Can I get you water?" When she nodded, he went to the washroom and came back with a full glass.

Samantha took it with two shaking hands, sipped carefully, shuddered. "We'll get Nathan to clean up the mess I made. But that tells us something. It is a seriously mutated bug. Who would manipulate poor insects like that?"

"A question I am afraid we are going to have to find an answer to. Let's get you upstairs to watch the girls so

Nathan and I can clean up here. Then, I'll call Jainyu."

"We need to find out who created these monsters." Samantha took a deep breath. "Give me a hand to stand, but I think I can handle the stairs now."

\*     \*     \*

Heading to the kitchen to make a late supper, Julie could hear that someone moved about. Sounded like Rickie, but something did not seem right. Stopping half-way down the stairs, putting a hand on Juniper's head to keep the dog still, Julie listened more carefully. Rickie's heart raced. He muttered under his breath. She hurried on to find out what was wrong. "Rickie, are you sick?"

"Sick at heart. Physically fine."

"I could hear you were upset from upstairs. A good thing Geoff is working late. Your emotion would drive him crazy."

"I know, but things are just so wrong."

"Tell me, but then promise me you will find a way to get a hold of yourself before Geoff gets home."

Rickie kept cooking while he filled Julie in. As she listened, Julie felt her own heart rate increase. Rickie's worry was contagious. Then, as he spoke about Samantha's reaction to the insects, she heard a loud crack. Juniper jumped to his feet.

"What was that?" she asked.

"Sorry. I hit the counter with a wooden spoon, and it broke. The spoon, I mean. The counter is fine."

"I wish Giovanni was here. You need to let go of that anger."

"I know. I'll work in the garden after supper."

Julie heard him pull two bowls out of the cupboard.

"Turns out I made lots," said Rickie. "You might as well share it. Let's eat out on the porch."

As they ate, Julie talked about her day at work. Rickie made appropriate comments, but she could tell he only half listened. Still, the warm sun on her face made her feel at ease and relaxed.

"If you're done," said Rickie, "I'll take the dishes in. I'll clean up the kitchen in a bit. I need some time in the garden."

"Supper was great. Thanks for sharing. And yes, get your hands on something green and growing. I think I'll stay out here and listen to a book."

"Thanks for listening to me first. I don't like putting the weight of this on you, but I feel better having talked about it."

"We're here for each other." Julie told her phone to call up the audio novel she had been listening to the night before.

A little while later, she heard the door open at the next house. The twins ran down their stairs, then stopped. Their parents came out just behind them.

"Can we pet Juniper?" Trinity asked.

"He isn't working right now, so sure. Phone, pause the book." Julie heard Juniper move to a sitting position while the girls whispered to him and rubbed him gently.

"The girls love your dog," said Samantha. "Nathan. Nathan, what are you looking at?"

"I don't know."

"Where is he looking?" Julie asked.

"Daddy is looking at the sky," said Gillian.

"He is always thinking about the sky," said Trinity.

"It's not the sky," said Nathan. "It's an object in the sky. Right over Metro."

"Lots of satellites now days," said Samantha.

"This one is new. I'll be back. I want to check this out."

Julie listened to his footsteps, heard the door of his house open and close, noticed Samantha sigh. "Is he okay?"

"He's a dog with a bone. And just when I got him out for some fresh air. Well, girls, say goodbye to Juniper, and we'll take our walk, the three of us. No sense waiting for Dad."

"Bye Juniper," the twins said together.

Julie started up her book again. On their way home an

hour later, the twins came and greeted Juniper and then disappeared inside with their mother. A short while later, footsteps told her that someone turned the corner and walked toward her. Listening, she identified Geoff by the shuffling gait. She waved, and the footsteps slowed. *He's worried!* "It's not terrible, Geoff. I just stayed outside to listen to a book."

"How's Rickie tonight?"

"Not great but he's outside in the garden. Won't be back in to clean up the kitchen for a while."

"Good thing I ate supper at work. I don't think I can handle being in the same house with him."

"You could sleep in the guest room near the twins. They exude such positive energy."

Geoff nodded. "And their worries when they have them are pretty fleeting. Except that Trinity doesn't think she's Gifted, but it is not hard to distract her from that."

"How was work?"

"Tiring." He slumped down onto the bottom step. "Exhausting really. I'll just go in and grab my things and sleep I think." Geoff paused. "Nathan is coming. He's got something on his mind. Seems more intrigued than upset though. Tell him I'm moving into their guest room, at least for tonight."

"Will do."

As Geoff went inside, the door to the other house opened and shut. Julie listened as Nathan walked slowly down the steps. "Did you learn anything?"

"There is no new satellite launch registered in the Canadian Space Authority or NASA. Nothing in the European, Russian or Japanese agencies."

"But you are sure it is there." Julie heard a shift in Nathan's stance, hoped he heard her words as a statement, not a question.

"I am sure. It's probably innocuous. It's not really any of my business. But the proliferation of objects in near space concerns me. Yes, we need them for the 10g networks. We need them for TV and communications. But every object has gravity, and the interactions of these are going to get complicated."

"Which is what you are working on during this sabbatical, right?" Julie heard a movement, thought Nathan put his hands on his hips.

"Yes. And tomorrow I'll follow up with a contact at NASA who monitors satellites. However, in this moment, I have been ordered to take two thousand steps. At least. Outside. In what Samantha calls fresh air. This is city air. Desert air is fresh and so clear that you can properly see the sky. Mountain air is fresh and thin, also good. This is thick city air, but I will do as I was told and walk."

"Your girls look after you. Oh. I almost forgot. I need to tell you that Geoff is going to use your guest room tonight. Rickie is having trouble containing his worry. Can you deal with yours?"

"No problem. By the time I get back from this walk I'll be well distracted."

# CHAPTER TEN

Biking to work, Jen checked two possible spots where the graffiti artist's painting could disrupt traffic and, finding nothing, headed for Monitor Central. The quickest route would take her up Elizabeth Street. Picturing that street in her mind, she saw in the intersection at College Street where just to the west was an old church with a new building towering beside it. That building crowded the sidewalk, a spot similar to the one the artist chose before. The main difference: College Street was a dedicated streetcar corridor.

*Girl, you are a fool. Why were you only thinking of cars!* A transit disruption would be much more of a headache. And more dangerous. Turning up the next side street, she rode east to Elizabeth and north toward College. Ten years earlier, the College-Carleton corridor became dedicated to streetcars and the tracks were lifted from Dundas Street. Two lines ran each way on College now. There were sidewalks, but no cars, trucks, or bicycles allowed. Unlike Queen Street, they had not put in overhead walkways. The streetcars were kept on a precise schedule so that passengers descending from the centre rails ran no danger from an approaching one on the outer rails. Disturbing the timing on those tracks would create a hazard.

At College Street, she bumped across the four sets of

tracks and dismounted at the sidewalk. People hurried toward the designated stops, checking their phones for the next streetcar's arrival time. Walking by the church, a brown stain was visible on the newer building with two smallish legs just behind it. She touched the wall. The paint was smooth, shiny, but dry. *Looks like a child running, but what is this brown thing supposed to be?* She traced the edges of the shape that clearly wasn't a person. As she ran her finger along the contour of the bottom, it hit her. *A dog. A big, fast dog chased by a child!* She snapped a picture and emailed it to Miles with the message, marked urgent, "meet me in transit in ten new graffiti."

Jen looked up. A cam pointed right at this spot. And this was not five minutes from Monitor Central. The choice of location felt like a deliberate, brazen provocation. And attacking the transit system raised the stakes. *What if the hacker could prevent Transit overseers from catching the disruption as well as the artist working?* Jumping on her bike, Jen dug in and sped the last few blocks north and west.

\*     \*     \*

Calling up his to-do list, Miles ran through the tasks pushed aside by the emerging urgent issues. Metro Social Services had renewed their request for better statistical analysis of the movements of homeless people. He moved it up the assignment list even though he found the request problematic. Yes, making sure to provide enough food at each soup kitchen was important, but people were not machines to be checked and calibrated. And the ethics of this kind of monitoring hovered near the border of illegal surveillance. One of the rules Monitor ran by was only watching what was essential for the public's protection. *And nothing on this list will get done until we eliminate these hacks.*

He called up the previous day's work logs. Before shifting attention to the taxi's AI hack, the team teaching Monitor to catch overlapping video feed had a program ready to be uploaded to specific cams. He would review that first thing. Scaling it to the whole system was today's task. The team working on teaching Monitor to identify anomalies had made some progress thanks to Tatiana's suggestions, but they had a long way to go before they could begin providing new data to teach the system. And two people had been pulled off that task to test their ideas for regaining control of a hijacked car.

His phone vibrated. An urgent message from Jen. Reading it, his whole body tensed. "Tatiana, I've been summoned to Transit. There is a new graffiti."

Tatiana whirled her chair around. "Hacking into Transit could be a nightmare. Same MO?"

"I'll know more in ten minutes."

"If this crew is shifting locations, we need that program to catch overlapping video scaled up this instant. I'll light a fire under that team. And let me know which cam to check. I'll want to take a look and see if the ghost was present."

"You will know as soon as I do." Miles told his phone to summon an elevator. A hack in Transit felt like an emergency. The elevator awaited when he jogged up. "Sorry if you're going down. I'm headed up."

Muttering, the four passengers stalked by him. As he entered, he caught rolling eyes and a fiery glare. "Unavoidable," he said. "Emergency in Transit." The doors closed on their disgruntled faces as he hit the button for the fifteenth floor. Hurrying into the office, the two Transit overseers looked at him with raised eyebrows.

"We didn't report a computer problem," one said.

"No Harry, but you and Guylaine will soon. Jen Sutherland from Traffic is on her way."

"What is up?" asked Guylaine.

"I have a guess, but I am not prepared to speculate. All seems on schedule and running efficiently here?"

"A planned power outage in the west end for scheduled hydro maintenance, but Monitor is running the signals on the Queensway lines directly. Things are running smoothly."

"Good." Miles walked over to the wall projection that showed subway, streetcar, and bus movements. All green in the core. *Not that the colour reassures me.* His hands clenched, as he wished he could see beyond the projection to what was really happening.

Right on schedule, Jen ran into the room with her bike helmet still in her hand. "Call up the cam one west of the corner of College and Elizabeth."

"Pardon?" asked Harry.

"Do it," said Miles.

Harry shook his head and grumbled under his breath. "There is a streetcar that has just picked up passengers."

Guylaine checked the schedule. "It is precisely on time. A westbound one is due in four minutes."

"Zoom in on the wall of the building just west of the church," said Jen.

Harry turned and glared, but Miles raised his eyebrows, and the Transit overseer did as instructed.

Jen pointed at the screen. "There. It's the start of a graffiti dog chased by a child."

"Indeed. Paint still wet?" asked Miles.

"Sorry, no."

"Fine. Make it harder for me." Miles moved to a vacant work station. He texted the location to Tatiana with a note that he would send the time of the hack as soon as he found it.

"Why bother us with a bit of graffiti?"

While Jen filled in the two operators about the incidents and the computer hack, Miles ran the program his team created to catch overlapping surveillance video. Given the paint was dry and assuming the artist worked in daylight, he ran a five-hour block from evening to sunset the previous day. Nothing. He set up the earlier five-hour block. Elbows on the desk, hands pressed together in front of his face, he waited. A ping, and the screen flashed.

"Here we are. Let me back up three minutes."

The other three came and watched from behind him. "There," said Jen. "The man with two kids disappeared."

"We fast forward, and yes, twenty minutes later, a different crowd on the sidewalk and the start of a picture."

"A wall painting can actually confuse the cars' AI pilots?" Guylaine asked.

"They are supposed to be smart," said Harry.

"They are supposed to be efficient and protect life," said Miles. "I guarantee that tomorrow or the next day, there will be another inserted feed. When the computer is returned to the real time video, you will find that the auto pilot on the west bound streetcar refuses to go ahead. Signal the car, and the pilot will tell you that a dog is about to race across the road with a child right behind."

"The driver will just override the pilot," Harry said.

"Aren't there protocols that would prevent an override that could cause an accident?" asked Jen.

"Yes, but..." Harry rubbed his chin. "If this is identified as a situation that could cause injury, the driver would have to call in so we could do the override. That would throw off the schedule."

"We'll send Maintenance to clean it off the wall," said Guylaine.

"No," said Miles.

"What do you mean, 'No?'" Guylaine glared at him. "If you two are right, this graffiti poses a danger."

"Administration has made it clear that catching the hacker is the top priority. The artist is a link to the person interfering into our system. I will put a trace on this camera to catch the moment it is hacked. We will have the artist detained and find out who is hiding their work."

"What if they succeed in disrupting the streetcars?" Guylaine asked. "Someone could get hurt."

"The tracer I'll install will set off an alarm here as well as in my office. You can monitor the real time situation from the cam east of this one and ensure no accidents."

"This can't be happening," said Harry. "There are

safeguards and protocols."

"Which do not seem to be working at the moment. Jen, you make the report to Admin Chan. I'll get back to my department and the task of tracing this hacker. And thanks for finding this at an early stage. You went out of your way to give us this advantage."

"The Traffic disruptions were a nuisance, but I hate the danger they are putting people in with an interference in Transit."

"How did you think of looking there?" Guylaine asked.

"The spot just came to me. I've been mapping the car roads for possible locations, but as I headed back here, I remembered that spot."

"You carry a map of the streets in that detail in your head?" Harry asked.

"Doesn't everyone?"

Harry laughed. "Not me. I let my phone tell me the best route to get where I need to go."

With a shrug, Jen ran her fingers through her cropped brown hair, twirled her helmet in her hand. "Whatever. I've a report to make, and Miles has a miracle to pull out of his computer terminal."

"Not a miracle. An extremely precise program that has already been installed on another cam." Miles walked Jen to the elevator still wondering about her ability to remember locations in such detail. Did she have a Gift for mapping spaces? Gift or not, finding the start of that painting gave them an advantage. When they got to Jen's floor, she stepped out with a quick wave goodbye. Miles pressed the button to keep the door open. "Are there more places where the artist might work?"

"A couple more between here and where I live. A few west of here."

"Can you email me the locations so that we can install the program to catch hacks on each of the cams?"

"Do you think it's necessary when we know they are working on this one?"

The elevator buzzer complained about the open door. "After the first," said Miles, "they waited a week. This time, the artist started the painting the next day. They might well go after two spots at a time. Keep upping the stakes as it were." The buzzer got louder. "And see if you can think of any other spots like this on Transit lines."

"You better let the elevator go before security comes. But sure. I can do that."

"You've given us a good lead, but we need to be vigilant and imaginative."

"You've got me worried, Miles."

As the elevator door closed, he realized Jen still watched him. He gave her a weak smile of reassurance, a smile that faded as soon as he was alone. He texted Darshani and Amanda asking if they could take a look at this graffiti. As he told the phone to send the message, his frown deepened. The first hack put property at risk. Would the artist and hacker risk human life?

\*   \*   \*

Nathan took a sip of coffee, almost spat it out. *That's cold as space!* He remembered Samantha bringing him the coffee, telling him she'd take the girls to their before-school program. He looked at the cup. How long ago was that?

"Nathan," said the House's unmodulated technical voice. "It is ten-thirty. Time for you to take a walk of at least one thousand steps. If not, I will be required to tell Samantha you reneged on your exercise program."

"Computer tattle tale. Don't you know that my mind has travelled millions of light years."

"Your body has not moved more than a few centimetres. A healthy mind requires a healthy body."

"Who taught you to nag? Don't answer that question." He knew the answer. Miles programmed the household assistant system for each of the Houses, here, in the core, and in Brampton, along with the intranet that connected them. Nathan had, with permission, borrowed firewall and encryption coding from NASA so that the security was spectacular. Despite that, Nathan made sure his own computer was not connected to any local network. His work with NASA let him connect to a high security satellite internet, but even that he only connected to when he needed to share or receive information from a scientific contact. His phone worked on a discrete network run by the International Space Agency.

"Which reminds me of a call I have to make, which I can do while I am walking."

"Please connect your step counter to my systems," said the House. "That will ensure proper record keeping."

"The connection to your system is not going to happen. Ever. Besides, you always remind me when I return. And don't make your usual quip about how I dive right into work as soon as I get back."

"I do not believe I am programmed to make 'quips'."

"Don't comment then." Nathan stretched. When his sabbatical began five months earlier, he argued with Samantha that they didn't need a nanny while he was on leave, that he would pick up the girls, prep supper, clean. Samantha simply shook her head and informed the nanny that the only thing that would change in her schedule was that she would inform Nathan when he needed to pick up the girls at school. She'd told him that it would save him time as this would count toward his daily walking total. He'd objected again, assuring her he could remember to get the girls on time. With fists on her hips, his wife declared that there were three females who would never forgive him if he forgot even once. The nanny kept coming. That is, until her grandmother died in the Philippines, and she left for her homeland for a month. Now, only the House's system nagged him. It never missed an opportunity.

Picking up his phone, he stepped out the basement door and climbed three steps to the back yard. "Phone, call Val, nickname Spacevalve."

"Afternoon Nathan," said Val, "at least it is afternoon here. You're at home?"

"Stepped out for a walk on completely empty streets, therefore close to home."

"Have you figured out a way to describe non-linear turbulence in gravitational forces yet?"

"Ever the optimist you are, Val. Not even close to a solution, though yesterday I did draft an equation to deal with gravity interactions of smaller objects in a larger gravity field." He rolled his eyes, and Val smiled. "Local space is so crowded with satellites now, keeping safe pathways out to the two space stations is a challenge."

"Tell me about it. Am dealing with a new one over Orlando. They got permission to place it just outside the flight path. If your equation would show that it would not take much to move it across the line or that the flight corridor should be expanded, it would help our injunction to get it removed."

"Might be a good test of the work. Send me the details. Satellites is why I called. There's a new one over Toronto. I couldn't find any authorization for it or record of its launch."

"They are proliferating like rabbits in Australia. Every company thinks they need their own. But launches are still highly controlled. There should be a record."

"Not in the places I looked."

Val nodded. "My clearance isn't much better than yours, but I've a contact in Geneva who is tracking new satellite placements world-wide. I'll get back to you. Meanwhile, if you don't mind taking some time off the super theoretical stuff you love and working on that equation, we'd be grateful here. The skies are getting so crowded, there is going to be trouble. It would be good to prove it ahead of disaster."

"My agreement with Samantha and the university is that mornings I work on theory; afternoons practical applications of incomplete theories. I do not like working in the dark. It feels like going for a space walk without a life line or not knowing if an aspect of an equation is a constant or a variable. But it is ever thus. We got to the moon without meshing the theories of gravity and quantum particles, and it looks like we'll get people to Mars before the question of turbulence is satisfactorily analyzed. I've accepted that working hypotheses can accomplish tasks."

"Good. Anything else?" Val asked.

"When we talked six months ago, you mentioned someone in Brazil working on air turbulence at the border of the old Amazon and the farmland that was forest. Can you send me their contact info?"

"Um. That was an article in Natural Physics or one of those popular magazines. I might have it at home, but the kids cut up anything with good pictures that I don't put on an upper shelf in my office."

Nathan's eyes went wide. "Thanks for that warning! My girls haven't started to do that yet, but I will keep what I need to preserve out of reach. I'll search out the article. And it was just a whim anyway. The question of small object interactions is more urgent. The one here in particular."

"Interfering with your line of sight, is it?"

"Not exactly. But it caught my attention, so it's a puzzle I want to solve. I'll let you get back to work."

"And you."

As the phone went clear, Nathan pondered Val's interest in his work on micro-gravity. Space was crowded with satellites now, some essential and some of uncertain value. Maybe he was making too much of this one. If Val could tell him where it originated, or that she knew and couldn't tell him, he would let it go. The idea he'd stumbled across to help track unexpected interactions in the upper atmosphere clearly needed to be pursued.

By the time he got home, however, a theory for the anomalous weather at the border of the Amazon rainforest gave him an idea to pursue for the main task he had set for this sabbatical. The question of micro-gravity would wait.

# CHAPTER ELEVEN

"Bingo," said Tatiana.

"What have you got?" asked Miles.

"I took a clip from the last hacked feed. Told Monitor to find all copies of it."

"Where did you say to search?"

"Everywhere. Monitor found the hacked feed quickly and the original almost as fast. I wanted to find where the hacker stored the video clip between lifting it and inserting it."

"That must have taken a while."

Tatiana glanced at her watch. "Eighteen hours and forty-three minutes."

"And where was it?"

"In an archive of obsolete passwords."

"Is the other video feed there as well?" Miles asked.

"That will take a few minutes to check. But first, I will find who has accessed this area of memory." Tatiana's fingers flew across the keyboard while her eyes stayed glued to the screen. Then she folded her hands together and leaned back. "And now, to identify our hacker." She banged her fist on the desk. "You are wrong, Monitor. The answer is not no one."

"They hid their insertion."

Tatiana stared at the screen. "They hid their insertion

from me. This hacker is too good." Her lips pressed into a tight smile. "But I am better. I will find you, ghost, so watch your back. I'm comin' for you."

Miles turned back to his terminal. "There should be a way to capture a record of who is active online the moment the hacked video is put in place."

"Good idea. You work on that while I go ghost hunting."

*We should stop calling the hacker a ghost. There is a real person intervening in Monitor's systems, disrupting Traffic and now Transit. But why?*

\* \* \*

Brindle's phone vibrated, then announced, "High Park. News Channel seventeen. Alert. High Park. News Channel Seventeen."

"House, turn on channel seventeen," said Brindle. "Phone, alert Rickie and Jainyu. Tell them to tune in to Channel Seventeen. Computer, save my work." *I will have to thank Miles for setting up this alert.* It had been Maria's idea that whoever was causing trouble in High Park might make the problems public.

On the screen, the developer E. D. Graham stood in front of trees with leaves turning brown. He held a small vial in his outstretched hand.

"And this creature is what is killing the trees behind me," said Graham. "How many of these strange creatures are there? And where will they go next?" Graham lowered his arm. "What if they get up to green roofs? What if they wiggle their way into the hydroponic gardens? Our food supply will be threatened. And that tree in front of your yard will turn brown like the ones behind me. I call on Metro to act now. Get this wild space under control before the creatures it generates destroy what we have worked so hard to build." He lifted his arm again. "Look carefully at this destructive insect." The camera focused on the vial, giving a closeup of the squirming insect. "And if you see one of these, call your councillor. Call Metro. Get someone to come and destroy them before they damage our food supply and set back our progress toward net carbon zero emissions."

The camera switched back to the news desk, and Brindle told the House to mute the screen. "Phone, call Rickie and Jainyu." They got an away message from Jainyu, but Rickie's face appeared. "Did you catch the news item?"

"We were pretty sure we got all the insects there were yesterday. Maybe someone released more. Those trees look even worse than yesterday."

"And how did Graham know about them? I don't see him as the type to take a walk in the park."

Rickie glowered, and looked away. "Someone tipped him off, or he is behind the scheme. Either way, Jainyu and I will go back and scour the trees and get the rest of those insects." Rickie turned back. "How did you know about the telecast?"

"I had Miles set up a search to alert me to any media, social or mainstream, about destruction in High Park. I tuned in part way through."

"Thanks Brindle. That was important. I wonder what Graham's role is in all this?"

"Another good question to add to the list of things we do not know."

\*   \*   \*

A buzz from Miles' computer announced an incoming call from Admin Chan. "Monitor, I accept the call." The administrator looked angry.

"Is what Ms. Sutherland said true?"

*Malformed memory circuits! Typical admin. Needs confirmation from a supervisor.* "Jen Sutherland is on top of this issue. It is her initiative, her ability to ponder the larger picture, that gave us this opportunity."

"Interfering with Transit is a major attack. What does Ms. Ricci have planned?"

"The name is Tatiana." She slid her chair over. "I concur with Miles that an alarm on the cam at this site will let us know when the hacker is active. At that moment, we will be able to trace them."

"Make sure you alert the police when the illegal painter is at work."

"Sending cops to arrest the artist is not a good idea." Tatiana leaned back toward the screen. "We need time to trace the hack."

"I did not ask your opinion," said Admin Chan. "I will request no sirens, but I will not risk losing the artist. That person is our only direct connection to the hacker."

"Fine. Expect us to perform a miracle." Tatiana pushed her chair away from the screen.

"I will not have our Transit system interfered with," said Chan. "You and Ms. Ricci will have the system working properly again. Immediately." The administrator ended the call.

*What do you think we are working on night and day?* Miles rubbed the lines between his eyes, tried to let go of the frustration. The administrator was doing her job, pushing to get ahead of these interferences. The trouble was that the people behind the problems kept shifting strategies and upping the stakes. Catching the artist might generate leads, but the police interruption would shorten the time they had to trace the hacker.

\*   \*   \*

In the enclosed consultation room, the only walled space in an otherwise open work area, Miles cued up the record of the man getting into the rogue taxi and the one where he got out. Officer Madison had requested a video conference so that he could demonstrate to the man the police had in custody how they identified him. The man claimed innocence, refused to acknowledge any responsibility. The computer told him he had an incoming video call. Officer

Carol Madison appeared on the screen with a stark white wall behind her.

"Thanks for giving me this time, Mr. Franklin."

"No problem, Officer Madison."

The officer widened the view on her tablet with view screens on both sides. Behind her sat a paunchy, balding white man sitting relaxed in a straight-backed chair, hands folded together on the table. He looked the picture of confidence. Miles found this disturbing. He expected that, innocent or guilty, a man in an interrogation room would be frustrated, angry, worried. This man seemed either supremely confident of not getting pinned with the takeover of the taxi's AI or extremely able to control his emotions.

"This is George Jones," said Officer Madison. "He's a retired teacher. Lives in a condo in the Don Valley. He claims to know nothing about the overriding of a taxi's pilot. I told him you would be able to demonstrate how we found him."

"Certainly. The woman in the taxi told us where she got in. The traffic cams showed you getting out just ahead of her. I will run that video now."

The man looked up from his hands to watch the screen. "Stop there. Focus on the face. Surely, you can see that is not me."

"As you know," said Officer Madison, "you used stage makeup to mask the shape of your nose."

"How would I know that this man disguised himself?"

"If you look closely now," said the officer, "you can see that the patches around the nose are a different colour than the rest of the skin. Also, you did not mask your body shape at all, and we were able to confirm the match through your teachers' union id."

"That identification is two years old. Things change about a body in that time, especially with retirement. And many people would match that body type."

"Not as closely as you might think. And I am sure I can find a more recent body scan to verify. Go on, Miles."

"You can see that you..."

"I can see that man. Please stop identifying me as him."

"Granted," said Madison. "For the moment."

"The man clearly tries to stop Barbara Ann from entering the taxi," said Miles. "That seems to indicate that he hoped the taxi would be unoccupied when it was taken over. That is a point in his favour, I presume."

"Lessens the possibility of a charge of reckless endangerment," said Madison.

"Lucky man," said Jones.

"The man continues to look dismayed as the taxi leaves and then makes a phone call." Miles paused the video. "Officer Madison, I presume you can check the GPS on Mr. Jones' phone and place him at that spot making that call."

"Done. Even have the number of the person he called."

Jones' eyes narrowed. "How many calls were in progress at that spot at that time?"

"Good point," said Madison. "Fifteen. We can check the cams, but I doubt we will find a picture of you that matches any better than this one. Go to where the gentleman in question got in the taxi, Mr. Franklin."

"The taxi company told us where the passenger began his journey. As I run the footage from that cam you can see that the man has a bag in his hand. The bag seems to hold something quite heavy. And I am sure you noticed that when he exited the taxi, he had nothing in his hand."

"You would have to show me the footage again," said Jones.

"Take our word for it," said Madison. "I should tell you that your fingerprints were found in the taxi." She raised her hand to forestall an objection from Jones. "It could have been that you happened to be in that taxi sometime earlier that day, but the evidence is accumulating. Now, if you will excuse me a moment, I need to speak to Mr. Franklin."

Miles waited while the officer took her tablet out of the interrogation room.

"I'm afraid the evidence is circumstantial," said Madison.

"And unless we follow the taxi through the whole trip, we can't prove that Jones did not hand off the bag he brought to someone else. Could someone else have left the device earlier with a set time to become active?"

Miles thought about what he found in the box. "The instructions were already programmed in. The car could only get to the Gardiner Expressway from that one spot. Also, the device was triggered by a phone call, so you can check Jones' phone to see if there is a record of that call."

"That's a help. I already have a warrant for his phone. I'll check before I let him go."

"What about the fake credit card?"

"The taxi company refused to lay a complaint about the fraud. They don't want news to get out that their system accepted a fake. And his phone was clean. If he had a fake card identification there, he erased it."

Miles rubbed the lines between his eyes. As he did, a thought surfaced. "You said you know who he called as the taxi pulled away."

Madison's fingers flicked across the tablet. "Hollingsworth. Martha Hollingsworth."

"That name. It's familiar." Miles tapped his forehead. Where had he heard that name? He snapped his fingers. "That's who started the social media call for protests. Maybe he called to tell her the taxi takeover had begun."

"That connects them, but her social media sites give no clue as to where she lives or works. And calling for a peaceful protest was not enough to get a warrant to dig deeper. Won't be able to until I can make charges stick for George Jones. We can keep an eye out for her in the meantime. Seems like too much of a coincidence for her not to be involved."

Miles nodded slowly, thinking hard. The media posts had not started the moment the taxi was hijacked but when the police stopped it. How had Hollingsworth known that? One more question to answer. "I have to go. We'll keep in touch."

"I'm afraid we will."

# CHAPTER TWELVE

*Two garden problems in one building. This building's manager needs help,* Jainyu thought as he headed from the basement hydroponic garden to the roof of the seventy-storey Metro-managed apartment building. He ran his tongue along the back of his lip, wondering how to get this manager assistance with the plants. It was ridiculous that Metro hired professional gardeners to plant in the spring, but expected building supervisors to handle the upkeep the rest of the summer. As if the person who knew how to manage stair-cleaning robots could automatically watch for pests in the hydroponic area and get the moisture levels right for the plants on the roof.

As soon as he stepped from the elevator, his phone vibrated. "Who is calling?"

"Timur Pachenko," said the phone.

"Answer, audio only."

"What isolated reception-less space have you been hiding in?" Timur demanded.

"A basement hydroponic garden. Just got to the roof."

"By an elevator not connected to any network?"

"I guess the Wi-Fi is out in the elevator as well. I knew it wasn't working in the hydroponic space." Without Wi-Fi surveillance, the water levels had gotten dangerously low, threatening a crop of salad greens that could supply this building for a week. Fortunately, the building manager was diligent if not knowledgeable. A routine check revealed orange lights through the whole complex. Hence, Jainyu's visit to check on the health of the plants while a technician repaired the water system and another worked on restoring Wi-Fi.

Timur took a deep breath, muttered a phrase in Russian. "Apologies. I am angry, but these monstrosities are not your fault."

"The insects?"

"They are not insects. Not properly speaking. They fit no natural genus. Their DNA makes no sense. They are a scrambled construction designed to destroy."

Jainyu stopped, took his phone out of his pocket and turned on the video. Timur paced in and out of view. "They are manufactured?"

"Such a mishmash should not live."

"But they do."

"Meaning the person who created them has a great deal of skill. And time and money. There would have been many failures before they came up with this one that will live months."

"At least, as technological creation, they would not reproduce," said Jainyu.

"Finding who made them is crucial. They are hungry bugs. Destructive and disrupting. And I cannot guarantee that the maker did not build in a way for them to clone themselves."

"Is that possible?" Jainyu asked.

Timur stopped pacing in front of the phone, breathed out slowly looking down toward his feet. "I should not have said that out loud. Forget my words. It is hard carrying secrets around in my brain. I forget when not to speak." His eyes came up and locked on Jainyu. "Promise me you will make certain you have collected them all while I work on discovering who made them."

"A colleague and I are going back to check the area later

today. There was a press conference about them earlier today. Only had one sample, but we're going to make sure more were not released. Any thought where to start looking for the maker?"

"Yes. It is a skillful abomination, and not many have the ability to create such a monster, at least not one that lives more than a few moments. No one will admit to the creation, however, because releasing a creature like this is highly illegal."

"Silence can be bought, however."

Timur seemed to be studying something in the distance. "Follow the money. Sounds like a line from a crime drama net-show, but someone spent a lot of money for a reason. Who released the news the bugs were in the park?"

"A developer I think." His eyes narrowed. "Metro has been totally committed to keeping the park out of the hands of those who build skyscraper housing. What would a developer think to gain?"

"Do you know what the exhibition grounds sold for five years ago?"

Jainyu rolled his eyes. "I get that Metro felt those one storey, cavernous buildings used only a few times a year were a waste of space. But the Royal Agricultural Fair was the only time most people got to see cows and chickens. The fair provided the only exposure to how meat is raised. Now that fair happens north of Barrie, beyond most people's reach."

"I agree. The virtual tours they run in the public floors of the housing complexes on the former grounds give little idea what farming requires. However, the animals at the fair were prettied up, in pristine clean stalls, little like life on the farm. But we are off track. The land sold for two *billion* dollars. What is left of the park is about half that size, but it's the next obvious place to build."

"But there would be a public outcry."

"Not everyone loves green spaces as you do. 'Dangerous new insects run rampant in High Park' is a headline that will grab attention, especially if someone hinted that all the city's trees and even the rooftop gardens would be at risk. Someone invested a lot in these insects. They are not going to quit just because you managed to stumble on the infestation."

"Thanks, Timur. Let me know if you get a lead on who might have made them." Jainyu looked up and realized that the building manager stood three meters away watching him. He waved to acknowledge him. "Duty calls, Timur. An infestation that I expect to be totally natural needs my attention. Thanks again for your work so far." He would have to fill Rickie in as soon as he was done here.

"Keep me informed if you find more."

"Indeed." Jainyu put the phone away and tried to bring his attention back to this rooftop garden and what he expected was a normal June problem. But he couldn't stop picturing those wriggling voracious creatures destroying the habitat of wild birds.

\* \* \*

"Miles, are you free?"

"I'm good," said Tatiana. "Give the man a hand."

Miles glanced over at the junior technician. "What's up, James?"

"I got an alarm from the program we put up to notice anomalies."

Miles rolled his chair across the floor. "What is happening?"

"I'm not sure, but at this subway station, one of the turnstiles is sending out a burst of unrecognized code. Repeatedly, but at odd intervals."

"Show me the code."

Typing in a query, James called up a copy of what the turnstile was sending. "I don't recognize what it is."

"How many times has it done this?"

"Five. No, now it's six."

Miles squinted at the screen. "There is a data recognition section. This looks like an instruction to erase."

"Share your screen," said Tatiana. A moment later, her fist hit the desk. "This is not good. And how is the instruction getting there?" Her fingers raced over the keys.

Miles' computer informed him of an incoming call. "Monitor, I accept the call. Miles here."

"We need you in Transit. Now."

"I bet you do. Before I get there, a turnstile at Spadina station needs to be taken off line. ASAP. My colleague will give you the information on which one."

"A turnstile? What does that have to do with... never mind. Just get up here."

"James, send them the ID of the turnstile."

As he hurried down the hall, Miles summoned an elevator. *I hope this doesn't become a habit.* At least, this time it was empty. When he got to Transit, the video conference screen showed the Spadina station supervisor with seven people behind him, all looking angry, two arguing with other employees. "Have you closed that turnstile?"

"As requested," said the supervisor. "You can explain why in a moment. First, these seven people all claim to be paid up transit users. Each of them tried to enter and were turned back. Their phones no longer show that they are legitimate customers."

"And they all used the same turnstile."

"I'm not sure."

"Check."

The supervisor turned around, managed to quiet the disgruntled group and ask the question. He turned back to the camera quickly. "How did you know? It's the one we were instructed to close."

"Have any of them tried to buy anything?" Miles waited while the supervisor repeated the question to the group. They all shook their heads no. Someone objected that they needed to get on the subway, not buy cigarettes. "Ask for a volunteer to go to the kiosk, use their phone for a purchase while we re-instate the record of their paid-up status one by one."

More grumbling from the group, but one of the would-be passengers put up her hand to volunteer and left the view.

"Invite the first one who had a problem forward," said Miles. A woman came into focus. "We are very sorry for your inconvenience. Please give my colleague Guylaine your name and Metro ID number." Then he crossed his fingers, figuratively, in his mind, not willing to give in to the superstition that such an action would affect the outcome.

Guylaine checked the record. "You are correct. You are paid up." She looked at Miles. "Why doesn't the phone show she's legit?"

Miles sighed with relief. The code burst only affected the information on the phone, not the record in the system. "Supervisor, you can do an override to indicate payment?"

"I can."

"Then, take her to a console and record on her phone that she has paid for this month and next."

"I haven't paid for next month," the woman said.

"It is a compensation for the disruption to your day."

"Are you authorized to do that?" asked the supervisor.

"Given everything, I'm prepared to explain to Administration. Give me a minute, then call the next passenger forward." He heard a man's voice arguing with the supervisor, claiming he was late for an urgent meeting. A couple other people grumbled loudly. *Everything is supposed to be instantaneous now. And work smoothly. These days those are false assumptions.* He called Tatiana. "The code burst erases the record on the phone that the user is a paid-up customer. Only on the phone though."

"And only Transit data?"

"I sent someone to make a purchase at the kiosk, so we'll soon know." Miles noticed a woman walk back into the area with a bottled juice in hand. "She succeeded."

"Good news. Now how did the hacker get through the

turnstile firewall? Bye."

The man who had been blustering stepped up to the video screen. "You. Get me on my way now."

Miles hesitated. He wanted to talk to the woman they sent to make the purchase. But this man was not stepping aside. "I need your name and Metro ID so that my colleague can check your status."

The man muttered his first name, then spelled the last. "No one gets it right, though it is a perfectly common name. But I am not going to have you tell me that I am not..."

"Your status as a paid-up Metro user is confirmed, Sir," said Guylaine.

"Now," said Miles, "we wait for the supervisor to finish with the first person."

"You're at Monitor Central. Fix this from there."

"I cannot," said Miles. "The problem is on your cell phone, and it has firewall protection." *The code burst had to get through that firewall!* One more problem to figure out, but that would wait. He pulled his attention back to the furious man. "The change needs to be done directly, not remotely."

The first woman left the payment console. "You can go over now, and you will be looked after."

Another man stepped tentatively forward. "I have a medical appointment. May I go next?"

"Given you are standing in front of me, yes," said Miles, "but if you would ask the woman who purchased the drink to come after you, I would appreciate it."

A check of the system showed the same paid up status, and this man went to get his phone information reinstated. The woman with a drink bottle in her hand came up to the video camera.

"Why did you want me to buy something?"

Miles took a deep breath, but decided to be open about his concern. "I wanted to make sure that nothing but your transit status had been affected on your phone."

The woman's eyes went wide. She gripped her phone more tightly. "My life is on this phone."

"It is the same for most of us. Run a diagnostic when you get home, but given that you were able to make that purchase, and given that we have a good idea how this happened..." Miles hesitated. All they knew as yet was that a burst of code came from a particular turnstile, not who had hacked the turnstile or how it got through the phone's firewall. "We will keep a record of today's problem, however, so if you discover other issues, be in touch with Monitor's Transit Department, and they will help you out. Now, if you would give my colleague your name and Metro ID, we will get you on your way."

Miles looked over the remaining would-be passengers. News that they were getting a month of free transit had spread, and the compensation seemed to make them less restive. Miles' phone chirped. "Answer."

"Get to that turnstile now," said Tatiana. "I cannot locate any signal going to it, so it must be a device attached to the thing. Get there before the interfering worm can remove the device. We need to examine it."

"If you can handle this Guylaine, I am out of here."

"I'm good. And thanks, Miles. You folks are sure on top of things."

"On my way, Tatiana." As he ended the call, Miles shook his head. He did not feel on top of these issues at all. "Don't hesitate to be in touch, Guylaine, if there are any other issues."

"Enough already."

*More than. But I'm pretty sure we are not done yet.*

\*     \*     \*

Miles flashed his Monitor ID to the security guard and asked which turnstile caused the problem. The supervisor who dealt with the problem joined him there. Miles ran his hand across the smooth top, felt a small spark of electricity. On the side, next to the sensor that checked for up to date payment, was a small device the size of a large watch face.

Touching it, he felt a set of electrical pulses.

"Phone, call Detective Madison." While he waited for the officer to pick up, he tried to identify the pattern of the pulses.

"You think that little thing caused this?" asked the supervisor.

"I don't see anything else different, and my office could not trace any unusual signal coming to this location." Miles' phone chirped.

"What has gone wrong now?" the detective asked.

"A subway turnstile that wipes phone data."

"You are sure making me doubt all the cyber security that I've learned to trust. Do you know how they did it?"

"There is a device attached to the turnstile which, I believe, caused this problem. Can you send an officer to collect it?"

"Good plan. Make sure the chain of evidence is clean. I'll get dispatch to send the nearest officer. Make that two. One can bring you to our lab. The other will take the report from the subway officials. We want to make sure this is on record. When we figure out who did this, we want the charges to stick."

Miles ended the call. Two trips to the police lab in as many days. This was getting to be a habit he could do without. "I know the passengers were all eager to get on their way, but officers may want to speak with them."

"We have their contact information," said the supervisor, "and we recorded the incident. How is the device attached?"

Miles felt around the smooth edge of the device. "Magnet I am guessing. It could be glue, but if someone stood here, applying the substance to the device, holding it in place while it set, other passengers would be anxious to get by them." Miles looked up over his shoulder. There was the surveillance cam. "We know when the device started working. Get your people to review the footage just before that moment. If they look closely, they may see the person placing the device." *Unless it was on a timer. Unless someone activated it remotely.* Miles rubbed the lines between his eyes. The surveillance cam might or might not give them data, but every possible lead needed to be followed.

Two uniformed police arrived. One took the supervisor aside to get his report. The other took pictures of the device. Miles rubbed his fingers together, then pulled gently, sensing the ongoing electrical pulses. The device didn't move. He reached for his pocket knife, pressed the edge of the blade between the device and the turnstile. The device released its grip with a soft pop. The electrical pulses ceased. *Malformed motherboards!* The device had died. Either it only worked when in contact with metal, or whoever installed it programmed in a self-destruct sequence. Looking closely, he found the line where the device opened. Even if the device was dead, he would at least learn how it turned on, and how similar the components were to the box that overrode the taxi pilot.

\*   \*   \*

Tatiana didn't look up when Miles arrived back at the office. James just grunted. Miles looked over his shoulder. "Repairing a firewall?"

"Rebuilding from scratch more like it," said James.

"Which one?

"The one that checks ID when we enter Monitor Central."

"Because that reads phone data." Miles nodded. "Do we know how the code from the device got through the phones' firewalls?"

Tatiana looked around. "No one says a word about what I am going to tell you. Not to anyone. Not a peep. I bet you didn't check which phones those people had?"

"It would make a difference?" asked James.

"And Transit employees did not notice that some people got through that turnstile just fine. The most popular phone right now has a firewall glitch. When certain apps are active, the firewall opens for information to travel both ways. There is a patch, so that if people update their phone systems as they should, they're fine. But most people don't bother. Whoever did this is as current with industry information as I am."

The implications hit Miles like a subway train. Knowing weaknesses increased the ability of an already smart hacker to wreak havoc. "That is bad news."

"Yup." Tatiana handed Miles a piece of paper. "Shred this when you are done. It's a list of known firewall weaknesses. Very confidential. Check it against Monitor's systems for possible entry points. Use your imagination. James and I identified the ones that read phone data. We'll get those." She interlaced her fingers and stretched her arms out, palms forward. "One more question. About the device you found. Same maker as the box in the taxi?"

"Very similar components."

"Good." Tatiana turned back to her screen.

Frustration clenched the muscles of Miles' neck. There was nothing good about anything taking place, only a small relief to think that the two types of devices were made by the same person. He glanced at the list Tatiana gave him. Firewall repairs were urgent given the scope of these attacks, but what about the hacker? And what could be the connection between these intrusions into Metro's systems? He rubbed the lines between his eyes. He had no answers. He went to his station to work out where Tatiana's list intersected with Monitor's systems.

# CHAPTER THIRTEEN

"Fifteen-minute warning," said Darshani.

"You usually let us work past the final bell," a student complained.

"I warned you that I couldn't stay today. I'll have the room open again at seven-thirty Monday morning and should be able to stay late that day." *Though the way things are going, I better not promise.*

The kids groaned but began the process of cleaning up. When they had the room as tidy as an art room ever gets, it was five past the bell. With her backpack already on her shoulder, Darshani locked the door and hurried to the bus stop.

Once the bus came, she calculated how long it would take her to get to the core, added fifteen minutes and texted Amanda her ETA. She pulled out the early twentieth century novel she was currently reading. Her students thought her old fashioned, reading physical books, but in art history classes, she liked to point out that to understand the art of an era, reading books from the period gave a sense of both the norms of a time and the accepted ideas that artists were embodying or pushing against. To illustrate the point, she would project images of famous paintings and read passages from equally famous novels. And physical books felt different from reading on her phone.

Arriving at the subway, she texted again that she seemed to be running right on schedule. This time Amanda answered that she would be waiting on a bench at the Firefighter's Memorial. That made sense. Set back from the road as it was, the seer would not have to watch the stream of pedestrians and cars, would not see all the things that could happen to them.

The ride went smoothly, and before she knew it, it was time to transfer to the University Subway Line. Five minutes later, she climbed up the stairs at Queen's Park station and into the cement parkette studded with statues. The statue to nurses felt inadequate to her, trying to represent the diverse profession with its founder Florence Nightingale. The one that honoured Doctors Without Borders annoyed her. The features of the doctors were generic enough, but the representations of the people they were helping were so clearly not European. As if DWB only worked in the Global South. What about the role they played after the nuclear catastrophe in Norway or the viral outbreak in the Canary Islands when the local health system collapsed, and these volunteers rushed in to fill the gap?

On a stone bench that faced one of the panels listing the names of firefighters lost in the line of duty, Amanda sat with her arms wrapped around her legs and her knees pulled up to her chin. Darshani slipped onto the bench beside her so that her shoulder touched Amanda's. She waited for her colleague and friend to shake off whatever held her attention.

"When you got off the Bloor subway, did you fall on the stairs or have your backpack stolen?"

"Neither. There was a commotion behind me, and when I looked back an older woman had fallen. Others stopped to help her up, so I kept going."

"You got out of the subway ahead of the pack of teenagers then."

"One of them was a former student of mine who made sure I got the right of way."

Amanda loosened her arms and looked over. "I did not see that."

"You can't see everything, dear."

"Thank whatever god there is."

Darshani hesitated. "I am surprised that you saw any of that. I was out of your usual range."

"I was tuned to you, knew approximately where you were thanks to your texts." Amanda stood and stretched. "This place relaxes me. It's about things that happened already. But as I let go of control, the focus on you was strong." A shiver ran through her. "Let's see what we can learn from this half-done graffiti."

Darshani took her arm and chatted about the day, starting with the antics of her Grade Nine class. These kids were strung so tight, so ready for school to be out for the summer, they could hardly pay attention. Then, she described the panicked excuses of two grade eleven students who had taken art as an easy credit to fill some hole in their timetable. As she rattled on, she felt Amanda relax. Her colleague focused on her stories, things that had already happened, keeping her attention off what might be.

Darshani squeezed her hand on Amanda's arm. "Almost there. The wall faces east so we can't see it yet." She felt Amanda tense.

"Somebody is there. There's a line of street cars at a standstill." Amanda stopped. "No, I can see that the rail line is empty." She bit her lower lip. "Police are coming! I think. I'm sure." Amanda hurried forward.

Beside the building, a lanky young man with a mask over his face stood with a paint brush in his hand. *That does look like John-boy,* Darshani thought. She opened her mouth to speak to him, then realized Amanda teetered. She got behind her, supporting both her shoulders.

At that instant, Amanda's phone chirped.

\*     \*     \*

A message flashed across the middle of Miles' computer. Monitor announced an overlap in the data stream coming from the transit cam on College Street. "The hack is live."

"Time to catch our ghost." Tatiana's fingers races across the keyboard, her forehead furled. "Damn they're good. We'd do better with direct access to the surveillance system and the backup feed. We'll have to go upstairs to the main computer room."

Miles summoned an elevator, while Tatiana grabbed her gear. They hurried down the hall just as an elevator door opened.

"Sorry folks," said Tatiana, "unless the twentieth floor is your destination, you're taking a detour."

Three people rolled their eyes and stepped out, but a woman in a trim suit looked her up and down. "What authorization?"

"You look smarter than your question." Tatiana grabbed the woman's elbow and pulled her out of the elevator, motioning for Miles to enter. As the door closed, she laid out precisely what she needed Miles to do. Then, she reached into a pocket of her pack and handed him a set of earphones. "We'll keep in touch by computer voice link. We'll have to hurry as I assume police are already on the way."

"That is Admin Chan's plan. Arresting the painter is a visible, concrete, action."

"As if the hacker isn't more important." At the guarded door to Monitor's main installation, Tatiana stepped in front of the scanner. The light above flashed green. She opened the door as Miles stepped in front of the scanner. When the signal flashed yellow, one of the guards moved forward.

Tatiana whirled around. "We don't have time. Have you ever seen a green light before? No? It means you let me in and my stuff and whatever else I need. I need him."

The other guard motioned them forward. "New guy. Following normal protocol."

"Teach him the difference between normal and now."

Inside, Tatiana headed to a surveillance work station, and Miles went to the backup for Transit. He called up the feed. A man with the same build, same tattoos and jacket was at work. "I see the artist," he told Tatiana.

"I've got the trace started."

The artist turned his head, staring up toward the camera, lips moving. "Tatiana, they might be aware of us."

"That means I'm getting close."

Tatiana's comment about getting close triggered the realization that Amanda and Darshani would be nearby. Miles told his phone to call Amanda. *Pick up! You don't want to be in the middle of this arrest!*

\*     \*     \*

Reaching into her pocket, Amanda handed her phone to Darshani. "You answer. I need to stay focused."

"Phone, answer," said Darshani.

"Where's Amanda?" Miles asked. "You can't go to the site right now."

"Hello to you too Miles, but we are there."

"Police are on the way. Don't land right in the middle. I've got to go."

A black car pulled up beside Darshani pointing the wrong way. There weren't supposed to be cars on College Street at all. A police officer threw open the door.

Two more police cars came from the east. Feet pounded the sidewalk beside the building. *We'll try not to,* Darshani thought as officers swarmed by her. She shoved Amanda's phone in her pocket. Amanda leaned against Darshani for support. A moment later, two officers led the painter towards one of the police cars. As they yanked his hands behind him to put on electronic cuffs, John-boy's face turned toward her. Fire sparked in his eyes.

"What are you doing here? You set me up?"

"Me? What do you mean?" Darshani thought fast. "If you don't have your licence with you, I can vouch for you."

He spat on the ground. "Like hell."

Amanda swayed, and Darshani put her arm around her to steady her. "What's wrong?" Amanda just groaned.

The police pulled John-boy toward the nearest car, but he looked back for an instant with a look of pure hate. One of the officers approached, mini-tablet in hand. "You know the vandal?"

"Pardon?" asked Darshani.

"He spoke to you. You must know him."

Amanda groaned again. "My friend isn't well," Darshani said. "I need to attend to her. We'll be on the church step there." She started to inch Amanda away.

"Don't leave until I get your contact information."

"Yes, Officer. Now let me get my friend to a place she can sit." Darshani heard Amanda's phone chirp again. "Okay, Amanda. Just a few steps this way. We can sit over here. Just one foot in front of the other." She wasn't sure Amanda was listening, but she responded to the gentle pressure on her arm. Helping Amanda sit on the step, Darshani sat just in front, took her hand and rubbed the palm. "Look at your hand. Feel my fingers. See my fingers."

"You can stop now, Dar. I'm fine." A shiver ran down her back. "The artist, he isn't evil, but he is deeply angry. He's furious at you for being here and for having his work stopped. He thought about destroying your art if he could find it, about getting back to finish this piece, starting another. But then, strained against the handcuffs, he realized he was helpless for the moment. All he could do was spit. I feel sorry for him."

"The number of police did feel like overkill."

"Who called?"

"Miles. He wanted to make sure we were not caught in the middle." She handed Amanda her phone.

"Small chance of that." Amanda held the cell phone in

the palm of her hand, frowning down at it.

"Here comes the officer."

The man studied them both in turn, then turned his attention to Darshani. "How does the vandal know you?"

"I teach high school art. I figured that one of the best ways to get kids interested in art was to teach graffiti. I have a licence and know quite a few in the community, at least a little." Darshani pulled up her business card on her phone. "I can send you this."

"Who is the man we arrested?"

"Goes by John-boy. I have only met him a few times. He's part of the legitimate west end club called 'Dragon Flight.' This is outside of his usual territory."

"Show your card again." When she lifted her phone, the officer transferred the image to his tablet. "These the best numbers to get you at?" When she nodded, he turned to Amanda. "You okay Ms.?"

"A massive headache that isn't going away anytime soon," said Amanda.

"That is what made you stop here?"

"Pretty much," said Amanda, the heels of both hands on her temples.

He reached his hand out toward Amanda. "I'll need your contact info too."

"Sure." Amanda pulled up the *contactme* screen on her phone and handed it over.

"What are you doing in the core?"

"It's a good place to meet my friend."

The officer looked back over his shoulder as the car with John-boy pulled away. The officer taking pictures turned from the wall and gestured for him to come. "Fine. I've your info." He studied Amanda. "You sure you're all right?"

"My friend will look after me."

As the officer walked away, Darshani sighed. Amanda put an unsteady hand on her shoulder.

"He didn't know what to do with us," Amanda said. "I think we looked too respectable to be part of a street art gang."

"Maybe he wants to take you out then."

Amanda gave a wan smile. "Thanks for that, but I don't think so."

"They're leaving," said Darshani. "Do you feel up to getting close to the painting?"

"That's what we are here for." Amanda pushed herself to her feet. At the wall, she pressed her hand against the still wet paint of a dog's head. "The streetcars are all stopped. One rear ends the other. No. I see her." Amanda's voice trembled.

"See who?"

"Call Miles. Tell him." Amanda ran her tongue across her lips, pressed her eyes closed. "She's in Monitor Central. She looks furious. She's going to break something. Or go to the window and get control of her anger. That's it. She'll be looking at the top of the new ROM building. Check how high that is. Tell him she's on that floor looking east."

"Who is?"

"The hacker. Tell him! God, she is raging."

"How do you know that is now?"

"She's planning, dreaming of what to do next. I can see all the... No! Fire!" Amanda sucked in a breath.

"What is wrong?" Darshani put her hands on Amanda's shoulders, felt her tremble. Then, the seer went weak. Darshani just barely had time to catch her and ease her to the ground. "Amanda? Phone, call Miles. It's okay, Amanda. You'll be okay." Her voice wavered. Nothing felt okay. And where was the fire Amanda saw?

"Yes Dar," said Miles.

"I know you're in the middle of shit. But, it's her, the hacker. She's in your building. At an east window looking over top of the ROM. The new building. It's eleven stories high, I think. That would put her on the twelfth floor." Miles started to object. "Amanda saw, that's how I know. But she's fainted. Find the woman. I have to look after Amanda." Darshani massaged Amanda's hand. "Amanda, wake up dear. Miles will find her."

\*   \*   \*

Watching the backup feed, Miles could see the painter working. No sign of the ghost. Miles asked Monitor how many were watching the feed. The reply came back that no one observed that particular feed. "Tatiana, I think they're watching but blocking access to who is viewing it. Their cover also hides the fact that I'm watching."

Tatiana swore. "They're in this building, damn them. I'm sending you code so we can triangulate."

A streetcar rumbled by on one screen, while Darshani and Amanda stepped into view on the other. Furiously typing, he followed Tatiana's instructions. Glancing at the real time images, a police car pulled up beside his friends. He chewed his lip. *They're right in the middle of this.* Hitting enter to start Tatiana's trace program, he watched as another police car pulled up. He felt like he was watching a movie, as powerless as a person sitting in a theatre to make a difference.

"The hack's been pulled," said Tatiana. "I'll be at your station shortly."

Miles turned his full attention back to the terminal. In the corner of the image, a spider blinked into sight and then disappeared. "Check your terminal first, Tatiana. Now that the hack has stopped, I see a trace of something."

"Got it. Now to trace it."

Again, the spider appeared and disappeared. Opening a back door portal, he nudged the system, trying to trace the watcher while Darshani led a wavering Amanda out of view. Police took pictures of the half-finished image. Every few seconds, the spider blinked into sight and out again. As the police left, he watched Amanda approach the wall, waver and faint. *Amanda!*

His phone vibrated. *Darshani?* "Phone, answer. Yes, Dar?" Her message threw him. Amanda had seen a woman watching the arrest. When Darshani disconnected, he rubbed his forehead. He couldn't leave this station, but he could not ignore the message either.

*I could ask Jen.* But how would he explain? No other thought came. *I guess I'll be telling her I think she's Gifted and hope she believes me.* "Phone, call Jennifer Sutherland." Jen picked up immediately. "Tatiana and I are tracing the hacker, so I need a favour. ASAP."

"What do you need?"

"I need you to go to the twelfth floor, the Accounting Department and take pictures of any woman looking out a window facing east."

"I don't get it?"

"The hacker is here, in this building, was watching the real-time feed. I know it sounds completely crazy, but I'll explain when you bring me the pictures."

He realized that the blinking spider had not reappeared. "Oh crap."

"No need to swear at me."

"Not you Jen. Can you just do it?"

"Raja can cover. But..."

"Just go Jen. I've a problem here, but I owe you."

"For what exactly you'll have to explain."

Miles watched Darshani help Amanda to her feet as pedestrian traffic got back to normal. The first few people looked at the half-finished image on the wall, then others ignored it. A moment later, Tatiana pulled in a chair beside him.

"What did you see?" Tatiana asked.

"Somebody masked who viewed the real time feed. Monitor couldn't tell that I was watching. Then, as soon as the hack ended, the ghost appeared."

"Back it up." Tatiana waited, zoomed in on the spider, then hit inspect. She leaned forward to study the code. "Nothing. Nada. Zip. Damn this ghost is good." Tatiana stood. "We needed more time. I hate relying on the artist to give up their accomplice, especially since we're hoping they'll be disloyal and a coward, but that's the choice administration made. I'll make our report directly to Admin Chan. That'll give me a chance to complain that we were not given enough time. I'll be back in your workspace within twenty minutes." She grabbed her backpack and left.

Miles smiled at her back, imagining the diatribe. Admin Chan's calm would just raise the heat for Tatiana. The smile faded though as he thought about explaining to Jen how he knew that someone on the twelfth floor mattered to this mess. If her photo allowed him to identify the hacker, he could put a trace on her login. But unless that trace gave concrete evidence, there would be no way he could use the identification.

# CHAPTER FOURTEEN

Back in his department, Miles sat at his desk, staring at the screen, waiting for Jen. He tried to figure out how to explain why he asked her to photograph a woman in accounting looking toward the new ROM building. He got up when she walked in and led her to the consultation cubicle.

"What did you find, Jen?" He raised his hand to forestall her questions. "I'll explain why I asked in a minute."

"I felt like I was looking for the last blue whale in the North Atlantic. Pretty well everyone was focused on their screens as if they had a deadline of some kind. Two guys were standing near a window looking at a tablet. You said a woman but I got a picture of them. A woman walked back from a restroom break still drying her hands, and then one more. This one matched your description, standing with her back to the room staring out the window." Jen folded her arms. "Now explain."

"Are you free for dinner?"

"That was to get me on a date? Come on."

"No, I just want to make sure you are free to meet a couple friends of mine who can help you to believe what I am about to tell you."

"No promises. Explain first."

"I have a friend who is connected to the street art

community. I think I mentioned I would show her the work and the disguised artist. She made a guess about who did the graffiti, but wanted to see the new piece for herself. But she brought along another friend, and it happens that they got there just as the police did."

"Did she know the artist?"

"Yes. But that matters less now that he's been arrested. It's the other woman, Amanda, that matters. At the first site, she sensed that there is a bigger plan behind these paintings."

"Working with an expert hacker suggests that. How do you get from there to a woman looking east?"

"Amanda has a way of sensing what might happen." Miles took a deep breath, forced his shoulders down, calmed his voice. "Amanda is a seer. She can sometimes sense the possible outcomes in a moment of decision. At the first site, she caught images of a city without car pilots."

"That's ridiculous."

"Getting rid of car pilots or seeing possible futures?"

"Both. No one sees the future. That's ancient carnival trickster stuff."

"A Gifted theoretical physicist who is part of our group thinks she's sensing what is happening at the quantum level, perceiving the divergent possibilities that become real for an instant. Quantum physics proposes that this happens."

"Theoretical physics is beyond me, but what you are saying sounds wrong. If the best minds can't describe what is happening at the quantum level, how does your friend see it?"

"That's her Gift. There are many kinds of them. Some of us sense emotions. Some sense weather better than any meteorologist. Julie hears better than a bat. Amanda senses divergent timelines."

"You've got to be kidding. You sent me to hunt down a woman at a window because your friend saw her in her head."

"Once you've met Amanda it isn't so hard to believe. Which is why I offered supper. You need to meet her to understand her Gift."

"Wait a minute. You said that your friend was on College Street? How did she see this woman on the twelfth floor?"

"A good question. I know the hacker had a bug on the cam and kept watching even after the art attacker was arrested. Because the hacker watched the arrest, still watched when Amanda and Darshani studied the partially finished piece, Amanda could sense her."

"I'm supposed to believe this magic trick?"

"It's a Gift, not magic, a kind of affinity or an extra sense. You do know that there are more than five senses?"

"High School biology. Had to know at least seven or eight. Forget the proper words for them. They had to do with perceiving heat, velocity, maybe position in space. Nothing about quantum divergence."

"For some of us, one of these senses becomes intense so that we can perceive the world very differently than most people. There are others with an affinity to some kinds of creatures, some things." Miles hesitated a moment. "You have an incredible spatial sense. I think you have a Gift."

"It's been a help, but it isn't that different from anyone else."

Miles shook his head. "Once it occurred to you that the graffiti attacker might choose another location, how long until you had a list of places that would work?"

"Maybe, ten minutes."

"And how long until you mapped the best route to check all the locations?"

"Five for those east of here. Longer to figure out how to check the ones to the west."

"Those tasks would have taken me an hour at least."

"But I missed the important one."

Again, Miles shook his head. "The first task you set yourself was within the scope of your work, traffic. Eventually, your brain added the question of transit routes, and then it took...?"

"The thought just appeared." Jen rolled her eyes. "Don't make such a big deal. It's just how I am."

"You see spatial arrangements in your head. Amanda sees alternative timelines. The ability to see into complex computer operations is what I do. That's why you came to me when you found the video had been messed with." Miles felt his forehead tense up, knew that lines had formed between his eyes as they always did when he worried. He rubbed the place with two fingers of his left hand. "Just come for dinner and meet a couple of my friends. Giovanni makes great Italian food."

"I'm vegan. But you already knew that."

Miles shook his head. "I read computers. People I find hard. On the other hand, Brindle reads worry and would have known as soon as you arrived that there might be a problem. I'll tell Giovanni, and he'll figure out what to make." Miles looked into Jen's eyes, hoped he'd convinced her to suspend disbelief, meet Brindle and Amanda. "I need to run that photo you took, identify the woman, and get a trace on her login. Agree to come, and we'll have time to talk this evening."

Jen studied his face. "You're serious. You really think that your friend saw the hacker." She shrugged. "I'll come." She pointed a finger at his chest. "But only because my Friday dinner partner bailed on me. Some stomach bug that you'd think we'd have gotten rid of by now."

"Sorry about your friend, but thank you for giving me the chance to convince you."

"I haven't agreed to be convinced, just to eat."

"That's all I can ask for. I will meet you in the front lobby just after five." Miles felt Jen's uncertainty and a hint of anger. She still looked worried that he had made this all up. If Brindle couldn't convince her, that anger would stay, making working with her on this problem more difficult. *One step at a time.* Right now, he needed to focus, run the photo, and get a carefully hidden trace on the woman's login.

Comparing the body scans of the people who worked in accounting against the picture Jen took brought up an instant match. Martha Hollingsworth. Same name as the person who started the social media blast calling for a protest against AI driven cars. Same name as the call from the man who initiated the taxi hijacking. Unless there were two people by that name, the connections were starting to fall into place. If she was the hacker who covered up the graffiti artist at work, she could have used the same technique to spy on the Traffic Department and know when the taxi had been stopped. That would explain the timing of the social media calls for protests. A trace on her login should give him the chance to prove she was the hacker.

\* \* \*

Maria set the heavy shopping basket on the floor. As usual, she picked up more than just the milk and bananas that she stepped into the grocery store for. She looked at what she put in the basket. The peanut butter could be put back, but with two sets of grandchildren spending Saturday nights with her and Juan, it was best to keep supplied. *I will text Juan to wait at the station to walk home with me and help me carry these.* As one of the express self-checkout stations became free and a mother and child hurried up to it, Maria pushed the basket forward with her foot. Given the length of the line, many people had forgotten items that they simply must pick up on the way home.

A burning blast of anger hit her. "Dios mio!"

"Sorry," said the woman in front of her. "Did I bang into you?"

"Oh no," said Maria. "I just thought of something."

"I can hold your spot in line if you need to run to get it."

Maria tried to smile at the woman. "Very kind of you. But not that sort of something." The heat of anger raged like a fire, and it was near. Looking around the busy store, two men in the next line over caught her eye. One scowled, and the other looked shocked. Moving up one spot in her line, she listened to their conversation.

"A stiff fine," said the man who scowled. "All she did was read a novel on her phone. Every subway driver reads. Such a boring job sitting in the front of a train while the AI pilot does all the work."

"Aren't the drivers there for safety?" asked the other.

"Eight years she has been doing this job. Never in all those years has the AI made a mistake. But all of a sudden, the bosses have launched a totally unnecessary hunt for people breaking the rules. It's a cash grab. Nothing but a cash grab. The city can't raise taxes because people would complain, but they can issue fines to ordinary working people. And Monitor will be praised for raising safety standards."

"That's what we get for letting machines take over. Your wife wouldn't be bored if she drove the train."

Maria felt the heat of anger increase.

"She'd be a terrible driver. She's always in a hurry. No, she's better just being there to get the train to the next station if the AI quits. Problem is how to cope with the boredom."

"She's never tempted to turn off the AI and drive the subway herself?"

"God no! The fine for that is more than a month's mortgage payment. Plus, two weeks off without pay. It's just this shitty attempt from that all-seeing Monitor to make sure everybody has two eyes on the track and all their attention admiring how good a job the AI is doing."

"Excuse me." Someone tapped Maria on the shoulder. "There is a check out free."

"Oh. Thank you." Maria lifted the basket and slowly walked toward the machine. The anger lost some of its energy but remained like a hot coal in her chest. She glanced over at the next line. The scowling man had put his items on the counter, and the other had walked away. She scanned her items and balanced the weight between the two cloth bags.

Miles said that there was tighter oversight of all Monitor's systems. It felt wrong, though, that ordinary people were being penalized when the real problem was the hacker disrupting the systems. But as she left the store, walking past a dozing security guard, she was tempted to trip over the woman's foot just to wake her up. As she rode down the escalator to the subway, it occurred to her that she would rather know that the driver of every train and bus stayed alert to the possibility of something going wrong. *Maybe we are getting lazy, trusting the machines to do the hard work.* As her train pulled in, she looked at the cab. The driver sat up straight and scanned the platform just as required. Stepping on board, she relaxed. Now, to text Juan and make sure he waited to help carry these groceries home.

\*　　\*　　\*

When Rickie got to High Park, Jainyu already had birds at work. "Hey bird man, do you think that your friends missed these the first time, that the bugs hatched overnight, or someone released more?"

"With the crew we had, I don't think they missed any."

Rickie laid his hand on the trunk of the nearest tree. Leaves in the canopy above swayed, brushing against each other with a gentle swishing sound. "You will be all right my friend," he whispered. "I promise."

"Not an easy promise to keep if these bugs continue to arrive," said Jainyu.

"We're just going to have to keep checking up on these trees until they stop coming."

"Given they are manufactured, natural reproduction is not possible." Jainyu put out his hand and a nuthatch landed with another insect, exactly the same as the others, in its beak. He did not mention, even to this close colleague, the possibility of cloning.

"So, someone released more."

"Seems most likely, though I can't imagine they are easy to produce."

"Once they have the pattern," said Rickie, "the hard part is done."

Quick footsteps on the path and a jogger came around the bend. He stopped, breathing heavily. "Hey, you have trained birds. What are they doing?"

Rickie blinked, opened his mouth, and closed it. *How do we explain?*

"Catching a type of harmful insect," said Jainyu. "Knowing the harm that pesticides can do to beneficial insects, using nature's control mechanism seems a logical choice."

"How do you get them to only bring you the harmful insects?" the jogger asked.

"A sample. Birds have incredible eyesight, you know."

"I did not know that. But good on you. Make sure you get them all. I love this park." The man stretched his right leg, then his left and jogged north.

"Trained birds?" asked Rickie.

"He suggested the idea. Should I have corrected him and said that I have a mental connection so that any bird will come when I call?"

"I just hope he doesn't talk about it too much, or Metro Green Spaces will be getting calls to loan out its trained flocks."

Jainyu smiled, head cocked to one side. "At which point, I will say that I was sure the man joked, and I simply went along with it."

"Given that is a more logical explanation, I am sure it will fly." Rickie looked up into the canopy. "Although explaining how we managed to catch the insects might be a problem."

"I think we've got them. The nuthatches have left, and the woodpeckers are dispersing."

"We have to expect that there will be more."

Jainyu closed his eyes. "I will forgo my weekly trip to Rattlesnake Point and come here tomorrow. Again on Sunday."

"I'd come on your behalf, but I would not do much good."

"Stick with your gardens. I'll come to summon the trained bird army."

Rickie laid a hand on the nearest tree, thinking healing thoughts. He looked at Jainyu. "You know, it is not such a bad idea."

"What idea?"

"Training birds. Not wild birds, but budgies or cockatiels for example. Have them live in a rooftop garden, take them to a hydroponics facility. They'd save Metro a ton in pesticides."

"Confining birds I am not in favour of."

"Those species are already living in confinement. This would open up their world."

"You aren't serious?" Jainyu studied Rickie's face. "You are serious. I refuse to be part of such a thing."

"Not you. It would have to be someone who isn't Gifted with connection, someone who just understands how you train a bird. Otherwise, it wouldn't be a scalable project."

Jainyu waved the back of his hand at Rickie. "Enough. Let's get these bugs dead."

# CHAPTER FIFTEEN

"Have you been to High Park lately?" Miles asked Jen. They agreed not to talk about the graffiti events while on public transit. Too many people listening on the crowded subway train. Listening ears also limited the stories about other Gifted that he could tell. It would be a long ride if they didn't find something to talk about.

"I ride through regularly, but I'd rather get out of town when I have a chance."

"It's still a lovely green space."

"No fields. No streams." Jen shook her head. "I still find it hard to believe that the city could channel the streams that once fed the park into underground conduits."

"Managed that, but still can't solve the flooding of the Don Valley Expressway. Filling in the gullies and ravines, building in all the green spaces just made that problem worse." Miles rubbed his forehead. "Sorry, that's a pet peeve of mine."

"Mine too as it's my department that has to get the cars out of there when it happens."

"You must have to go a long way to find wild places."

"Most Saturdays, if the weather is at all decent, I put my bike on the commuter train and head north. If I get off at the Holland Marsh, there are acres of vegetables and a trail up beside the Nottawasaga River. Sometimes I go to the last stop beyond Barrie. Terrain is hilly and forested out there. A challenging ride but beautiful."

"So, you're not a city girl?"

"Toronto downtown born and bred. Still live near where I grew up with my mom and gramma. They still live in the first house my grandparents bought."

"Your dad?"

"Is Anishinaabe. Couldn't handle living in the core. He worked as a wilderness tour guide, mostly in the Arctic, so he'd be gone for months. Coming home to the core when he had time off, he found hard. No open spaces. Crowds. Cars and noise. Eventually, he built a house on his reserve north of Wiarton and stopped coming to Metro. I'd visit spring and fall for weekends, Christmas for longer. He taught me to snowshoe and canoe, showed me how to set up a camp and take it down without leaving a trace. I can't imagine not living in the city, but I still escape when I can."

"How did your parents meet? They sound very different."

"University. Mom found him fascinating. She enjoyed weekends away with him. But when he found the asphalt and concrete too much, she could not imagine leaving Metro. They still get along okay, and there were never fights. They just don't live in the same world."

"The world your dad loves is getting smaller."

"Don't I know it. You should hear him on that topic. He's one of the oldest guides still working in the north. I can't imagine him ever giving it up."

"Have you been to the Arctic?"

"Three summers when I was in university," Jen said. "Dad got me hired on. I had the time of my life. The night sky in late April astonished me. And the long days were amazing. But summer work is not enough to pay for life in Metro. Now, I content myself with visits to him when he comes home to what he considers the south."

"Your father is not quite a man of this time."

"He's got some pretty intense ideas. Visiting him is like

leaving the world where I work for a different planet. Mom hasn't even tried. They talk via computer video chats, but they haven't seen each other in person for ten years. She can't handle the gravel road that leads to his place or the lack of people. And he can't deal with the lack of green in the core."

"Aren't they divorced?"

"Separated. Neither has ever hooked up with anyone else, so the expense of a divorce never seemed worth it. Strange family dynamic I know."

"That's okay. Family takes a lot of different shapes. My relatives in Jamaica can't believe what has become the norm here." Miles smiled as he remembered the uncle who railed against children who lived more than three hours from their parents.

"Mom never minds when I take off to see him. Clear nights at his place the sky is beautiful. Not like the far north, but still so different from the city. Have you been north?"

"Never been north of Barrie except for one cottage stay in the Muskokas. Big trips were and still are back to Jamaica to catch up with family. Night sky over the ocean is pretty spectacular."

"Stars are what I miss most in the city. There's a farm family I got to know. During spring planting and then harvest, I spend a few weekends with them helping with the work. The rhythm is so totally different. The nights are amazing. And they always send me home with a great stock of veggies."

"Nice arrangement. I think you'd like Rickie. He's got a real green thumb. It's his Gift." Miles noticed Jen stiffen up. Referring to Rickie's Gift brought them back to the reason he talked her into coming to the Houses for supper. He shifted away from that topic. "Like you, he doesn't like how much of the park was taken away, so he lives in Scarborough but works on our garden as well."

"You have a yard where you live then?"

"We have both sides of a duplex, so yes."

"Such a luxury. All I have is a balcony, and what I can grow in pots." Jen shrugged.

"Next stop is the one we want."

Jen swung her backpack over her shoulder and got her bike out of the rack. Her deft manoeuvring onto the subway platform and up the stairs to the road impressed Miles. "Cycling is your preferred form of transport I see."

"Except in the snow." Jen hesitated. "A question?"

"Sure." Miles looked at her profile, watched as she ran her fingers through her hair.

"Did you figure out who I took a picture of?"

"Yes. A senior accountant. Martha Hollingsworth. Someone with the same name started the social media call to protest AIs after the first rogue taxi. I'm hoping the detective working on the case can figure out if it is the same person."

"Did you talk to her?"

"I put a trace on her computer. This is a carefully planned operation with computer hacks out of proportion with the actions they are hiding. No sense tipping her off until we have proof. Here's our street." Jen said nothing, and Miles wondered what she was thinking. "And that's our house."

Jen cocked her head. "Nice ground cover. No lawn mowing for you folks."

"There is a bit in the back, but a push mower does the job."

"The garden is lovely. Is that basil?"

"Enough that we won't buy any. Told you Rickie has a Gift with plants."

"One that isn't quite natural."

"A different kind of natural." Miles hesitated. "As long as you are still willing to work with me after tonight, anything else you conclude will be a bonus. We can park your bike around back out of sight."

"Not just out front? Couldn't your friend see if it would

be stolen?"

Opening the gate to the back, Miles decided to ignore the bait. "It's an expensive bike. And I'd hate to have you endure the trip back on transit."

Jen bit her lip. "Sorry for the comment. I'll be nice to Amanda when I meet her. Guess I'm being defensive because I just don't know what I will believe when I head home."

\*   \*   \*

Looking through the open doorway into Darshani's room, Samantha shook her head. Sketch books were piled on the dresser. A paint splattered cabinet with drawers was crowded in between the bed and the cupboard. An easel stood in a corner with the beginnings of a street scene, and Darshani sprawled on the bed with a tablet and laptop in front of her.

"Hey Sam. What have you got there?"

Samantha lifted the bottle in her hand. "Diet pills."

"You carried twins. Of course, you are rounder than you were. And chasing them doesn't really count as exercise. You've a lovely shape."

"What? No. I'm fine."

"You aren't bringing them for me." Darshani frowned.

"No, mate," Samantha said in a hurry. Darshani was sensitive about her well-rounded shape. "I didn't bring them because they are diet pills. They're just the most accessible form of chromium picolate."

"And why are you interested in Chromium pico something?"

"Because it was the one unusual ingredient in the paint sample you found."

Darshani sat up on the bed. "Diet pills in paint. To make it thin?"

Samantha laughed. "Chemist I consulted said it's used in commercial grade metal paint. Improves rust resistance.

Enhances lustre. And it increases the reflectivity index of the paint."

"Now that's interesting. I'd like to see how much the compound changes the paint. How much gets added?"

"There was quite a bit in the sample. Three times as much as would be in commercial metal paint."

"So, John-Boy made it himself. I wonder if he always uses this mixture?" Darshani went to her paint cabinet. "I could try to find a painting of his and scrape off a sample, though I hate to disturb a finished piece." She pulled out a large tube of red paint. "Let's experiment."

"We'll have to crush them. You've a mortar and pestle, or we head for my workroom?"

"No South Asian kitchen would be without." Darshani gathered a couple different brushes, and the two descended to the kitchen where she pulverized a small pile of the pills. As she mixed them into a large glob of red paint, she whistled at the result. "It shifts the surface look a lot. Doesn't change the tone, but the texture of the colour feels quite different. Let's see what it looks like on a wall."

"Outside on the brick?"

"I'm thinking the concrete foundation. We'd need more paint to cover brick. We'll try it at the back of the house. Out of sight. We can always scrape it off later." Darshani smiled. "Who would complain? But this is an important experiment."

"Just don't tell my girls we painted the house wall. They'll claim they have an important experiment to make with crayons and markers on the wall of their bedroom."

"Good thing they are out of the way then for our rule breaking."

Slipping out back, Samantha felt like a teenager trying an illicit experience rather than a scientist testing a theory. Her heart raced, and she looked around to see who watched, then tapped her forehead. *This is an experiment,* she told herself.

Choosing a place in the sun, Darshani sat on the ground

and with deft strokes created an image of a ball cap with the regular paint. Then, she shifted to the treated paint and created a matching image. "What do you think?" she asked, leaning away from the wall.

"The colour is the same, technically, but they look different."

"I liked the feel of the paint going on," said Darshani. "The quality of the colour really does change. Do we wait for it to dry?"

"Don't think so," said Sam. "Cars stopped on the spot when your John-Boy finished."

Darshani got out her phone. "Phone, camera mode. I'll grab a pic to show Miles the comparison." She touched the screen and frowned. Stretching the phone to its maximum size, she touched the screen again. "That's weird."

"The image is different on the phone?"

"I keep trying to centre the image between the two caps, but the camera keeps moving the focus to the one with the modified paint."

"Better tell Miles. Might be part of the reason the image could confuse the car pilots."

"A fascinating effect," said Darshani. "In the street scene I'm working on, I could use this technique to draw certain objects out of the background." Darshani dipped her brush in the paint and studied the colour on the bristles.

Sam smiled. "Send me that pic. You experiment. I'll call Miles."

\* \* \*

"I'm sorry Rickie didn't drop in this evening," said Brindle. "I think you'd have a lot to talk about."

Jen laughed. "I manage a decent balcony garden, and do what I am told when I stay at the farm."

"We also are good at doing what we are told," said Giovanni, "at least as far as the garden goes. We water and weed when Rickie tells us to."

"As if you are good at doing what you are told," said Amanda. "You're too busy telling the rest of us what we need to do."

"For your own health," said Giovanni.

When Miles' phone beeped, he pulled it out of his pocket. "Sorry. I set it to vibrate. A beep means urgent. Phone answer. Hi Sam. What can I do for you?"

"I've talked to Darshani, and we've a picture to share," said Samantha. "You'll want video for this. Oh sorry. You have company. "

"This is a colleague from work," said Miles. "You can go ahead."

"Right-o."

A picture of two red ball caps came up on Miles' phone. "Baseball?"

"The paint the graffiti artist used has a special additive. It's in the cap that is in the centre of the picture."

Miles looked down at the phone, frowning, trying to figure out what this meant. "You recreated the formula?"

"Not precisely, but enough to show that an electronic camera sees the two differently."

"Can I see?" Jen moved the phone so she could get a good look. "The only difference is that one is more centred and clearer."

"On the dot. Camera couldn't take its focus off the modified paint."

"That might affect how the car pilots interpret the image," said Jen.

"Thanks Sam," said Miles. "This gives us part of the explanation."

"Okay. Gotta get the girls ready for bed. By the way, Brindle, they are asking when you are coming out our way. They say it has been forever since they hugged you."

Brindle smiled. "Assure them I will come soon."

"On my way then." The phone went dark.

"I should probably be heading out as well." Jen turned to Amanda. "Will I have a safe ride home?"

Amanda shrugged. "If we were riding together, I'd see an accident coming just before it happened, maybe giving you time to react if I spoke up fast enough. And if you heeded my warning. And made the right decision. I see divergence as it develops."

"Except today." Jen laid her palms on the table.

Taking a deep breath, Amanda looked down at her folded hands. "Earlier in the day, because I knew Darshani's route and focused on her, I saw what might have happened when she got off the subway. This was similar. The woman was using surveillance to look at the same thing Darshani and I were. Her anger focused her whole attention on that spot. The choices that flew through her mind were bizarre. She chose to back away, to take time to think." Amanda looked up at Jen. "I am glad you helped figure out who she is."

"Miles will have to prove that this Martha Hollingsworth is involved. My picture based on your..." Jen ran her tongue across her teeth. "Based on what you sensed doesn't count for anything."

"But the fact that Miles could put a trace on her computer login makes you feel a bit more confident," said Brindle. "You want to stop these interferences."

Jen shrugged. "The artist has been arrested. Feels like a good step." She got up. "Thank you for a great dinner Giovanni."

"Come again," said Giovanni. "You have a good appreciation for my cooking."

"I'll see you out." Miles led the way to the back yard. "So? What do you think of the company I keep?"

"Nice people. Brindle is passionate. Giovanni seems so Italian I can't believe he's fourth generation Torontonian. And Amanda is nice, though intense."

Miles' mouth quirked into half a smile. "And?"

"I don't know. I can see that they believe they have senses that other people don't, but I am not sure that I accept their belief."

"Or mine."

Jen sighed. "You've always seemed quirky, in a good way. And a magician around computers. The idea that you actually have a Gift seems weirdly believable."

"We are good going forward?"

"If your trace on Hollingsworth gets us an advantage, we're fine." Jen rubbed her shoulder. "And this is such a difficult time at Monitor Central, we have to be fine."

"All about results then?"

"What do you want, Miles?"

*I want the hacker stopped. I want to know what is behind these attacks and what is coming next.* Miles took a deep breath. "I want to be sure you and I can work together, and be friends, once all this is settled."

"Okay. So how about dinner on Toronto Island one night next week?"

"That sounds like a date."

"It sounds like dinner at a place where there is a little bit of open space. I've a fave Thai take out place there. You can rent a bike, and we'll ride over together."

"What makes you think I don't have one?"

Jen looked around the yard. "An invisible one?"

"You're right. Transit is just so easy here. But I remember how to ride."

"Tuesday then?" Jen got her helmet in place. "Let me know if anything pings from your traces."

"And you will check locations west of the office for graffiti?"

Jen raised one eyebrow. "Why? The artist was arrested."

"Just in case, Jen. What if someone besides John-boy knows how to do this? There is a serious motivation underpinning this. They've gone to too much trouble to just quit."

"I thought your team set an alarm to notice hacks."

"We've scaled the program to catch overlapping data streams across Monitor's systems, but I would like every possibility covered."

"I can do that on Sunday." Jen tilted her head one way

and then the other. "I need to get out of town tomorrow, to shake off some of this tension. But Sunday, I'll check them all."

"Thank you. Enjoy your country ride."

"Enjoy your weekend." She hopped on and rode at speed down the road.

Giovanni came out on the porch. "Well?"

*She asked me out on a date.* That still surprised him. "She isn't going to report me to HR as needing a psych evaluation."

"A good thing. She does not believe she has a Gift?"

"Doesn't yet believe there is such a thing. But she'll work with me. The issue has her attention."

Giovanni nodded. "A deeply caring person, this Jen. I liked her."

"And what did Brindle think?"

"Always feels frustrated when Gifted people don't want to believe in their strength. But my love is now thinking about Rickie. They're going to call and check in with him."

*I'd forgotten about the park issues.* Focusing on the problem at hand was one of his strengths. And a weakness when his vision got too narrow. Right now, he needed to let go. "Hope you both get a chance to relax after that call."

"And you." Giovanni went back inside.

Miles crossed to his side of the duplex. A good read this evening to give his thinking brain a break, and then tomorrow he'd maybe trek out to Scarborough and borrow one of Angelique's bikes. Gifted with an ability to read weather changes, Angelique was also an avid cyclist. *Hope I can remember how you balance one of those things.* And he could check what she thought the weather would be like next Tuesday, though four days ahead, it would be her meteorologist's guess rather than her Gift's sense of imminent patterns.

# CHAPTER SIXTEEN

Turning the tap counter-clockwise, Deena watched the flow of ice-cold water increase. *Guess I forgot which way it turns off.* She turned it the other direction. The flow slowed. *Almost got it now.* With a gurgling sound in the pipes, water gushed from the tap. Her whole body shook as she pulled herself out of the dream.

Glancing around even though she knew there would be no water, she began the meditation technique that an old water dowser, Sophia, had taught her. She had met Sophia in her late teens, when a difficult dream pulled her from her bed. That night, unable to get back to sleep, she had slipped out of the house without waking her parents, drawn by the sense of water moving. At the back of a nearby school yard, she found the place where an underground stream had shifted from the path Metro determined for it. Standing in the dark, wondering what to do, she'd seen a light approach. Startled and afraid, she backed away. Then, she saw that a small old woman carried a flashlight. The old woman laughed and hugged her, named her a water dowser, then called her contact in Metro's water department.

That night, Sophia took Deena by the arm and led her to a nearby all-night cafe, telling stories as they walked. Putting a dose of something from the flask in her pocket into Deena's coffee, she assured Deena that there were techniques to help her sleep when she could not follow a dream and to get back to sleep after finding a flood like the one they found this night. Sophia gave her phone number, told Deena to call when she was ready to learn more, then walked her home. It had taken two weeks and another intense dream, but Deena made the phone call. Sophia not only taught her meditation and relaxation, but also taught her to understand the images of her dreams. Then, she introduced Deena to Brindle. Now, the Houses were home, a place where her gift was cherished. Sophia had died a few years after they met. Deena still missed the old woman.

A meditation on drifting desert sand and a warm breeze sent Deena back to sleep. An annoying drip caught her attention. Surely, she would be able to stop the sound. She moved the tap slightly, and the water flowed quickly. She spun it the other direction. Water poured out of the sink and onto the floor. She stepped back as water rose to her knees. *Something's wrong!* The water tore a hole in the floor and flooded downward, pulling at her knees. She slipped and fell, water dragging her toward the hole. Her eyes flew open. Sleep would elude her this night. Something was seriously wrong.

Knowing there had been no rain in the forecast—she constantly checked to be ready for a rain-inspired dream—she ran over what happened. *A water main break, I think. A bad one and nearby.* She rolled over and shook her partner's shoulder. "There's a problem. And no way I can sleep through this one."

Ruth opened her eyes slowly, met Deena's gaze with a gentle frown. "Are you sure?"

Deena started to argue, but Ruth put a finger on her mouth to stop her. Deena's eyes strayed to the wall.

"I don't mean there isn't a flood building," said Ruth softly, "but Monitor's surveillance will catch the problem. It's two in the morning."

"But Monitor overseers missed the sewer blockage I sensed last week because someone hacked the system. They wouldn't have found it in time without me. And Miles says the hacks are continuing. In this dream, I couldn't even slow the flow from the tap. A hole opened in the floor. It is a big one."

"Where?"

"Near here. South, I think. That's where the sink appeared on the wall."

"Damn." Ruth threw her legs over the bed and grabbed the jeans and shirt hanging on the chair near the bed. "High Park area. We'll go. I need a coffee though."

Deena was already out of bed, grabbing the clothes she wore the day before. "We need to hurry."

"I'm moving as fast as I can. House, start the coffee machine."

Deena wrapped her arms around her chest. "The flood almost pulled me into the sink hole."

"You also need something hot to drink. Come on."

In the kitchen, Deena looked outside, trying to calm her racing heart. Lights shone on the lawn. "Someone else is awake. House, who is up?"

The dry, technical voice of the house management system spoke. "In Scarborough, Trinity is in the bathroom. Rickie is in the kitchen. In Brampton, no one is out of their room. Here, Miles is on the stairs."

"Wonder why Rickie is awake," said Ruth. "I'll check in with him."

A bleary-eyed Miles stepped into the kitchen. "What has you two up and dressed?"

"A dream," said Deena. "A water main is going to fail. South of here."

"Misshaped motherboards. And the hacker is covering it. Monitor set off an alarm that a hack is active. House, call the nearest taxi." He poured coffee into a travel mug.

"Taxi is on the way," said the house.

Ruth's phone pinged. "Rickie had a nightmare about the trees that were infested. I'll tell him we're on our way to check it out."

"House," said Miles, "wake Giovanni. Tell him to check his phone. Phone, text Giovanni the following message: hacker alarm went off deena had a dream go with her to check it out."

"We're fine," said Ruth. "You didn't need to bother him."

"Maybe no one is on site. But maybe is not good enough given all the effort going into these attacks. I have to head for Monitor Central, but I don't want you going alone."

"Okay." Deena shivered. "As long as Giovanni hurries."

"I'll grab our jackets," said Ruth. "It's going to be chilly."

"Giovanni and Brindle are awake," said the House. "They will be at this front door in five minutes." A moment's pause. "A car has pulled up in front of the house."

"That's my cab," said Miles. "Be careful."

\*   \*   \*

Once in the taxi, Miles connected his laptop to the car internet and accessed his account. Facial recognition let him in immediately. He needed to know which system had been hacked and where. Deena's certainty of a water main break did not justify calling in a damage crew. As soon as he got into the system, he found that the hack did indeed cover a section of the water mains at the south end of the park. He called the water department. As the computer call connected, he watched a man rub his eyes. The voice sounded sleepy.

"This is Miles Franklin from Tech. You've a water main leak near Parkside Drive and the Queensway. Get a crew out there."

"Miles who?"

"Franklin. And don't bother checking your surveillance feed. It's faulty. That's why I know about it, and you don't."

"The lights are all green. Not even a slight drop in pressure. There can't be a break."

"If you want to explain to Administration and the mayor why the whole street has to be dug up, shutting down three lines of the Queensway streetcars, and apologize to the whole neighbourhood when they don't have water in the morning, keep believing the green lights. But if you want to be ahead of this, send a crew out."

"You're sure the display is faulty?"

Miles clenched his teeth. He was assuming that the hacked feed meant a problem. But with Rickie and Deena both on the alert, the signs were strong. "I know the data you are getting is false. And false data means a problem. Send a crew."

"Where are you?"

Miles rolled his eyes. "I'll be in the office in fifteen minutes. I'll happily tromp on your toes in person."

"Tromp away after you have given me proof there is a problem."

Miles stared into the man's eyes. "If you prefer a call from an administrator, so be it. You will face her anger at being awakened at this hour just to order you to send a crew to check an emergency report from a credible source."

"What makes you credible?" The man shook his head. "Techies. You folks all think your computer info is better than eyes in heads and ears tuned in. I'll send the crew, but if you're wrong, you owe them and me dinner."

"Fine. Now I've got work to do." The next thing to check was his tracker on the possible hacker's login. The wait sign circled as the car shifted from one network to another. Then, a message indicated that the script he searched for could not be found. "Damn ghost."

"Is there a problem?" asked the mechanical voice of the taxi pilot.

"Not with your driving."

"Of course, there is not a problem with my driving," said the pilot. "May I assist you?"

"No. Thank you." Miles refocused his attention. The hacker had noticed his trace and removed it. Made sense that with the artist's arrest, everyone involved would be more careful. At least, when he got to Monitor Central, he could check if Martha Hollingsworth logged in just before 2 a.m. That would be something.

\*     \*     \*

After Deena and her companions crossed Bloor Street, the narrow roads that wound between the high-rise apartment buildings were almost empty of car traffic. A woman walking her dalmatian crossed the road to walk on the other side, kept her head down, talking to the dog. No other pedestrians were out, but a few lights were on in the buildings they passed. Someone was always awake in Metro.

"Miles' message did not give details," said Brindle. "Tell us about your dream as we walk. It'll help to know what we are looking for. There was water of course."

Ruth glanced at Deena. Her lips were pressed tight together, her eyes watching the ground. Ruth took her arm, but Deena pulled away gently.

"I have to concentrate," said Deena. "It's hard to distinguish between the underground streams and the water mains."

"She couldn't turn off a tap," said Ruth. "The flood knocked her over, almost pulled her into a hole that appeared in the room."

"Not a good sign," said Brindle. "And Miles had an alarm go off."

"Yes. The hacker is at work," said Ruth. "Which means something is being hidden."

"Phone," said Giovanni, "text Miles this question: do you have more details."

Deena sped up. Ruth hurried to keep up with her.

Giovanni's phone pinged. "Text from Miles," said the phone, "hack begins at Parkside Drive and the Queensway extends to Ellis Ave."

Deena shook her head. "Parkside Drive is too far east. I'm sure it's just south of us."

As they walked closer to the Queensway, the rumble of traffic began. Streetcars ran all night on that route, and the Gardiner Expressway was never quiet. At the sidewalk, Deena did not hesitate, turning west.

"There are flashing yellow lights to the east," said Giovanni.

Deena just shook her head. Now, she walked slowly, moving from one circle of light beamed from the streetlights, into shadow, back to the light. Deena kept cocking her head one way and then another. The lights of a streetcar blazed, then it rumbled by them.

"Here!" Deena stopped, turned slowly in a circle. "Something is wrong here."

Giovanni stepped off the sidewalk onto the grass. "It feels spongy." He moved forward. Crossing into the dark beyond the reach of the streetlight, making his phone into a flashlight, he looked around. "Here it is. Water bubbling up from the ground. We found it."

"How do we get the crew's attention?"

"I can jog back to where the flashing lights are," said Giovanni. "You call Miles."

He had gone a couple hundred meters when two trucks turned onto the streetcar tracks. He stopped, waved his arms to get their attention, The first stopped right beside him, and he pointed to where the others waited, moved his hands as if describing a fountain. The trucks rumbled forward, and four workers jumped down.

"Over here!" Ruth pointed. "We found water here."

"What are you four doing here at this hour?" asked one of the workers.

"I couldn't sleep," said Deena. "I wanted to see the water."

"At the pond," said Ruth quickly. "We're going to the pond in the park."

One of the workers swore. "Call the office. We need this section of the main shut down." She turned with fists on her hips. "How did you find this?"

"An accident," said Brindle. "My friend stepped off the

sidewalk and felt spongy ground."

"I don't know what to think." The worker pulled out her phone. "What are your names?"

"Leave it. We found the leak," said another. "Let's get to work. You folks get out of our way."

"We're going." Ruth took Deena by the arm. "Come. We can walk by the pond, and get out of the way of this repair crew."

Giovanni joined them, and they hurried along the sidewalk toward the path by the pond. "I called Rickie. He's pretty upset. This is right near where he and Jainyu found the insect infestation. Fixing the leak is going to disturb the roots of trees and shrubs. Hard on already stressed trees. But he said thank you, Deena. If it the main had blown, the resulting flood would have done a lot more damage."

"Someone is investing a lot to cause trouble in this park," said Brindle. "Why?"

# CHAPTER SEVENTEEN

Another yawn and Miles rolled his neck. *A nap or a coffee?* A glance at the clock said a trip to the cafeteria for a coffee would have to do. It was almost eight a.m. Tatiana had promised to pull herself out of bed and join him for eight-thirty. He had texted her when he got to Monitor Central, got a reply almost immediately asking if the ghost was online. There had been no sign of anyone watching. It seemed that this time, the hacker set the loop in place and went offline. *Why is this person hiding the work of a street artist and threatening serious damage with water and sewer systems? Or do we have two hackers?*

Getting off the phone with Tatiana, he had emailed Admin Chan and marked it urgent. Then, he asked Monitor to generate a list of who had logged in that was not officially on duty. While Monitor worked, he took a nap. The list of twenty-five people was ready when he woke, and sure enough Martha Hollingsworth had logged in for ten minutes right at the time the hack began.

He yawned again. Something to eat would also help. Grabbing his portable coffee mug, he pushed away from his desk and headed for the elevator. As it arrived, he decided not to go to the cafeteria and rooftop garden, but hit the button for the ground floor. He needed a chance to stretch his legs and really wake up. At this hour, there wasn't much of a line at the coffee shop. He bought a fruit cup and croissant to take back and a large coffee. Heading down the street, he decided to take a walk around the block north of Monitor Central. *Jen would be able to say exactly how far that would be.* He hadn't heard from her except for a text early the night before to say she got home safe.

The phone in his pocket vibrated. "Phone, who is calling?"

"Administrator Chan."

Miles pulled out the phone. "Phone answer, with video." The administrator looked serious. "Good morning."

"I regret the need to call so early on a Saturday."

"I'm at work. I have emailed you a report marked urgent."

"I will read the report. What matters is that the artist will appear in court this morning for a bail hearing. I want to know what happens there."

"Did we learn anything when police questioned him?"

"He asked for a lawyer immediately. Refused to answer any questions. The lawyer argued that the only relevant charge had to do with where he painted. Should have been a fine only. The prosecutor refused to drop the other charges, so they held him overnight."

"That suggests he'll have a lawyer who will get him out on bail this morning." Miles decided he better forgo a walk and turned back to Monitor Central.

"The prosecutor promised to make our argument that the painting was a serious hazard to city order. If he does not make bail, he may be more willing to give information. No mention will be made, however, of the hacks into Monitor. That cannot be made public. People are already upset that a taxi could be hijacked. Can you go to the court house and observe?"

"Not this morning. You'll understand once you read the email I sent."

"Get someone else there then. It is essential that we know what happens."

"It is Saturday." *Brindle would be a great observer. Maybe*

*Amanda would go too.* Miles smiled to himself. Admin Chan did not specify someone from the office. "I think I know just who to ask."

"Perfect."

"Do read that email."

"Before breakfast?"

"I believe that you will regret it if you wait." The silence on the line was as eloquent as a string of profanity.

"Fine."

"Call ended," said the phone.

"Phone, call Brindle," said Miles.

"Still awake Miles," said Brindle when the connection opened. "How are you feeling?"

"I had a nap. I feel good that we caught the problem early. I am worried that the hacks are ongoing. I am hopeful that clues are starting to add up." Miles shrugged. "I'm tired, and I know I'm not getting a rest anytime soon. But I didn't call you to mope."

"I've never seen you mope."

"Call it rant then. But I called for a favour. The artist's bail hearing is this morning, and I wondered if I could impose on you to attend and see what happens."

Brindle looked away for a moment. Lines of concern spread across their temples when they turned back. "I think that would be a good idea. Deena did not sleep last night. Finally, Ruth got Giovanni to come over and help her relax. These problems are pushing my community hard, too hard. I am worried. So yes. And I'll see who is available to come along. Juan might be able to read the artist's goals. Maria could figure out if anger is a motivation. We'll be there." Brindle pointed a finger at Miles. "And you get some rest. You'll be running on empty soon."

Miles rolled his eyes. "I'll sleep when I can, but it isn't just our community that is suffering from these events."

\* \* \*

"House, what time is it?" Rickie asked without opening his eyes.

"Ten minutes after ten o'clock in the morning."

Rickie rubbed his shoulder. The gardens needed work, and he'd lost hours of daylight. *I really should get up.* It had been a difficult night though. He had sat up until Giovanni let him know that a repair crew had begun work at the water main break. He texted Jainyu what had happened before heading back to bed. Once there, sleep eluded him. Thanks to Miles and Deena, the break was found, but the risk to the trees had been serious, could still be depending how badly the tree roots would be disturbed by the repair work. Finally, near dawn, exhaustion took over, and he slept again.

Sitting up now, he picked up his phone from the table beside the bed, checked for messages. Jainyu had replied. "meteors and asteroids! could have been disaster" Rickie flicked to the next message. "we have to find out who is attacking that park land"

*Well duh,* he thought. "any idea how," he texted.

Rolling out of bed, Rickie pulled on work clothes. As he made a fresh pot of coffee, the reply came in from Jainyu: "that's the question will check in with timur first thing Monday."

Waiting for his toast, he went through his task list for the day. Overnight, the irrigation system automatically provided water to the drip lines he had laid out, but he needed to check that things were damp enough. This extended dry spell, though not unusual for Toronto in June, meant some daytime watering would likely be needed as well. He sniffed. Ironic that last night he worried about too much water, and today it was not enough. *That's city life for you. All this concrete and super heating means the natural systems are out of whack.*

Once outside, the smell of green wrapped around him. Meandering through the vegetable garden, he checked the moisture content as he went. Leaf beetles were chewing holes in the lettuce and brassicas, but the damage was not dramatic. No need to chase the little bugs away. Folks in the Houses were used to a few holes in their greens. Tomatoes were growing well, and the peppers he started inside in February had their first flowers. Then, he toured the front yards. Zinnias and petunias raised under lights in their basement were now blooming. Lilies had flower buds. Crocosmia was getting tall, still looking like a decorative grass. The bright colours of the long, delicate flower spikes would come later.

He leaned on one of the dwarf apple trees in the yard, could feel the yearning for water. The apples were starting to form, but the tree felt the stress of June heat. He could set a slow drip around the trees for the afternoon. A shiver ran up his spine, across his scalp. Worry for the trees of High Park returned. "Phone, call Miles." He waited six rings, started thinking he would be leaving a message.

"Rickie. How you feeling?"

"I finally slept some. You?"

"Still at work. Tired but focused. You called because?"

"I was going to ask you to slip down to the park this afternoon and check how the repair has gone. Maybe you could do that on your way home. Jainyu will be by this morning to look for more insects, but he'll be too early to see much of the repair work."

"I should be able to go that way."

"Thanks. I just keep visualizing destruction."

"Let it go. Deena found the spot sooner than anyone else would have."

"I know. I'm just worried."

"As am I, Rickie. But first things first. If Tatiana and I can track the hacker, we have a chance to shut this all down."

"I get it. I'll pay attention to what I can do." Rickie got a hoe from the shed to work his worry out on the ground.

Geoff threw open the back door and stalked across the yard. "Stop it. Green things are supposed to calm you down."

"Stop what?"

"Worrying." Geoff jabbed at the bridge of his glasses, pressing them against his nose. "How am I supposed to get through the day with you spouting worry about this tree and that one? Where even is that one?"

"High Park."

"Kilometres and kilometres from here. And that's your weekday job. It's enough that you are worried about no rain here."

"The trouble there is serious, Geoff."

"But not my problem, and here you are bombarding me with it."

*He's really upset.* Breathing in the fresh air of the garden, Rickie leaned on his hoe, studied the empath, while relaxing his shoulders, calming his heart rate.

"That's a bit better." Geoff poked his finger at Rickie's chest. "But don't start worrying about me now. That won't help."

"I am sorry. It's been a tough week."

"For you. For me. For Samantha. I felt how upset she was when you brought those bugs home. And Trinity is again worried she has no Gift. As if being an empath, getting bombarded by everybody else's stuff is a good thing."

"Geoff, would it help if you had a task, say picking snow peas?"

Geoff glared at him. "Just don't worry that I am picking the wrong ones."

Rickie laughed. "If I delegate the job to you, it is yours to do as you please. Even eat some as you go."

"Fine. I just can't seem to shake off all the stuff I felt this week." Geoff's hands flew to his hips. "And don't worry about me. I know very well how uptight I am. Think herbs and flowers. Now!"

"Right." Rickie pushed aside the thought that he really should let Brindle know how on edge Geoff was. "I'm thinking of coriander and basil. I'm thinking nasturtiums."

"Not nasturtiums. You'll try to make me eat one of the silly, peppery flowers. Think lettuce. I will fill my thoughts with peas."

\*   \*   \*

At the court house information desk, Juan asked for directions to the room where bail hearings would take place while Maria greeted the security guard. A few years earlier, she and this young man used the same agency to find work. Maria thought that he had a slight empathic sensitivity for truth-telling.

"Here for a family matter?" the man asked.

Maria blushed slightly as she thought how to answer truthfully, as he would know if she did not, without revealing too much. *I consider the people of the Houses family.* "It is a family concern, but gracias à Dios my children have stayed away from the law."

"Hope this matter works out for you then."

Maria followed Juan to the elevator where Giovanni, Brindle, and Amanda were already waiting. Amanda was pale, with a slight twitch in her eyebrow that she kept rubbing.

"What did you say to that guard?" Amanda asked Maria. "He considered asking for details about why you are here, but I think someone came in who has caused trouble before. He made the choice to pay attention to that person not you."

"I knew him pretty well at one time," answered Maria, "encouraged him when he did not get much work. He called me his work mom. A nice boy."

"This is our floor," said Juan. "We sit separately?"

"No need to look like a phalanx of investigators," said Giovanni.

The elevator door opened, and a woman with tears running down her face stood with a man's arm around her shoulder. Maria stiffened. The man was furious, though trying to comfort his wife. He pulled her a bit to the side to let them out. As they slipped by, Giovanni's shoulder brushed against the woman's. She glanced up startled, then wept more loudly.

As they moved down the hall, Brindle took Giovanni's hand. "Sometimes pain is so real you can't just ease it away."

"I know. I wonder what happened?"

Amanda shuddered. "The man is considering not posting bail."

"He is furious," said Maria. "You folks go in first. I will find a washroom."

When she and Juan slipped in, others had taken seats in the back row to the right. They moved farther in and found an empty bench on the left. There were people scattered around the room, some clearly family, a few in suits whom she guessed were lawyers, two uniformed police officers. As each case ended, a few people left. A few more would arrive, quietly slipping in between proceedings.

Maria studied the people brought in by the bailiff, a couple in orange jumpsuits, most in the rumpled clothes they were wearing when they were arrested. The duty lawyer represented most of the accused, though she stepped aside for another lawyer from time to time. Maria glanced back. Amanda had a troubled look on her face. Pain and tension marked the faces of her other colleagues. She gave a half smile of encouragement and turned back. *This is not something we empaths will ever agree to do again.* Raw emotion flowed through the room.

The judge pressed a button on the bench and a chime sounded. "Next case."

The prosecutor looked at the computer screen on his desk. "Chong Bai charged with mischief, endangering the public, interfering with Monitor systems, and street painting outside the area he is licensed for."

With hands folded on the bench, the judge watched a lawyer in a stylish suit step forward. "You are not usually here on a Saturday for minor offences bail hearings, Ms. Henry."

"When a client comes before you, your honour, I appear."

The judge raised one eyebrow. "Take your place."

A door opened. A bailiff brought in a scowling young man in jeans and rumpled T shirt. Ms. Henry spoke quickly and quietly to him, and the two were seated. Maria sensed that as the lawyer spoke, the young man's anger diminished a little.

"Your request for bail is?" the judge asked.

"Two million dollars," said the prosecutor.

There were gasps around the room as people sat up to attend to this case. Chong Bai stiffened. His lawyer put a hand on his arm and whispered something.

"You clearly don't want him on the street. " The judge studied the accused for a moment, then turned back to the prosecutor. "The charges mentioned do not seem to me to warrant that hefty an amount."

"He is a danger to public safety," said the prosecutor, who proceeded to describe the three incidents of graffiti. "If you turn to the evidence screen, you will see the chaos he repeatedly caused." On the screen appeared a block with pictures of the stopped traffic and the masked painter.

"You caught him doing this picture?" asked the judge.

"No. Police arrested him working on the next disruptive painting, this time on a busy transit corridor."

"Judge Baker," said Ms. Henry," may we focus on the first picture of the painter?"

When the judge nodded, the clerk switched to the requested slide. Ms. Henry motioned for her client to stand. "There may be some resemblance around the eyes, but the build is quite different. I suggest that a connection between my client and the earlier paintings is merely guesswork on the part of the police. The only charge the prosecutor can connect him with is practising his art outside of the area where he is licensed."

"Prosecutor?"

"It is believed he disguised his physique to hinder recognition software. The parts of the tattoos that are visible match the tattoos on Chong Bai."

"Again, your honour," said the lawyer in a quiet, confident voice, "so little of the painter's tattoos are visible that it is hard to be sure that the painter is my client. Also, if I may ask, was anyone injured in the other two alleged events, which you have not yet connected to my client?"

The judge turned to the prosecutor with narrowed eyes. "Was there?"

"No one was injured. There has been other interference, however."

"Other graffiti?" The judge waited.

"No."

"With due respect to my esteemed colleague," said Ms. Henry, "unless this interference is described, and clearly attributed to my client, it has no bearing on this proceeding." She turned to look at the prosecutor. "I repeat that the only charge that we see evidence of is one count of painting in a part of Metro for which he is not licensed."

The prosecutor looked down at his screen. Maria could read tension in his shoulders and anger brewing. "I have no other evidence to be presented at this time."

The judge studied the prosecutor and then folded his hands together under his chin. "A man was held in jail overnight for an offence where the fine is under a thousand dollars. This feels totally out of proportion to me. Do you have any more to add?"

"Traffic snarls may seem like a nuisance, but it is these unexpected events that can cause tempers to flare and problems to erupt."

The judge held up his left hand. "No need to object, Ms. Henry. In this court, we only deal with events that have happened. In this case, nothing took place except that a bit of paint was placed on a wall." He pressed the button on his desk and again a chime sounded. "Chong Bai is free to go. No bail. And because he was held in jail overnight, let the record show that the fine is considered paid in full."

"Thank you, your honour," said Ms. Henry.

"Ten-minute recess," said the judge.

Chong Bai got to his feet looking a little dazed. The lawyer spoke softly. The young man listened and shook his head. The lawyer gave a reassuring smile and led him down the aisle. Half way down, he looked up, and, as if for the first time, realized that the proceedings had an audience. Maria felt Juan's full attention on the young man. The young man's gaze skipped over the crowd. With a jerk of his chin, his eyes narrowed, staring toward the back corner. His anger flamed so that Maria felt as if her chest burned. Then, the lawyer gave his elbow a light tug, and they moved out of the courtroom.

A moment later, Maria and Juan got up and slipped out of the room. The lawyer and her client were nowhere in sight. The others came out a short while later. Amanda looked totally twitchy.

"Can we get out of here?" said Amanda. "Now. This place is horrible."

"I saw a cafe with an open patio just down the street," said Juan.

"I'll text Miles," said Brindle. "He'll want to know Chong Bai is free."

"Tell Darshani too," said Amanda. "He's still furious that we were there when police arrested him."

Juan took Amanda's arm. "That was incredibly interesting."

"Incredibly difficult," said Amanda. "You would not believe how many divergences I saw during that hour. And when Chong Bai recognized me." She shook her head. "There were too many flares of revenge for me to be sure what I saw."

# CHAPTER EIGHTEEN

Maria and Juan brought cold drinks out to the table where Giovanni massaged Amanda's shoulders. Maria sat down and placed a hand on Amanda's. "None of us empaths will ever want to come to that place again, but the place seems to have hit you hardest, Amanda." She glared at her husband. "Juan found it very interesting."

Amanda rubbed her temples. "The timelines just would not settle. The judge constantly tested options, considered different choices. At the same time, the people asking for bail were trying to imagine what they were going to do, how they were going to pay. A woman in the crowd was deciding whether or not to mortgage the house to get her child's bail money. I could see that if she did that, she was afraid she'd lose her home."

"Dios mio. What did she do?"

"No idea. She had not yet chosen."

"It was exhausting," said Giovanni, "but we learned a fair bit for Miles. First, Chong Bai has wealthy back up. That is one high-priced lawyer that showed up to represent him."

"Esposo, husband, with your gift, could you see his plans, Chong Bai's place in the world?"

"I got a good look at his horoscope." Juan lifted his hand to stop Brindle's objection. "What else do we call what I sometimes see about a person's life story? What matters is that I sensed he is working toward a great accomplishment and is connected to a larger network."

"More than just the hacker accomplice?" asked Brindle.

"I believe so. I sensed a community reinforcing him. And that he has a big plan."

"The lawyer knows that more is going on," said Giovanni. "She taunted the prosecutor to say more than he had permission to."

"She knows who paid her to represent him," said Juan. "I read her as well, and she is pretty sure that today will help push her toward her goals. Better money. A partnership in the firm maybe."

"All because a young man has a special talent with graffiti." Brindle tapped the table. "I sympathize with the judge trying to figure out what was behind all this."

"That's why he called a recess," said Giovanni. "Needed to clear his mind. Otherwise, his lingering questions would have carried over to the next cases."

"A judge who is seriously committed to justice," said Juan. "From what I sensed, I'd want this judge if I ever came to court."

"Basta!" Maria pushed back from the table. "Don't even think something like that. You do not want to be arrested."

Juan put a hand on her shoulder. "I trust the system here much more than what we knew back home. But no. I will stay on the right side of the law."

Maria squeezed Amanda's hand. "That street artist recognized you, didn't he?"

"I'm pretty sure." Amanda closed her eyes. "There was a flash as he chose between going home to nap on a real bed or getting a hot breakfast. Then, he saw me. It was like a shot gun of possibilities then. Some of them included Darshani, but I can't imagine how he'd get at her. She usually sticks close to home on a Saturday, given her long weekday commute."

Brindle rubbed their temples. "Your worry is going to give

me a headache. Let's call her."

Giovanni laid his phone on the table. "Phone, call Darshani and put her on speaker. Voice only." One ring and she answered. "Hey Dar, just checking in. Amanda wants to make sure you are home and safe."

"I'm on the train headed to the core," said Darshani.

"Why are you coming to town?" Amanda's voice was tense.

"A street art clash. Should give me a chance to find out what people know about John-boy."

"I don't like the word clash," said Maria.

"We think you might see him," said Giovanni. "He's out on bail."

"Oh." Darshani hesitated.

"And he considered taking out his frustration on you, Dar." Amanda touched the phone. "I don't think you should go."

"At least, not alone," said Juan. "Is there a place for observers at this event?"

"I'm fine. There won't be any trouble. John-boy's part of this community. He knows the rules."

"But Chong Bai was thinking about you, Dar," said Amanda. "Pointed, angry, vengeful thoughts."

"I can go," said Juan. "I would like to see the art Darshani does when none of us is watching."

"I can go with Juan," said Giovanni.

There was silence from the phone. Maria could imagine Darshani pressing her lips together. The girl had an independent streak which showed up even stronger when she worked on street art. She'd had a lot of practice standing up to her South Asian parents and challenging their ideas of appropriate behaviour for a woman.

"Juan and Giovanni will keep out of your way, Dar," said Brindle.

"Where is the event?" Giovanni asked.

Again, Darshani paused. "If you must come. Shuter and Church Street. Just try to fit in with the crowd. Please."

"We'll just be there to keep an eye out, Dar. While you have your eyes on your art. Take care." Giovanni broke the connection. "It's too public a setting for there to be trouble, don't you think?"

Amanda got to her feet. "Thank you for taking me seriously. Public space or not, Chong Bai wanted something from Darshani."

Brindle stood slowly. "Dar is right though. It is a place where she might gather information. Someone with big money is causing these disruptions. They feel like a nuisance, but there must be a purpose behind them, the big accomplishment Juan sensed."

After giving her husband a kiss on the cheek, Maria took Brindle's arm. "You and I will go home with Amanda. The three of us need a rest after that harrowing morning." Turning again to Juan, she shook her head. "I suppose you will enjoy reading the aspirations of these artists. Just remember, you are there to look after Darshani."

"And if Chong Bai shows up, I may get an even better sense of what he is hoping to accomplish."

Maria sighed. "What is that boy up to? It is so confusing. And disturbing. I need the peace and quiet of home."

"So do I, Maria." Amanda rubbed her temples. "That was a difficult morning."

\*   \*   \*

Satisfied with the outline of her design, Darshani started in the centre, filling in the leaves of the tree while making sure the pattern of branches could be traced. Working from the trunk to the outer leaves, she switched colours for the branches, deepening the brown, trying to hint at the age of the tree. That would be most evident in the size of the trunk base and the gnarls in the bark, but for the design to be integrated, she had to build in hints up above.

The toe of a running shoe appeared right beside the outside leaves. People were not supposed to get this close!

She sat back on her heels and looked up. John-boy! He wouldn't dare disturb her design, but he was so close and standing over her. He looked intimidating. She swallowed. "You're in my light."

He moved his toe to point to a section of leaves. "This colour, it lets me see that the sun is behind the tree. Where did you get it?"

"I made it."

"How?"

Darshani shook her head. "Trade secret. Too often chalk work feels flat." She put her hands on the ground and pushed to her feet.

"We work with flat surfaces." John-boy shrugged.

"So does an oil painter. Their work suggests depth and space."

"Why were you on College Street yesterday?"

"Taking a walk with a friend. I am glad to see the police didn't hold you." *What do I say that won't tell him how much I know?* "What happened?"

"It was a coincidence that you were there when police arrested me?"

Darshani tried to force a small smile to her lips. "What else could it be?"

"I thought I saw your friend in court this morning."

Darshani could think of no answer except distraction. "They held you overnight? That's terrible. Street artists are supposed to be respected as long as we follow the rules."

John-boy turned his eyes away, gave a small shrug. "I was out of my district."

"There are fines for that. Are we all going to get hassled now? We'll have to get the clubs to band together and petition Metro."

"I may have angered the cops. Some say I have attitude." John-boy studied her work, reached for a piece of chalk. "Another colour you made?"

Darshani nodded.

"You have skill. Maybe..." He handed her the chalk. "Good

luck today." He turned away.

"You don't have a piece in this clash?"

He turned back slowly. "I have a mission, and it's behind schedule." His eyes narrowed. "Stay out of my way." He turned and walked away.

Darshani shivered as she watched him disappear into the crowd of spectators. A moment later, both Juan and Giovanni were beside her.

"You okay?" Giovanni put a hand on her shoulder.

"What did he say?" Juan asked.

"That people better not interfere with his work. And he did recognize Amanda in court today." Darshani looked down at the place John-boy had put his toe, so close to the first leaves of the tree. "You better tell Miles to expect another piece of his art."

"Will do," said Juan, "but what did you do to your hair? Part of it is green? And those jeans look like you paint walls with them."

"The jeans came this way. The colour will wash out of my hair tomorrow, so don't worry. I will look like a proper teacher by Monday." Darshani twirled two pieces of chalk in her fingers. "I'd better get back to work. This is a pretty ambitious design. I hope to wander at some point and see if I can run into anybody else from his club. But I have to finish first."

Juan looked down the street at artists kneeling on the street and observers milling on the sidewalks. "I find this quite fascinating. We'll take a bit of a tour, check in with you before we go."

"Just watch where you walk." Darshani knelt, then looked up. "Get too close, and an artist will have you thrown off the street." *John-boy got way too close, and he knows better.* He'd been interested in the colours she'd created. Given his own experiments with paint additives, that kind of made sense. But a threat had been there in his last words. As a shiver went down her spine, she was glad that colleagues from the Houses had been nearby.

# CHAPTER NINETEEN

"Finally Monitor spat out the list for us," said Tatiana. "Now we know who was logged in for all of the incidents. And thank you Monitor for separating out those who were not officially on duty."

"How many?" asked Miles.

"Twenty."

"Who logs in to work when they don't have to?"

"People with a deadline—and given that six are from accounting I'm guessing their department has a big one coming up. People with a work obsession. Somebody awake in the night because they forgot something crucial. People like you with an emergency."

"Monitor," asked Miles, "how often did these people log in when off duty during the last two weeks?"

"Working," said Monitor. Five minutes later another list came up on both their screens.

"This guy from security logs in twice a day from home," said Tatiana. "Something is up there. We'll put a special tag on his id."

"And a trace on the others." *Though it will have to be a carefully hidden one, given that Hollingsworth erased my first one.* "It would also be good to know whether they entered a different department of Monitor than where they work."

"Good idea." Tatiana called up a spyware program on her

laptop.

Watching over her shoulder, Miles marvelled at the code she had written to make sure the spy would not be detected. "You know, working with you is the best professional development I've done in years."

Tatiana swung her chair around and stared at him. "That's it. Something has been trying to surface in the back of my brain, and you've triggered it. Three years ago, somebody from accounting took my white hat hacker course. It didn't feel right, but they claimed to be working toward a management position, thought this course would broaden their resume." She opened her laptop. "Let me call up the course list." She tapped her finger nail on the edge of the computer. "And there we are. Martha Hollingsworth. You, my dear, get a special spy tag. Now, Miles, you are half asleep. Go home."

"Don't think I'd do good work if I stayed."

"This was productive, but if you yawn one more time, I'll physically throw you out of the room. Goodbye." She waved the back of her hand at him.

Tired as he was, Miles felt he owed it to Rickie to check on the damage from the water main break and repair. Once on the westbound streetcar, he set the alarm on his phone. Even a fifteen-minute nap would give him a boost.

A soft ping woke Miles from a surprisingly deep sleep. The streetcar's automated system announced that the next stop was Parkside Drive. The stop after would be his. *They should have changed that street name when they clear cut the eastern part of the park.* Miles got to his feet. Rolling his shoulders, stretching his back, Miles tried to slough off the tiredness that made his arms and feet heavy. He wondered if he should have just assured Rickie that Metro employees knew their job.

Heading west from the stop, he could see the heavy equipment at work. A man held the hand of a boy who looked about five. The child kept leaning toward the yellow tape that marked off the repair area, entranced by the big machines. The street was wet, and the ground looked soggy, but no water pumped from the hole in the ground. The crew had the leak under control.

Watching the efficient team, he let himself relax and headed home, enjoying the walk in the cool shade under the trees. Sheltered by the lacy green canopy, the air smelled fresh. At a branching of the path, he turned northwest, back toward the upper part of the pond. At the edge of the trees, he found a shrub with half the branches stripped bare. He moved closer. Ants swarmed all over the leaves that remained. Huge ants. A line of them carried pieces of leaf along a path. *Leafcutters don't live in Toronto!* With their voracious appetite, they'd finish this shrub and start on the trees. How had a tropical ant, a whole nest of them, gotten here?

"Phone, call Monitor Central." When the switchboard operator answered, he asked for Metro Green Spaces. A quick explanation to the person on duty generated colourful swearing, and the promise that somebody would be over to deal with the ants immediately. Disconnecting, Miles studied the line of industrious creatures. *I do not like ants.* An irrational fear of the insects had stayed with him ever since stepping into a nest of fire ants as a young child visiting relatives in Jamaica. Still, he forced himself to bend over and study the creatures. They looked normal to his eye, but he wondered. Given the constructed bugs that had been found here twice, it might be best to have them checked out. Samantha would be able to tell in a moment.

Looking at their line, he wondered how to collect some. Glancing around, Miles found a blue can brimming with recyclables near the pond. In it, he found a few compostable take-out containers, coffee cups, and pop cans. He chose a coffee cup and lid. Placing the mouth of the cup in the middle of the path of the ants, he waited while several walked straight in. He considered messing up their path with his foot, but that might redirect the whole nest and make it harder for the Metro Green Spaces crew to locate them. Putting the lid on the cup, he made sure it was a tight fit. Still, he found himself carrying it with two fingers well away from his body. On a Saturday, Samantha was almost certainly at home, but best to check. "Phone, call Samantha." She picked up on the first ring.

"Hey mate," she said. "What's up?"

"More bugs. Are you at home or at the university?"

"Home. What kind of bugs?"

"Ants that should not be in Toronto. I collected a few. I'll come out with them right away."

"High Park again?"

"You got it. Let Rickie know."

"Will do. Text when you get off the train."

"See you in an hour." Miles pocketed his phone and headed for the subway. This day just got a whole lot longer.

\* \* \*

Joining the crowd exiting the subway, Miles walked to the escalator that would take him to the light rail train and on into Scarborough. Waiting on the platform, Miles looked down the track to check the signal lights. They looked right. He tapped his foot on the concrete platform thinking he was starting to get paranoid. As the train approached, the driver scanned the platform. Miles breathed a sigh of relief. Once aboard, he found a seat and leaned back, resting his tired head.

The train travelled through the deep shadows of the hundred and fifty storey apartment buildings that crowded the rail line and each other. The sudden bursts of light between the complexes created a staccato effect. This part of Scarborough, where there had been malls with huge parking lots, had been taken over by high-rise housing with stores moved to the street level of the buildings. It felt exactly like the core. All cement and asphalt. Green roofs were legislated for all new buildings, but those were out of sight, and only people who lived in the buildings were allowed access. Not until the train passed the fifth stop on this line would there be houses with lawns and gardens. In those neighbourhoods, the parks were scooped up by developers, but at least the yards of individual houses and duplexes had been left.

Despite the changes, visiting the Scarborough Houses felt like going home. When his grandparents moved from Jamaica sixty years earlier, both sets came to Scarborough where housing had been more affordable. His parents stayed on in the community when they married, but when Miles and his siblings grew up, they all moved to new lower cost condos and apartments at the edge of Scarborough or in the core. Of them all, only he lived at road level with a yard. On his own, he could not have afforded the luxury.

The train passed the station before his, and he texted Samantha to say he was almost there. Once off the train, a short walk along Kiriakou brought him to Jenkinson Way. The quiet out here in this sheltered neighbourhood soothed his over-extended brain. As he turned the corner, he saw Rickie sitting on the front step of the house where Samantha lived, a sign of how upset Rickie was. He never sat still outside.

"You have to figure out who is attacking High Park," Rickie said. "Those trees must not be injured more."

"Just be glad we are right there to keep an eye on things."

"I am. Let's go see Samantha. She's in the workroom."

At they came down the stairs, Samantha wrapped her arms around herself. She stared at the cup in Miles' hand and her whole body started to shake. "Show me."

Rickie put a hand on her shoulder. "You don't have to do this. Jainyu can take them to his contact at the ROM."

"On Monday. Your colleagues need to know today if pesticide will kill them." Samantha uncurled her fingers, released her arms. She pulled a sample jar from a drawer.

Miles lifted the lip of the cup and poured the ants into the jar.

Samantha reached down to touch one of the squirming

ants and breathed a sigh of relief. "Theses are normal, ordinary ants."

"Destructive ants that don't belong in Toronto." Rickie shook his head. "But if they are ordinary ants, an ordinary pesticide can kill them. The folks on duty at Metro Green Spaces will get this under control. I'll let Jainyu know." He instructed his phone to send a text.

"Guess one of us is taking the long way home every day for the time being," said Miles. "But while I'm here, I might as well see about trying out one of Angelique's bikes." When Rickie raised an eyebrow, Miles gave half a smile. "I'm meeting a friend to go riding on Toronto Island, thought I better see if I remember how a bike works."

"You can get ones that drive themselves," said Samantha.

"Not for a ride with this woman. She is quite the feet-on-the-pedals type."

"You might as well ride Nathan's," said Samantha. "No need to figure out Angelique's specialized racing bikes. I'm sure the girls would go along to give you a few pointers."

Miles rolled his head, stretching out the tension. "I'm not going far. Too tired. But I might as well check that I can keep my balance on the thing while I'm here."

Rickie's phone vibrated. A text from Jainyu. "need a sample for timur to identify"

Rickie wrote back. "why samantha said they're normal"

"to figure out where they came from"

"Samantha, will these critters stay alive in a jar until Monday?" Rickie asked.

"Likely. But an expert can identify them and where they come from dead or alive."

"Perhaps he can help figure out how they got to the park," said Rickie.

Miles stretched his arms. "Figuring out the bicycle is about all I can manage today."

# CHAPTER TWENTY

*Water,* thought Jen. *What I want this Sunday morning is rippling, blue water.* Cycling the bike path along the lake would satisfy that desire, though sky-high condominiums now crowded the once open paths. Still, with the lake to the south, this provided the most open space in Metro.

Coffee first though. Telling her phone to start the espresso machine, she took a quick shower. Back in the kitchen she frothed the milk and with latte in hand, stepped onto the balcony. Before settling into her favourite comfy chair, she checked the potted plants—tomatoes, salad greens, and snow peas. They would need water before the day's excursion. Then, she settled into the spot where sun poured through the gap between nearby buildings. When moving to this tower five years earlier, there had been two vacancies, one on the fourth floor facing north and this one on the twenty-second facing east. The fourth-floor option tempted her as she would not have to always use the elevator, but the potential for natural morning light won out. Bathing in this early sunshine, she again thanked her younger self for the choice.

Wrapping hands around the warm cup, sipping the rich brew, Jen closed her eyes and planned her cycling route. *Lakeshore first, I think.* Last thing Friday, Miles had asked her to check the possible graffiti locations west of Monitor Central, but that was work. This was Sunday. A day off. She could check the locations on the way back. She didn't mind winding through city streets—there were always interesting things to notice in the neighbourhoods—but Saturday's ride had been all farmers' fields and forests. A few good hills. Only a couple stream crossings. Not enough water. That she craved. Her stomach rumbled, reminding her she needed breakfast next.

Putting an everything bagel in the toaster, she unwrapped the phone from her arm to check messages. Saturdays she wore the phone in case of an emergency, but did not look at it. As usual, a pile of emails and texts waited for her attention. Scrolling through, she saw three texts from her mother, an email from her dad, and a text marked with flaring orange from Miles. As she swiped it open, she felt her chest tighten. Reading carefully, she learned that there had been another hack, though not in an area Traffic supervised. And the artist was out on bail. Miles added an apology for asking, but hoped she would check the potential locations for the artist's graffiti this morning.

*Damn. Water comes second.* Jen wrapped the phone back around her wrist. As she put roasted soy butter on the bagel, she mapped in her head a way to check all the locations she had identified, east and west of Monitor Central. *Take me an hour and a half, get me to Bathurst. I can slip down to the Lakeshore trails there. Go west to Mississauga and come all the way back along the water.* She put down the knife. She could see the exact route, including backtracking twice to get a good look at two locations. Lips curling into a rueful smile, she knew what Miles would say about the map she'd just drawn in her head. Couldn't everyone do that?

She knew the answer to that question. Her mother needed a navigator even in the city. Jen never got lost, never needed a map after she had been to a place once. *Miles calls this a Gift.* Jen thought about Amanda and Giovanni, remembered Brindle's intensity and awareness. They all seemed quite special. *And I am very ordinary.*

Taking her bagel back to the balcony she sat in the bright sun, watched the shifting light on the buildings around her. Her father would disagree with that last thought. He always told her she was special, one of a kind, but she'd been sure he would say that about any child of his.

What Miles talked about was different. Felt like magic to her, though he argued these were natural abilities that were just stronger in some people than in most. *Does the graffiti artist have that kind of magic gift?* That thought got her moving. Time to get on the road.

The sidewalks were empty of all but dog walkers and a few purposeful pedestrians, but the streets held a steady flow of cars and delivery trucks. Pushing aside the questions Miles' talk of Gifts raised, Jen followed the map she had drawn in her head. There was nothing on the wall where she'd found the painting of a pedestrian. That figured. The next possible wall was clean. Jen backtracked along a bike lane busy with cyclists out for a hard ride before the day got hot. Nothing at the next two locations.

A side trip occurred to her. The best croissant in Metro could be found at a bakery nearby. She seldom came this way, and the treat would be worth it. A purchase at this cafe allowed access to the rooftop garden, but she did not want to leave her bike. The best lock available should protect it, but there were not enough people around yet. She leaned against the wall savouring the buttery flakes. Water from her bottle, and she headed out again to check the rest of the locations east of Monitor Central. No sign of unusual graffiti.

Heading further west, the next stop was on Queen Street's dedicated streetcar route near Spadina. With no cycling allowed on that road, she took back streets over to Augusta. At Queen, she walked her bike along the sidewalk. There, on the other side of the road was the kind of graffiti she sought: a bicycle with no rider. Again, the wheels of the bike seemed to be in motion, and she could picture the image of the rider that would be added, leaning over the handle bars, racing on to the road. The streetcars would stop.

She sent a text to Miles marked urgent with a request to be notified when he read the text. If he didn't pick up the message, she'd call. Then she emailed Traffic to be on alert. *Now to the water?* But the next five locations were in interesting neighbourhoods that she seldom rode through. *Might as well be thorough.* At the next side street, she turned north. Half an hour later, she had just one more location to check.

A man flew backwards out of a shop onto the street. Braking quickly, the auto-car beside her also stopped. A store keeper brandishing a phone stepped from the store yelling at the man. The man raised his hands and kept backing away. Cars approaching on the other side of the road also stopped. When the shop keeper stepped onto the road, the man put his hands on his hips, shook his head, and threatened to call the police.

Someone in one of the stopped cars pressed the horn and leaned out the window. "Get out of the damn road! You think you own this street!"

*If he stays much longer, Monitor will notice the stopped cars.* Jen considered calling up her id on her phone and intervening, but this was a day off, and the two men seemed really angry. A distant siren caught the first man's attention.

"I'm leaving. But don't think I'll ever darken your door again."

The shopkeeper pointed his phone at the man. "If you, your partner, your child crosses my doorstep, I will call the police."

The two men cleared off the street in opposite directions, and the cars started to move. Jen shook her head, wondering what transaction might have gone wrong in the shop. Some things were better not known.

She wove her way through back streets heading north

and west. In the small yards of these houses, there were patches of green grass. Bright flowers grew along pathways, against house walls. Driveways were paved with brick laid in interesting patterns. A basketball escaped across the road, and a teen dashed in front of her to grab it. Another driveway was blocked with a hockey net swarmed by three young girls. Houses here cost a pile of money, completely unaffordable for ordinary people. So far, thanks to the incomes these people made, this neighbourhood survived. The money developers offered so they could tear down the houses and build high-rises did not tempt them. She wondered how long that would last. So many neighbourhoods had been taken apart and converted to high density housing.

Turning north on Ossington, she headed for College and the last location on her list. She stopped her bike. A big beach ball had been painted onto the wall right at the road's edge. A small arm reached for it. *This is going to be a child chasing their ball. A classic the auto pilots were taught to watch for.* Checking her phone, she saw that Miles had not picked up her first message. "Phone, call Miles." The phone on her wrist vibrated slightly, then she heard the ring.

"Hello?" said a groggy voice.

"You sleep late." There was a pause. He was probably looking at the phone to see who called.

"And you don't, Jen. But I don't imagine you were up most of Friday night."

"What happened?"

"Long story. Why are you calling?"

"Two graffiti are started. I texted when I found the first on a transit line, but with two, I decided I better call."

"What! I got no warning!"

Jen looked around to find the surveillance cameras. This section of wall shouldn't be outside the camera's view. "Wonder why no hack covered the work. Looks like the paintings could be finished in one more stint. Should I call a clean up crew to get rid of them?" A long pause on the other end of the line. She wondered what Miles considered. The silence stretched on. "You there Miles?"

"Leave it with me. Don't think I should decide that on my own. Damn, I wanted today off."

"I suppose as a manager, you don't get overtime pay."

"I'll be taking a week of lieu time when we solve this." Another pause. "But thanks, Jen. For looking for them."

"Happy to. You need anything else from me?" Again, a pause.

"No. I'll go in and see what the camera shows. Likely the same artist, but when it isn't the same MO, I need to be sure."

Another pause. Jen imagined Miles rolling himself out of bed. *Wonder what kept him up Friday?* Can't have been an issue in Traffic, or he'd have told her. "Are we still on for Tuesday?"

"As long as something else doesn't blow up."

Jen winced. "Don't even mention an explosion."

"Right. There is no telling what might happen next. But I better go figure this one out."

"Bye then. Phone, disconnect." Jen studied the beach ball. What did it mean that this work had not been hidden by a computer hack? Was the artist feeling more cocky? That did not feel like a sensible reaction to being arrested. She shook her head. Enough worry. Time for water.

\*  \*  \*

Adrenaline got Miles as far as Monitor Central, but as he rode the elevator, tiredness seeped back in. He felt his feet drag. Arriving at the department, Tatiana was already at her work station.

"I thought I told you to stay home," she said. "You look like something the dog threw up."

"Nice to see you too."

"Sorry, but it's true."

"The truth does not always need to be spoken."

"I suppose." Tatiana turned back to her screen. "But you haven't said what you are doing here."

"Jen found two places where graffiti has been started."

"Your alarm failed?"

Miles rubbed the lines between his eyebrows. "No alarm went off."

"You could have called, and I would have checked them out."

"I wasn't sure you would be here. You have other priorities, and if the alarm failed, it will be hours of work strengthening it."

"In which case, two heads are better. Take a look, and let me know."

Calling up the cam at the first location where Jen found the partially finished image of a cyclist, he snapped a screen shot and emailed it to Darshani to confirm the same artist had painted it. He skipped back through the record to identify when it had been started. He found a blank wall Saturday noon, ran the video at high speed forward. His eyes hurt with the speed of motion. He rubbed one eye closed, and then the other. And there was the painter. He set the speed to normal, and watched as a man with a baseball cap worked deftly to create the image of a moving bicycle. There were the same tattoo marks on neck and wrist. It seemed that, released from jail, John-Boy had gone right back at it.

*Without being hidden.* He wondered what that meant. Did John-boy work alone now? Or now that he was known to be the artist but had been released without even a fine, he wasn't worried. Miles rubbed his temples and switched to the second site. Nothing Saturday afternoon. Nothing Saturday evening. But there just after dawn, a completed beach ball. Backing up at high speed was even more dizzying. He jumped back an hour and fast forwarded. There, just as the day began to brighten, John-Boy walked up to the wall and started painting.

Tatiana slid her chair over. "At least the alarm didn't fail.

The artist is there in plain sight."

"I can set up a physical recognition program on these cams so we get notified when he comes back to finish the job."

"And arrest him all over again."

"That answers the question of whether we should have a clean up crew get rid of them," said Miles. "I wonder how many times we'll have to arrest him before he gets tired of the experience." Miles wrote a quick report and emailed it off to Admin Chan marked important. *At least this one isn't urgent.*

Tatiana rolled her chair back to her work station. "If you have enough energy and brain power to handle the recognition program, I'll get back to what I was working on."

"That much I can do half asleep."

"Good. Then do it, and go sleep. And no matter what else happens, don't come back until tomorrow."

Miles turned to meet her eyes. He could not make that promise. He tried to think of something that would require him to return, though that felt like tempting fate. "Yes, boss."

Tatiana rolled her eyes. "I am not your boss. And I'm not your mother. But I want you at your best tomorrow. Now get busy, and get out of here. I only ordered lunch for me."

\*   \*   \*

A steady buzz from Miles' phone broke his concentration. Samantha had marked her call urgent. "What's up Sam?"

"I hate to ask you to go into Monitor Central on a Sunday."

"I'm already here."

"One bit of good news. Geoff has gone missing. It's been four hours, and we can't find him in any of his usual hideouts."

"What happened?"

"He worked a night shift. It must have been bad. Julie

heard his erratic breathing from inside her house as he walked by. He planned to sleep at our place, but there was Rickie at work in the front yard. And you know how upset he is these days. He called out to Geoff, promised to go out back, but Geoff crossed the street and started to run. Rickie let him go, which seemed like the right thing, but after two hours, he told Julie and me. Another hour, and a couple of us went looking. Can you track him on the cams?"

*It's against policy,* thought Miles. "What time did he get home?"

"About seven-thirty."

"Hang on." Calling up the record from the cam outside the Scarborough Houses a little before that time, Miles could see Rickie in a corner of the picture working.

"What's up?" Tatiana asked.

Miles took a sharp breath in. *Admit breaking protocol or lie?* "A friend has gone missing. He's…" How to describe Geoff? "Fragile. Kind of on the autism spectrum."

"Aren't we all?" Tatiana asked.

Miles looked at her sharply then turned back to the cam's record. Geoff crossed the street.

"I mean not everybody, but any of us with an obsession like me or an intensity like you. Maybe ASD isn't the right thing to call it, but our focus affects our ability to interact with other people the way they expect us to. I'm always setting people off."

Miles shifted cams. It was a couple seconds before Geoff appeared in view. Cams were less frequent in the quiet suburb. "Geoff is sensitive to other people's intense emotions. Other people set him off, like today."

"Well find him, and get back to the task you are here for."

Shifting cams again, Miles saw that Geoff crossed the road into the high-rise complex that had once been a neighbourhood park. More cams in this densely populated area meant it was easier to keep track of him. Passing four of the buildings, the running man slipped between two. Miles shifted to the street at the other side. Geoff did not come out. "Sam, I think he's between two buildings in the complex east of you." He gave the addresses.

"I'll take Julie to the spot, let her go in to get him. Thanks Miles."

"Just get him home and rested. Tell him to take tonight off if he's booked to work."

"Already thought of that. Have a call into Brindle and Giovanni too. Bye."

Miles shifted back to real time on the cam that had showed Geoff enter the alley and got back to his task. When Julie and Juniper with Samantha hanging back appeared on the screen, he shut down the feed. He'd done his part. He needed to get his task done so that he could get home and sleep.

\*    \*    \*

"I'll wait here, Julie," said Samantha. "Giles trusts you completely."

"He likes you a lot, Sam," Julie said.

"Not the same. You've got way better control of your emotions."

*Just breathe slowly,* Julie thought as she stepped onto the laneway between the two buildings. The air was significantly cooler in the shade of the the two apartment complexes. They had not thought of looking for him in this complex with its thousands of people and their psychic noise. Julie knew there would be deep shadows here, places to hide. Rank smells filled her nose. There were garbage bins in this alley. *Good thing smell isn't my Gifted sense.*

Listening, she heard someone breathing farther down the narrow alley. At least, the rhythm sounded fairly calm. As she got closer, the sound echoed. The person sat in a narrow space. Juniper whined softly.

"How can you stand the smell, Geoff?"

"Hello Julie. How did you find me?"

"Miles. He tracked you here. We were worried."

"Great. And that's supposed to calm me down." Geoff took a ragged breath. "You don't feel worried."

"Because I knew you were here. What are you doing in this awful spot?"

"Pretending to be homeless."

"Why?"

"Because people consciously avoid thinking about the homeless people they see. Most, at least. They carefully think about something else. It's great."

Julie thought about that, wondered if she so studiously avoided paying attention to homeless people in the core. "Sounds like a good strategy. Only problem is that the longer you were gone, the more worried we were going to be at home."

"I had not solved that part yet."

"Fortunately, Miles did that for you. Once we knew where you were, everybody relaxed."

"What about Rickie?"

Julie sighed. "His anxiety is based on real problems that seem to be multiplying, not decreasing. But he's practising meditation right now so that he doesn't drive you away."

"I need a rest."

"We know. We'll call the hospital and tell them you are ill. Take tonight off."

"My supervisor won't be surprised. I didn't do well last night."

"Oh Geoff. Yours is a hard Gift."

"On the way home, tell me how you learned to sift the sounds you want to hear from all the rest. Might help me learn to filter."

Again, Julie sighed. "Sure. It's a pretty personal technique though." *I think you just need less psychic exposure.* Stepping forward two paces, she reached her hand down. Geoff took it, got to his feet, and together they walked slowly back to the sunlight and to Samantha.

# CHAPTER TWENTY-ONE

A huge machine built like a high-hoe but with a saw on the end carved its way through the trees of High Park. The grinding whine was like a garbage compactor and an airplane engine all at once. Drenched in sweat, Rickie pulled himself out of the dream. Another nightmare about the devastation he feared would become reality.

Sitting up in bed, he heard the pre-dawn songs of robins, a cardinal, and the song sparrow who built a nest in the thirty-year-old maple outside his window. The sky was two shades less than black. Only four-thirty or so. Lying down again, he closed his eyes, pictured an acorn falling to the ground, buried by a squirrel, slowly softening and swelling. Hearing a truck rumble down the road outside, remembering the roar of the clear-cutting machine, he began the meditation again.

The clock read 6:07 when he woke. An hour before he needed to get up. No more dreams that he could remember. He lay looking at the ceiling, painted a rich green like the walls of the room. Darshani said the colour made the room seem smaller than it was, but she did acknowledge that it spoke of life. He had asked her if she could create the effect of leaves against the sky on a bright day, but Darshani told him that would be more than a month's work, and he might as well just lie down under the maple tree outside.

That tree he could protect. He clenched his teeth. *And I will protect High Park with all my energy, all my heart.* Getting up, he headed to the shower. Starting his day now would give him time to check out the park himself before meeting up with Jainyu to pass him the sample of ants to show the entomologist at the ROM. It crossed his mind that he would have more time to explore if he took the Bloor subway line all the way to High Park Station, but he shook his head. The more roundabout route, down the University line to the Queensway, would have to do. He would not walk the streets which had once been rolling hills, streams, and forests.

An hour and a half later, getting off the streetcar, he walked the sidewalk beside the spot where the water main had been repaired. The ground had been levelled, and sod laid. The Green Spaces crew had done their part.

Where the forest began, thick shrubs created a wall of green. They had, so far, survived the repair work. Time would tell how much of the root systems was disturbed. Taking a path inward, he touched the trunks of trees that arched overhead. In the first few, he felt stress. These ones had roots that ran toward the busy roadway. He lingered on these, pushing energy into them, encouraging them to draw what they needed from the earth. With the next few, it was more like an echo or a memory. Rickie leaned in to these trees with the thought that they could draw their energy from the roots away from the stressed trees, perhaps share carbon with them.

As he wandered the path, he wondered what more he could do. High Park received its quota of compost in early spring when it would be most helpful. Roof-top gardens were now the priority as they produced essential fresh food for the city, but he could check if the compost facilities had extra this season. He didn't think that the budget would allow for artificial fertilizer; that went to the hydroponic facilities because they also produced essential food. Perhaps one of the manufacturers or a big retailer could be talked into making a donation as long as the gift came with a high-profile appearance and lots of social media uptake.

Cheered by that possibility, Rickie circled back toward the pond. Coming across the place where Miles found the ants, tears welled up in his eyes. Five dogwood shrubs were stripped bare. Above them, the lower branches of an oak were also devoid of green. What would it have been like if Miles had not happened by this way, if the Green Spaces crew had not raced to the location, if the ants had been resistant to pesticides?

Rickie shook off the feeling of despair. The ants had been exterminated. The oak had greenery to spare and the dogwood would put out a secondary growth of small leaves, enough to get it through the growing season. But a fist tightened around his heart. Someone was working really hard to show that High Park was not thriving.

\* \* \*

After meeting up with Rickie and checking to make sure no more of the manufactured insects had appeared, Jainyu returned to the ROM. A different security guard staffed the admission desk, and patiently, Jainyu went through the same careful security routine to get the admission code and entomology key put in his phone. Effective security felt comforting given all that was happening. At the lab, the intern greeted him with the information that Timur was in his office before he said a word. Timur welcomed him with a serious look on his face.

"I hope you have not found another technological infestation."

Jainyu shook his head. "The staff that dealt with it used a strong but normal chemical pesticide. It worked."

"They will likely need to do a second application. Some ant colonies will bury larvae to protect them at the first sign of danger. Let me see these voracious little things, and I will tell you."

Jainyu removed the sample jar from his pack. Several of the ants still moved around the edge as if looking for an escape route. Timur reached for a magnifying glass.

"I think we are in luck. But come let me take a closer look before we gloat."

*Gloat?* Jainyu thought, as he followed the entomologist to the photographic microscope. *You just told me they may be hard to get rid of.*

When Timur stunned the ants, they stayed stunned. "That's a good sign they are natural insects." He placed one under the microscope. "Five times magnification. Picture. Eight times magnification. Picture," Timur said. He studied the images on the screen closely. "Eureka. These are a common Asian ant not found in North America."

"Why is that *good* news?"

Timur smiled. "Because someone imported them."

"Insects can arrive on produce, can't they?"

"At one time they did, but we have found a microwave that does not harm the vegetables and fruit or live plants but does deal with almost all insects. Ants are not the exception. Luggage and materials at airports and goods arriving at the ports are also treated in this way to prevent accidental arrival of hazardous insects. These had to be imported intentionally, and what has been imported can be traced."

Jainyu felt the tension in his chest relax. "And as the head ROM entomologist, you can find out who got the permit."

"Indeed, I can."

"Which will get us close to who is attacking the park," said Jainyu.

"The federal department that looks after such imports will be very unhappy these were released. Nail down the culprit, and we will pin these murder hornets to a sample board."

It was Jainyu's turn to smile. The image of this Timur as a predator differed greatly from the man who could be gentle with the most poisonous of insects. *If he is right, we'll be able to put a stop to these attacks!*

\*   \*   \*

"But if that is true, then the equation $e=mc^2$ would be missing a variable," said Nathan to the computer terminal inches from his face.

"You wish to know if there are eggs equal to what in one of the House's kitchens?" asked the House in a voice that almost sounded irritated.

"What? Is it lunch time?"

"No one is eating lunch. Geoff is in this kitchen making his first meal of the day."

"Geoff? Right. He stayed in our guest room the last three nights." Nathan pushed back from his desk. A break might help figure out where his thinking took a wrong turn. And Samantha had urged him to check in with Geoff, pointing out the fragility of the empath. He headed upstairs.

"Do not enter until you clear your mind of that stupid problem." Geoff stood with his back to the stairs, tension rippling through the muscles.

"It isn't a stupid problem," said Nathan. "There are still things to work out around Einstein's theories. And my work on gravity has been making progress. With quantum divergence..."

"Don't drag Amanda into your physics stuff."

"You can see into my brain?"

"It's like you've dragged her all the way out here from the core. I can almost feel her."

Nathan sat on the edge of a stool. "If I could see quantum divergence as she does, then..."

Geoff whirled around, pointed his bread knife at Nathan. "Don't you ever try to explain how I know what I know."

"You don't want to hear my theory?"

"Your theories do nothing but confuse me." Geoff stepped closer. "And when I get confused, you get impatient, and you just try harder. So just don't. I've enough to deal with." He slammed the knife on the counter.

Nathan folded his arms. "Geoff. There is an explanation

for everything. When it seems like a mystery, it means that we simply don't see the process clearly yet."

The toaster popped, and Geoff rescued the bread that flew up. "Why do you have this old-fashioned thing? I can never get it to work right. And don't answer that. I want to complain, not get an explanation." Geoff slammed peanut butter onto the toast. "You don't understand her Gift, or your own more than I can explain or stop mine."

"Would you like to? Stop, I mean."

"As if that is possible." Geoff jabbed the knife into the peanut butter jar.

Nathan's phone vibrated. A call from Val. "I should take this. Are you okay?"

"Fine." Geoff grabbed his breakfast and strode down the hall. The back door slammed.

Nathan answered the call. "Morning Val. You found something?"

"Indeed, I did. Is it okay to fill you in now?"

"I happen to be alone all of a sudden. Go for it."

"The satellite was registered, but through the space program in India. Not a place you would normally look."

"Someone can register a satellite for Toronto airspace on the other side of the world?"

"One space agency world wide. Different branches but one organization. No one owns the stratosphere."

"Do you know what the satellite is for?"

"There are four science projects being run through it. One is measuring electromagnetic variations in the atmosphere and trying to locate the source of the variations. One is measuring water temperature fluctuations in the lake beside your city. That one is tied to some weather channel in Canada. A university group is trying to map fish migrations from the sky. The last is a pair of scientists measuring carbon capture in the city core."

"Carbon capture, not carbon emissions."

"Right."

"Why?"

"The friend who gave me the clue to look in India had a hunch. Two years ago, satellites went up above New Delhi and Beijing. Both registered in India. Both paid for by the same company. Both measuring carbon capture."

"And this one is sponsored by that company."

"You got it."

"Does not sound like a coincidence. What is this company's interest?"

"My friend has an interest in climate change mitigation. The scientists used the data from those two satellites to prove that urban farming, including green roofs and hydroponics facilities, are reducing carbon emissions in the cities they monitored."

"Woo. That's good news."

"In and of itself, yes. However, the evidence from those studies was used to influence development policy. They succeeded in taking over land in Beijing that had been designated for new park spaces and completely derailed a plan to limit urban development in New Delhi."

"And now a similar study is taking aim at Toronto."

"One more thing," said Val. "The two scientists running the carbon capture study were on leave from their university. At the time, they were employed by a company owned by a developer with interests in both cities."

"That's conflict of interest. How come nobody noticed?"

"It took my friend some digging to make the connection. And it happens that the developer is based in your city. E. D. Graham. Heard of him?"

"Who hasn't? One of the wealthiest. Thanks Val. You really went to town for me."

"Not just you, my friend. She's worried that Toronto seems to be the new focus for this research. As much as she appreciates urban farming, she is afraid that less utilitarian ways of capturing carbon—tree-lined streets, parks, forests, even rural farms—are in danger if we count on urban farming to promote carbon capture."

Nathan nodded slowly. Given the money spent to attack

High Park, Val had a good lead. "Can you email me the names of the scientists who ran that project? I'd like to learn a bit more about them."

"Already sent. Anything else?"

Nathan rubbed his chin. "This feels like important information that Metro should have. If I get you the name of the administrator who has been following these issues, would you give them a call? It would sound more credible coming directly from NASA."

"I can do that. Just get me the name."

"Will do. And thanks again." Nathan saw that Geoff had come back in, arms wrapped around his body.

"One of these days," said Val, "we'll sit and chat about how you found that satellite. It's a small one, given the simplicity and similarity of the measuring equipment."

"We'll talk. Bye Val." Nathan disengaged the call. "You okay Geoff?"

The empath shook his head rapidly. "Looking at Rickie's gardens brought back all his worry. I couldn't stand it. Now, you reek of racing ideas. I may have to move to a hotel."

"Remember how badly it turned out the last time you tried that." Nathan took a deep breath. "With that call, I actually got good news. I'll take a walk now and get my mind out of your reach. I'll make my calls while I'm walking. Then, I will start thinking about gravity, and I guarantee that by the time I get back from my walk, I won't be thinking about carbon capture at all. Unless I decide that carbon atoms, given their size and complexity, have a gravitational influence on neighbouring atoms."

"I can always depend on you to get distracted. Makes you a reasonably comfortable person." Geoff held himself more tightly. "Sometimes. Not now. Get out of this kitchen."

On the way out the door, Nathan decided to also call Brindle, ask them to come out to see Geoff. The empath was much more on edge than normal, and the problems setting off the people around him were not getting any simpler.

# CHAPTER TWENTY-TWO

"Alert," said Monitor. "Contact with taxi 07TW34 disrupted. Initiate protocol Ricci four."

"Ricci four! That's the program we're supposed to use if a car gets hijacked!" said Raja.

"Call Miles!" Jen called up the program that the tech team designed. It had been installed in the system late the previous day.

"911 Emergency," said Monitor. "Fire. Police. Ambulance. 911 Emergency."

Jen glanced at the board where a red circle flashed on and off. Calling up the cam, her hand went to her mouth. She had not been quick enough. A car sat with its front end in a shop window. People screamed, shouted words she could not make out. A woman came to the door of the shop yelling, waving her arms. A police car appeared, and two officers jumped from the car.

"I've got Miles," said Raja.

"Tell me something didn't blow up." Worry lines marked Miles' forehead.

"By all that is holy," said Jen. "Another car went rogue. We need to find out if there is the same box in the car. How do we make sure the police check? And what if someone was hurt. The car smashed a shop window. Shit. There is an ambulance. And they are looking under the car. Someone may have been hit. That can't be. Not in our day."

"Take a breath, Jen. Did the program to recover connection work?"

"There was no time. Just seconds between the alarm and the car hitting the store window."

"Tell me where this happened so I know which police detachment to call."

"Why do you sound so calm! This is horrible. You can't imagine. There is a second ambulance now and two more police cars. One of the paramedics has gone into the store. Do something, Miles."

"I am not calm, Jen, but panic from me won't help. There is information I need. Where did this happen?"

"Shit. Yes. You need to know. It's near the corner of Harbord and Ossington, just west of the corner, I think. I'll double check. Yes. That's where it is."

"One more thing Jen. What is the make of the car?"

Jen zoomed closer, told him the make and model, heard Miles swear. She typed a flurry of commands that would tell all car pilots to take an alternate route. Then, as the fire truck arrived, she watched as they ensured no one had been pinned under the car, turned it off, and went inside to help the paramedics. Pieces of glass littered the sidewalk.

"How can this happen?" Raja put a hand on her shoulder. "And if two cars go rogue, who knows how many others might. What are we going to do?"

A fourth police car came from the opposite direction and stopped right beside the crash. The officer opened the back door, took a photo with her phone. Then, she reached in, pulled out a metal box, held it up toward the camera. She returned to her car with the box and drove away.

Jen breathed a long sigh. Miles had gotten through to the police. And they found the same kind of box. This meant that not every car would go rogue, just the ones with this particular box placed in it. *I hope those are so rare, so impossibly expensive that there were just the two.* Jen closed her eyes. That wish had no substance. She had no idea how many more cars might get hijacked. But she could find out who placed this box by tracing the history of this taxi. "Raja. We need to prepare an email for the night shift. They need to know before they get here what might happen. The usual shift change won't be enough to explain this." As her co-worker took up that task, she began to trace the movements of the car backwards.

\*   \*   \*

After a trip to the police station to examine the box, Miles settled back at his work station. Everyone else had left, but he wanted to check progress on each project before heading home himself. A few minutes later, an alarm went off. Hollingsworth had signed in. *She is like a virus that just won't quit!* Mentally crossing his fingers that she would not find the new spy program, he watched what she worked on. The water system again. He leaned closer. High Park area. *Damn her all to hell.* Studying her key strokes, he saw a new kind of hack. Made sense. She would have realized with John-boy's arrest that someone at Monitor figured out how to spot the type of hack she used. But what was she doing? Miles followed her work. Ingenious. She seamlessly joined two surveillance streams.

Still watching, Miles called security. A quick check, and they let him know she was not in the building. *Where is she?* First things first. The spyware recorded every move, gathering the evidence that it was her who hacked the system. But what did she cover up this time? He put in a call to the water department.

The overseer who answered had clearly heard about the incident on the weekend, immediately accepting Miles' concern, agreed to call up the backup feed. When Hollingsworth logged out, he undid her work, restoring real time surveillance data. Then, he saved the record from the spy program, left a copy on his laptop, sent one to the cloud, and emailed another to himself.

Writing an email marked urgent to Chan, he explained what he had seen and how he documented the hack. He added that Hollingsworth was not in the building. He went back to checking the day's work log but found he could not focus. Checking his email, he found a reply from the administrator saying that security would detain Hollingsworth as soon as she arrived the next morning, asking that Miles attend that examination. As he closed down his work station, he decided to check in with the water department. The same person answered.

"Things are under control," the man said. "Thanks to you. I don't know how you knew, but pressure dropped shortly after you called. A leak right into the pond at High Park. Would have flooded in no time."

"We are on high alert in Tech right now."

"Ground crew is on site and will have it under control shortly." The supervisor looked away. "Gotta go."

As the video closed, Miles wondered what else had happened. But as long as the supervisor knew about it, Monitor's systems were working, meaning it was an issue he did not need to worry about. Time to go home.

# CHAPTER TWENTY-THREE

*Another day, another possibility for disaster,* Miles thought as the subway neared the Monitor Central station. Then, he rubbed his temples, told himself that pessimism did not help. Progress had been made. He had given Admin Chan proof that Martha Hollingsworth hacked the system at least once. And Nathan might have figured out the reason for the attacks on High Park. *Which leaves the reason for the graffiti a mystery, though maybe Hollingsworth will clear that up.* As he got out of the subway, he faced a large, noisy crowd of protesters. Police were scattered around the crowd that now blocked all eastbound traffic on Bloor Street. Clearly, the mayor's office had decided not to break up the protest, simply to make sure it stayed peaceful. Jen and the others in Traffic must have cleared another eastbound route to keep vehicles moving. Police held open a corridor through the crowd to the front door.

A woman stepped in front of him. "Join our campaign to limit machine interference," she said as she pushed a pamphlet toward him.

"Keep your propaganda." Miles pushed by her. Two men stepped in front of him, shoulder to shoulder, blocking his way.

"The machines are a danger. You must understand this,"

one of the men said, pushing his face closer to Miles. "People are in hospital because of them. "

*And a woman didn't die in a taxi.* Pushing aside the thought of what could have happened if Monitor employees, Jen in particular, had not been on top of the interferences, Miles straightened his back and met the eyes of the man who had spoken. "Human interference, not AI mistakes caused the accident."

"No one was in the second car. The car that injured people. It was the AI."

Miles breathed deep. "It was people who compromised the normal working of the car pilot. Let me by."

"You work here! You are one of the scum who is leading us into a robot takeover!" The other man raised his fists.

Taking a step backward, Miles spread his hands wide, trusting that the angry protester would not punch him.

A police officer appeared at Miles' side. "Let's keep this protest calm, and let these people do their work. This way, Sir."

With the officer's hand on his elbow, Miles was led to the protected corridor into the building. He felt rattled. The protesters were so wrong. It wasn't the AIs that were causing the problem. People planned the incidents and carried them out. As he glanced at the protesters glaring at him, he straightened his shoulders and kept moving. As he got to the door of the building, his phone vibrated.

"Text from Admin Chan," the phone said.

"Read it to me."

"in my office now"

*I take it Hollingsworth has arrived and been detained.* Miles texted his department that he was in the building but occupied and took the elevator up to the administration level.

A security guard at the door to Admin Chan's office checked his ID. Inside, security personnel guarded Martha Hollingsworth who stood, arms folded, glaring at the administrator. Chan sat behind her glass topped desk, leaning back in a large leather chair.

"Good morning, Mr. Franklin," said the administrator. "I have been explaining to Ms. Hollingsworth that she will be charged with technological invasion, a serious crime, as well as intention to damage public and private property, among other charges. I have also informed her that if she explains why she is illegally entering Monitor's systems, and agrees not to do so again, I have a proposal for her, a way for her to serve her probation. She seems to think that she has nothing to confess. Explain to her that she does."

Miles turned to the woman who met his eyes with a cold stare. "We cannot prove you hacked the system to cover the graffiti artist's work, although you were online for each of them. However, we know that you logged in at 2 a.m. when the system was hacked to cover a water main break. More important, when you logged in yesterday after hours, I traced your work. You again interfered with the surveillance of a water main. That we can prove.

"Also, we found four social media posts originating in your accounts, calling for people to protest the use of AIs in cars. The claims that a taxi had gone rogue were posted immediately after that taxi was stopped, long before the news became public. This connects you with an invasion of an AI that could have caused injury to the passenger."

Hollingsworth lifted her jaw, pulled back her shoulders. "There is nothing like that in my personal accounts. I repeat 'personal,' because what is there is none of Monitor's business."

"I agree the posts were deleted," said Miles. "But they existed. I have copies. Given the speed with which they went public, it appears that you had inside knowledge of the taxi override."

Hollingsworth turned away and stared out the window. "Appearances get you nothing."

"The protests give us some clue what is going on," said Admin Chan. "The graffiti makes something of the same point: AIs are not as smart as our society thinks they are."

The administrator stood, and placing palms on the desk, leaned forward, spoke with a voice like ice. "The second car takeover was horrific. We will have to come back to that. Mr. Franklin, explain to her what her water system hacks put at risk."

Miles thought Hollingsworth flinched, but she continued staring out the window. "Would you like to know what would have happened if I had not caught your hack last night? The pond at High Park would have flooded, spilling over into the nearby housing complex. Those are older buildings with electrical rooms in the basement. You know what happens when water and electricity meet? Imagine hundreds of families with no hydro for days."

Slowly, Hollingsworth turned her head to look at Miles. "You cannot charge me with what did not happen."

"But the hack took place." Chan sat back down. "Before I can offer you probation, there is the question of the second taxi hijacking. People were injured. Why did you go ahead with that?"

Folding her arms across her chest, Hollingsworth looked at the floor, bit her lower lip. "If I knew about these rogue cars, I might know that the second hijacking was cancelled because a passenger ended up in the first. Someone may have gone ahead without adequate planning."

"Do you know who?" Chan asked.

Hollingsworth shook her head.

"No, you don't know, or no you will not say?"

"I do not know who set up that override."

"We will need to know as much as you do know about where the hijacking devices originated." Chan placed her hands flat on the desk. "If I read you correctly, you did not know what your interference in our system hid at the park. You could have guessed, however, and yet you went ahead. Police will be here in ten minutes. If I do not have your agreement by then, you will simply be arrested. I see that smile. If you go that route and get the same high-priced lawyer your graffiti artist got, we will have a lead on who is behind this. We won't need you to stop the attacks." Chan stood and looked out the window as if studying the skyline of the core. "Metro has become extremely reliant on AIs. It has lowered the vigilance of the human workers. And the people of our city came to think that Monitor was impregnable. You have shown that it is possible to hack into the system. The people whose transit status was wiped off their phones were quite unsettled."

"I don't know what you are talking about."

"Perhaps," said Chan. "To get to my point. People are asking questions of us, and I want to tell them that Monitor has a new department of Cyber Security with the most skilled whitehackers, a department staffed by people who are suspicious of AIs, making them alert to any and all potential problems." Chan turned to meet Hollingsworth's eyes. "I would like you to head that department. This job would constitute the terms of your probation. The price is that you are charged, you plead guilty, and you tell us who is behind the High Park attacks. "

Hollingsworth bit her lower lip, never took her eyes off the administrator. "Why not have the woman who ran your white hacker course head the department?"

"Ms. Ricci has already refused the position, wants her independence and the opportunity to work in multiple locations. She suggested you." Chan studied the accountant. "I was skeptical, of the suggestion, but she pointed out that you have the right amount of suspicion. And I have to acknowledge that you have credibility in the community that is suspicious of Monitor."

"What if I refuse?" Hollingsworth asked.

Chan shrugged. "You go to trial and hope the judge does not give you jail time. I doubt, however, that you will find a better way to spend your probation."

Miles clenched his teeth. He would have to develop a working relationship with Hollingsworth given how close his department was to this new one. It was not going to be easy to trust this woman. He wondered if Tatiana and Chan were right to suggest she head up this work.

Chan looked at him as if reading his thoughts and gave a small shake of her head. "But before we talk any more about that new job, who is behind the attempts to destroy parts of High Park?"

Hollingsworth hesitated, looked down at her hands, moved her fingers as if counting. "What if I tell you, hypothetically, that someone might have contacted me anonymously, that the payment for the High Park attacks came by email from an account that even I could not trace, that our group used the money to fund the projects that demonstrated the weaknesses of the AIs?"

"A group. Well. What if I asked you to tell us who is in the group?"

"I wouldn't."

"The police may insist, but we already have some idea who is involved," said Chan. "We have a photo of the man who is suspected to have initiated the first taxi hijacking, and police have identified a potential suspect. We know who picked up your posts calling for the protests." Chan folded her fingers together. "Coming back to High Park, it seems that you were paid to hack the water and sewer systems so that the damage would be well underway before anyone caught the problems. What about the other attacks there?"

Hollingsworth's chin rose. "What other attacks? I did nothing else."

Chan's eyebrows went up. "Nothing else. That is quite close to an admission. If you were paid anonymously, I suppose you don't know who it was. Two additional conditions then: you will email the person who contacted you informing them that you will not hack for them again; then, you will provide a copy of the emails in which you were paid—don't bother to claim you deleted them as we both know deleted items can be retrieved. Police can get a warrant to follow that trail. Now, if are you ready to acknowledge that you hacked Monitor's surveillance system five times, describing what you did and how, I will turn on the voice and video recorder. Before you give your testimony, I will lay out the terms of your probation so that there is a record of my offer. The charges are serious enough that without our advocacy on your behalf, jail time is inevitable."

Miles' phone buzzed. Monitor recognized the physical description of the artist at one of the graffiti sites Jen found. "The graffiti artist is at work, Administrator. The police have been alerted."

"This time I want you to take part in the interrogation. Show the artist how deep a hole he is in. And that we have his co-conspirator caught between our fingers."

Hollingsworth folded her arms. "He's on his own today."

"An interesting development. Still, he knew that other times you were hacking into the system to hide his work. Make him squirm, Mr. Franklin. I think we have an agreement here."

"Agreed," said Hollingsworth quietly.

Leaving the office, Miles found two police officers chatting with the security guard.

"How is it going in there?" asked one of the officers.

"She's about to give a recorded confession," said Miles.

"Perfect. Chan should signal us to rush in shortly then," said the other officer.

Shaking his head at the extent of Admin Chan's planning, Miles called Detective Madison, checked that officers were on route to arrest John-boy. "I'd like to be part of the interrogation," he told her. "I'll head right over."

\*   \*   \*

In the enclosed consultation cubicle of the Metro Green Spaces department, Jainyu laid out for Rickie what Timur found out and what he hoped to discover. "There are two companies in North America with the capabilities to create the bugs we first found. Talking to his contact in one, Timur found the horror that entomologist expressed genuine. The second conversation was more interesting. In the video call, the first emotion Timur read was fear. Horror yes, but it felt different, as if there was some other thought, maybe guilt, as well. Timur guessed that the bugs had been created in that lab, but the creators did not know they would be released. The federal Department of Genetic Engineering is following up."

"A guess is not enough." Rickie shook his head. "And he already said that department is underfunded."

"Timur pushed them a bit saying that if they are able to uncover a serious crime, they would prove the need for better funding."

"What we do to get the money we need. What about the imports?"

"Those were traced to an entomology professor at the university. The professor looked frightened, claimed the ants had been stolen. A police report was filed a few minutes after Timur's call."

"What now?" Rickie asked.

In silence, Jainyu studied his notes on the table, and Rickie paced the narrow room. After two circuits, he laid his palms on the table. "We go see the administrator that Miles has been dealing with."

Jainyu looked up. "You think we can get a hearing?"

"We have to try," said Rickie.

"When?"

"Now. Come on."

Taking the elevator to the level beneath the cafeteria, Rickie knew he was being impetuous. Their supervisor, always concerned about protocol, would be furious they had not sent the request up the proper chain of authority. That could take a week, and with the rate of attacks on the park, he would not risk waiting.

The receptionist motioned them to stand back until he finished his call. When he signed off, he looked them up and down. "Who is your appointment with?"

"We need to see Admin Chan."

"No appointment?" The man's voice was both icy and disdainful.

"Information has just come to us about the two insect infestations that attacked the area of High Park where a water main broke on the weekend. Admin Chan will want to know." Rickie thought the disdain on the receptionist's face grew stronger.

Jainyu stepped forward, laid one hand on the smooth warm wood of the desk. "Given that two federal departments are now investigating these infestations, we thought the administrator would rather be up to date before getting calls from Ottawa."

*That got his attention,* thought Rickie.

"Take a seat," said the receptionist.

Moving to the large leather chairs against the wall, Rickie chose one. The chair pulled him in and down. Uncomfortable, he pushed himself up so he could sit on the edge. On the shining wood table between him and Jainyu were news magazines and an urban planning journal featuring a picture of the Monitor Central building. Watching the receptionist turn away and speak quietly into the microphone, he began to feel nervous. Would Chan see them?

Removing the headset, the receptionist turned to them with lips set into a tight frown. "Follow me."

Rickie glanced at Jainyu, eyebrows raised.

"I guess Chan will see us," Jainyu said quietly, "and the receptionist is offended we get to interfere with the orderly schedule he set up."

The receptionist glared back to ensure they followed. Opening a carved wooden door, the man ushered them into a bright room. One whole wall was windows. Behind a glass topped desk, Chan stood looking outside.

"Tell me precisely how you know about the water main problems." Chan did not turn to look at them.

Rickie swallowed. *I am not going to tell you that my*

*colleague Deena dreamed it. We'd lose credibility for our main point.* "Because Metro Green Spaces had to repair the damage from the heavy equipment used in the repair. And it is an area we have been watching closely due to two extremely unusual insect infestations."

Jainyu took one step forward. "We thought you would like to know that two federal departments are concerned about those infestations. As we told your receptionist, we believe you would rather be in the loop when they call."

At that Chan turned, sat in the leather chair behind the desk, and motioned for them to take the two stiff backed chairs in front. "Which departments, and why are they interested?"

"The first infestation was found in a routine check." Rickie held his gaze straight, though he was sorely tempted to glance at Jainyu. *Found thanks to Amanda.* "We did not recognize the insect and took samples of those we collected to experts at the ROM and at the university." *No need to mention Grandfather.* "The university professor suspected they were a construction, not natural."

"Which the head entomologist at the ROM confirmed through DNA. The insects were technologically created. Dr. Pachenko reported the infestation to the Federal Department of Genetics. Releasing anything genetically manipulated into the environment is strictly monitored. Whoever did that is in significant trouble."

"You said two departments." Chan's palms rested casually on the glass desktop.

"The second infestation was reported by a community member walking in the park." Rickie swallowed. *Is Chan astute enough to notice we aren't telling everything, like the community member was Miles?* "Samples taken to Dr. Pachenko confirmed that these ants are native to Southeast Asia. They were imported and released, again a serious crime."

"Who made the first insects, and who imported the second?"

"There are two companies that could create the first bugs," said Jainyu. "Dr. Pachenko could not determine which. Neither admitted to the manipulation. The federal department is following up."

"A university professor imported the ants," said Rickie, hurrying to add, "not the one we consulted."

"Fortunately for you," said Chan.

Rickie nodded quickly. "The federal department that deals with live imports is very concerned that these ants were stolen, though the police report was made only after Dr. Pachenko called the professor who brought them into Canada."

Admin Chan looked from one to the other. "You think the professor released them in the park?"

"There are serious penalties for releasing exotic creatures," said Jainyu. "Dr. Pachenko does not believe that a reputable scientist would risk their status, their freedom to work, their job."

"Dr. Pachenko does not believe."

"You are welcome to speak to him yourself," said Jainyu. "We felt it our job to ensure that you knew what was happening before being contacted by the federal government."

"Gracious of you."

Rickie felt his hands tense, forced his fingers to relax. "The employees of the Green Spaces Department are concerned about High Park. It is the last significant..." Rickie took a deep breath. The park was not the significant forest it had been. "High Park is the last natural space in our city. It's our job to ensure its health."

Chan stood and walked to the window, gazed out for a long time, then turned back. "I received an interesting call from NASA about a project that may show we don't need these kinds of wild green spaces, that our urban farming is accomplishing a significant amount of carbon capture. Along with your information, I think I am beginning to see the shape of this puzzle. Would your Dr. Pachenko give me his contacts with the federal offices?"

"I am sure he would."

"It is time to take the offensive here. I do not like being forced into a corner I have to defend. I can see that the two of you are naturalists, that is, you love the park for its wild things. I am not. However, with Central Park in New York gone along with so many other natural areas in the cities of our neighbour to the south, High Park is a place that draws tourists to our city. And I am not prepared to have our policy determined by people outside Metro's administration. Get me those federal contacts."

# CHAPTER TWENTY-FOUR

Miles took a short detour to see John-boy's latest graffiti. In part, he wanted to study for himself the image of the racing dog. Mostly, he had not been inside a police squad room since he was thirteen years old. The lab where he investigated the hijacking technology had felt as familiar as his lab at home. This time he would enter the space where people were booked, investigated, interrogated. A shiver went down his back as he remembered his thirteen-year-old self. His friend had dared him to steal a package of gum so that they could try out the cigarettes he had taken from his dad. A store clerk had seen Miles pick up the gum, followed him out the door, and grabbed him by the shirt collar. The police officer had been frighteningly stern and taken him to the station. His mother was in tears when she picked him up, though the officer had not laid shoplifting charges. When his father got home, he took Miles alone to the living room and lectured about how dangerous it was for a young black man to get picked up by police. Miles stayed away from that friend for a week and from anything that might get him arrested the rest of his life.

Telling himself that this time he had been asked to come to the station to help the police, he picked up his pace and shook off the old memory. At the building, the image of a racing dog was almost complete. How did an image like this confuse the AIs? Touching the wall, he ran his fingers through the still wet paint. He touched something sharp. Pulling his hand away, he found a micro circuit stuck to this finger. Studying the image more closely, he found three more.

Getting out his phone, he pointed the camera toward the circuits in his palm. He felt a small electrical pulse. The sensors on vehicles would generate a similar reaction from the circuits. That could be enough to complicate the data that the AI read. Combined with the qualities of the paint that seemed to attract visual sensors, this helped explain the dramatic effect on the car pilots. Getting out a handkerchief, he cleaned his fingers, then wrapped the circuits in it. The detour had proven worthwhile. Now to the harder task of convincing John-Boy to give up this project.

At the police station, Miles was taken down a corridor to a window into an interrogation room where Officer Madison waited. Through the glass he could see John-boy alone, tapping his fingers on the table. "He's pretty stubborn. Seems to think that we'll slap his wrist and let him go."

"Will you?"

"May have to. No computer hack. No stoppage. There will be a fine, but illegal graffiti is a misdemeanour."

Miles studied the young man. What did he have besides threats to get him to stop making these disruptive paintings? He pulled out the circuits. "I found these embedded in the paint."

"What do they do?"

Miles thought for a moment. Officer Madison would not believe that a person could sense the pulse that Miles could feel because of his Gift. "We'll need to examine them to be sure. But their presence is a clue. As they are evidence, I'll be stuck examining it in your lab I guess."

"Not clean evidence as you found it."

"I can testify that I accidentally removed it from the wet

paint."

Madison shrugged. "Maybe. At least, we can show them to the artist. Might help open him up."

Inside the room, Officer Madison pulled up a chair for Miles. "This man is from Monitor, Chong Bai. He has some information about the trouble you are in."

Miles laid his palms on the table. "We caught Martha Hollingsworth hacking into Monitor's systems yesterday. She has admitted to interrupting the video feed in order to cover your work. She will be charged. She will not hide your work again."

Chong Bai lifted his chin. "I don't need her. All I've done is paint outside my licensed area."

"Repeatedly," said Madison. "The fines go up each time."

"I've a job. I can pay the fines."

Miles laid his palms on the table. "Keep disrupting Traffic and Transit, and one of these times, you are going to cause an accident."

"People have to learn how stupid those machines are."

"If you prove that they are stupid enough to hurt someone, the charges will be different. Officer?"

"Even now, a charge of nuisance would make sense. Reckless endangerment is possible. Given the potential for an accident, I will ask the prosecutor to consider adding those. If you cause an accident and someone gets hurt, one of the charges related to causing bodily harm would be automatic. You could see jail time."

"I haven't hurt anyone." Chong Bai folded his hands and looked down. "My skill is getting the cars to stop."

"It isn't just skill," said Miles. "It's the paint you use, the chemicals added to it." He laid the chips on the table. "And these helped."

Chong Bai's head shot up. He glared at Miles, fire in his eyes. He opened his mouth then shut it again.

"You may make that paint, but you certainly bought the micro chips," said Miles. "Was this a benefit of the funding Martha Hollingsworth secured?"

Officer Madison turned to Miles so that her shoulder, almost her back was to the artist. "I should call up a photo of the man who left the disrupter in the taxi. Chong Bai might know him."

"I had nothing to do with that." Chong Bai half stood, leaning his hands on the table.

"The group that is planning these disruptions seems pretty tight knit," continued Madison, as if Chong Bai had not interrupted. "The protests show careful planning. Charges of conspiracy to commit a crime seem to fit the circumstances."

"I'm not in a gang." Chong Bai's voice got higher in pitch.

Miles turned his chair so that he faced Madison. "We were able to trace the posts that called for the protest. Hollingsworth put up the first ones, but the shares were so immediate that it looks like people were waiting for them. That gives us the identities of some of the central people in this conspiracy."

"It's not a conspiracy," Chong Bai objected.

"A conspiracy that includes threats to High Park," said Miles.

"High Park? What are you talking about?" demanded Chong Bai.

Madison brought her fist down on the table so that it shook. "Damn your stupidity. This most certainly is a conspiracy. You and Hollingsworth conspired together to make sure no one stopped you before your graffiti did its job. And she conspired with others, dragging you into two extremely dangerous car hacks, one that put people in hospital."

"I had nothing to do with hijacking cars. I just stop them."

"That's the problem with joining a conspiracy." Officer Madison smiled. "You never know for sure what else your partners are up to. Once you're in the gang, you're all in."

Folding his arms, Chong Bai slouched in the chair and looked at the table. "I work alone."

"You may have in the past, but once you let Hollingsworth give you a head start, you're in with the rest of the group." The officer stood. "I'll send someone in to book you."

Miles turned back to Chong Bai. "You won't get much done. Monitor has been programmed to recognize you." *A slight exaggeration. Only those two cams are programmed.* "That's how the police caught you at work today."

"And we'll just keep catching you." Officer Madison stood. "Let's go."

Out in the squad room, Madison led the way to her desk. "I told the booking officer to add nuisance. I'll speak to the prosecutor, but until he actually causes an accident, I'm not sure that any other charges will be added."

Miles rubbed his neck. Without Hollingsworth covering Chong Bai's work, he could program Traffic and Transit cams to recognize Chong Bai at the potential locations that Jen had identified. *Shoot. Today is Tuesday. We're supposed to going biking on the island!* Miles pulled his mind back to the task at hand. "We'll do all we can to prevent anyone from getting hurt, but I sure would like to find a way to convince him to stop. The threat of stiffer charges will only work if they stick."

\*      \*      \*

Riding the elevator back up to the Technology office, Miles ran through the to-do list on his phone. A couple urgent items really should be assigned now that the hacker had been identified. With the physical recognition program ready, James should be able to install it on the cams where the graffiti artist might work. Stepping into the Technology office, Miles stopped short. Martha Hollingsworth stood stiff and tall behind Tatiana, who stared at a screen.

"What's up here?" he asked James.

"Admin Chan sent her down to see if Tatiana could trace the emails from the person who funded her."

"Any luck?"

"From the way Tatiana's been muttering, not so far."

"There we go," said Tatiana. "Trashed, and deleted, and I found it. I'll send it to the police so that they can get a warrant to identify whose account it came out of." Tatiana flicked her finger at the accountant. "Now get out of here so we can get back to work. Go set up your new office."

"Which I suppose will have to be somewhere on this floor," said Miles, "as we are going to have to coordinate efforts." He studied the tension in her body, not certain he trusted the arrangement Admin Chan had made.

"I am wanted at the police station." Martha swallowed. "To be formally charged."

"And fingerprinted with a court date." Tatiana turned and grinned at the woman who had gone pale. "The leash Chan put on you is real. Without it, none of us would trust you to do your new job. Tomorrow, once the collar is in place, we will tell you how we caught you."

*Most of how we caught you,* thought Miles. *Amanda's part you never need to know.* "Phone, text Jennifer Sutherland this message: things calm enough here. biking at 5?" Meanwhile, he should be able to get some normal work done.

# CHAPTER TWENTY-FIVE

A message from Admin Chan flashed across Miles' computer screen. "Rooftop helipad. Now." Miles was on his feet, though his legs were stiff and sore from the unfamiliar work of riding a bicycle the night before. As he summoned an elevator—this felt like an emergency even if he had no idea what the context was—he tried to imagine what the administrator needed him for. No guesses came to mind. On the roof, he made his way through the gardens and found the helicopter already running. The pilot motioned him to climb into the front seat, buckle in, and put on a headset.

"Fifty-two division, Pilot," said Chan through the intercom.

Miles' stomach sank, then flipped as the helicopter rose and banked. Why did they need a helicopter, and why go to the police station?

"Mr. Choe tells me that you two are acquainted," said Chan.

"Morning Miles," said Rickie.

"Morning," was all he could manage as his stomach rolled. He closed his eyes, shutting out the dizzying view of rooftops flashing by just meters below.

"Once we have picked up Detective Madison," said Chan, "we are going to High Park. Mr. Graham has called another of his news conferences. This time, a friend at the CBC gave me notice. We are going to interrupt his party."

As the helicopter descended, Miles felt his stomach in his throat. Detective Madison hurried across the helipad. The helicopter rose as soon as she climbed inside. Miles leaned back into the seat, decided he would take transit back to the office once this press conference finished.

Five minutes later, the helicopter landed in an open area beside the pond. Climbing down, Miles felt his knees give way for a moment. He steadied himself against the door frame.

"Not your favourite mode of travel, I see," said Detective Madison.

Miles just shook his head, then smiled weakly at Rickie. "You don't seem to have minded."

"It was fascinating to get a look at rooftop gardens from that perspective."

"This way," said Chan. Walking quickly, the administrator led the way through the trees toward the Queensway. A cluster of people with tablets and cameras stood by the road.

"That's where the water main break was," said Rickie.

"Detective, tell the reporters to keep their cameras and recorders off until I am done." Chan strode by the curious group without glancing at them, walked straight toward a man in a suit flanked by two men and two women dressed in formal business attire. "Mr. Graham, I believe you want to cancel this news conference."

"Administrator Chan," said Graham. "A pleasure to see you, but the public cannot be kept in the dark about the danger this wild park presents and the things that are slipping through Monitor's control."

"I am quite prepared to let the public know the affairs that you have set in motion, if that is what you want."

"I have no idea what you are talking about. This water main break for example. None of you acknowledged the potential disruption of the important Queensway transit line."

"Given how many people travel the Queensway even on a Saturday morning, be assured that thousands of people saw the repair vehicles. More saw the muddy ground and the crew that laid sod. Fewer know that the break was engineered, but many know of the issue itself."

"But you kept it out of the news. I am prepared to let our city know how much danger this area presents to the smooth running of Metro."

"Are you? In that case, it is good we are here to make sure the whole story is told. Mr. Franklin, how did the repair crew get here so fast?"

Miles stepped forward. "My department set up an alarm that let us know that the system that tracks water pressure had been hacked. That told us that false data hid a problem in this area. The crew found the leak before it got out of hand."

"Monitor has been hacked?" said Graham. "I did not think that possible. What will the public think if news of that gets out? I don't think you should have told me."

"I have only told you what I believe you already knew. And the public will learn today. A press release has already gone out announcing that Monitor has a new department of cyber security led by Martha Hollingsworth, a woman I believe you know. We intend to eliminate all vulnerabilities."

"Hollingsworth? Name isn't sparking any memory, but I do meet a lot of people."

"Mr. Franklin," said Chan, "what did you learn that night?"

"My department noted who was online that night and for each of the other hacks."

"More intrusions! Tsk, tsk. And here I thought Monitor had even better cyber security than I do."

"Which would be why you hired the best." Chan raised her hand. "Don't object yet. We'll get to uncovering who hired her. Continue, Miles."

"We put a trace on each of the people who were logged in to Monitor for each of the hacks. When she logged on at a time she was not on duty, I traced her actions, found she substituted false data about another water main near here. We identified our hacker."

A tight, predatory smile came to Chan's face. "Once we secured Ms. Hollingsworth's cooperation, Mr. Franklin and Ms. Ricci, who unfortunately was summoned to Ottawa for an emergency late last night, traced the payments made to Martha Hollingsworth. They all came from a company you own."

"I have the warrant to look at that company's records." Detective Madison patted the satchel she carried. "Judge agreed it would be important to know who authorized the payments."

"I'd like to see that," said one of the women beside Graham.

"My lawyer is so careful. You don't mind?"

"Sure thing." Detective Madison stood right beside the lawyer as she perused the document.

"And the other warrant, Detective?" asked Chan.

"Right. Served first thing this morning. The two scientists studying carbon capture through satellite data are in Graham's direct employ." Madison handed another folded document to the lawyer. "You can look over this copy of that warrant."

"Why don't I know about this invasion of my privacy?" demanded Graham.

"You will have to ask your staff that question," said Chan. "Do you want to know why it matters who paid the scientists?"

"You are going to tell me whether I do or not."

"You are starting to get the drift of this," said Chan. "Mr. Choe."

Rickie took a step forward. "The anomalous insect infestations at the park were caused by human intervention. These have been reported to the appropriate federal agencies who are very concerned. But we got curious about the water issues and did some research with the department that deals with underground streams. Several once ran through the old park and were diverted underground. Turns out that one has shifted. It now runs under the apartment complex between the pond and Ellis Avenue. The second water main break would have added to the threat already posed by that shift. The damage would have been devastating."

"That is terrible," said Graham. "Housing is already tight in the city. We cannot lose a whole complex."

"We'll come back to that complex in a moment," said Chan. "One step at a time. The study on carbon capture will prove that we can afford to lose the park. The scientist I spoke to confirmed that their study proves that the combination of rooftop gardens and hydroponics are helping lower Metro's carbon footprint."

"Such a study hardly seems illegal," said Graham. "It is good to know that the mechanisms that secure our food supply help with our climate mitigation goals."

Chan nodded. "However, we know that you paid for similar studies in New Delhi and Beijing. Anti-corruption agencies in both places are now looking at the development contracts you gained. Seems there may have been bribes involved and pressure from organized crime. It was on the basis of those investigations that the judge gave us the warrant to check the scientists' employment status."

"Get to your point, Chan. I have a news conference to hold."

"You may want to postpone that." Chan glanced at her watch. "Two teams are arriving shortly from Ottawa to investigate the releases of genetically manufactured insects and imported hazardous ants."

"I don't have those warrants for you to check." Madison smiled. "They are bringing federal ones."

"As far as I know," said Graham through clenched teeth, "I don't own an insect manufacturing or importing business."

"True," said Chan, "but when the people responsible learn how serious the charges are against them, they may admit who they gave the insects to. Whoever released them faces the stiffer penalties, and I hazard a guess that we will find they are in your employ."

A shadow of doubt cross Graham's face. Then, with a raised chin, he met Chan's eyes. "You clearly intend to interrupt my effort to keep Metro informed. The news conference is cancelled." He motioned to his team and turned away.

"You might want to stay and hear my announcement," said Chan.

Graham swung his head back. "What?"

"No point wasting these busy people's trip to High Park. I had planned to wait a couple days to make this public, but I think the announcement can go ahead. High Park will be expanded."

Graham turned and took two steps back, arms folded. "This dangerous, uncontrolled, free-growing area has proven to be a hazard."

"You have proven to be a hazard. Not the park. But yes, we humans cannot completely control nature and that underground stream is posing a problem. Mr. Choe, please inform the media that I will speak to them about a bold initiative in just a moment. You see, Mr. Graham, the owner of that apartment complex knows that his buildings are not up to the standard of the new ones. He was already weighing his options when Metro informed him of the shift in the stream's path. He has decided to donate the complex to Metro on the condition that we demolish the buildings and integrate the land into an expanded High Park."

"You cannot displace tenants. That's the law."

"You are right. Unless we have alternative accommodation that is better than where they are. Fortunately, he allowed the vacancy rate to climb a little over the legal limit knowing there were problems in the buildings. At the same time, the group that Martha Hollingsworth is part of has a plan to move to a new community north of Highway Nine. Seems you can drive your own car in that area, and that is important to them. In exchange for leniency on the interferences with Monitor which did not pose a hazard to human life, the group has agreed to make their current housing available to people from the complex. Along with units that Metro's housing department has available for emergencies like the ones your water main attacks might have caused, we can house them all."

"You value wildness that much?" Graham asked.

"With all the green spaces gone in cities of our neighbour to the south, places like this park, Montreal Mountain, Vancouver's Stanley Park are attractions that draw people. Losing them would be a blow to tourism." Chan took a step forward and leaned toward Graham. "And I do not like having Metro's decisions made by people like you."

Graham laughed. "This is all about your ego, your ability to be in charge."

Chan straightened and smiled. "I know what is and is not in my power. For today, I believe I got what I want. Good luck avoiding the consequences of your actions." Chan turned her back on the developer. "Now, I have a press conference to give."

"Impressive," said Detective Madison quietly to Miles. "I better go make sure we make these potential charges stick. You staying?"

"I think so," said Miles. "I need a bit of time to let this sink in." Following Chan to where the media were now gathering into a tight circle, he turned to Rickie. "Did you know this was the plan?"

"Just when I got into the helicopter. Amazing isn't it?"

"It will be years before the new park amounts to much."

"But think about it, we get to nurture a new forest from the ground up. New trees. New undergrowth. New creatures. School kids can learn what it takes to grow trees right here in their backyard." Rickie looked north at the trees gently swaying in the breeze. "Instead of losing what we have, we get more. Just amazing."

\*     \*     \*

"Alert," said Monitor. "Identity confirmed."

"Another alert," said James. "I thought Chan had solved the issues. Monitor, what is it this time?"

"Graffiti painter. Corner Bathurst and Palmerston."

"Camera number?" asked Miles. When the identification appeared, Miles called up the feed. Sure enough, Chong Bai worked on a painting on the newly installed hoarding that would protect a demolition site. "Police alerted?"

"Affirmative," said Monitor.

"But how did you know to look here?" muttered Miles. "This isn't one of the places where I put the surveillance in place."

"Affirmative," said Monitor.

"That does not answer my question," said Miles. On the screen, the painter turned his head as if listening. Then, Chong Bai grabbed his backpack and slipped around the building out of sight. A minute later, a police car pulled up. The officer touched the wet paint, looked in all directions, and shrugged, returning to the patrol car.

Miles rubbed his temples. "Chong Bai is going to be hard to catch now that he is alert and shifting to a different kind of location. There are a lot of construction sites like this one." Which still did not answer the question why an alarm had been placed here. "Monitor, show me the code that sent the alert." It was an exact copy of the code installed on cameras at each site Jen had identified. "Team, did one of you add locations for the physical identification program?" One by one, they said no.

"It makes sense to look at these locations," said James, "but we thought he worked on buildings."

"People change their modus operandi, but who thought

of this possibility?" Privacy rules required that surveillance only be put in place where need justified it. Watching for Chong Bai on cams that were not specifically designated as potential graffiti spots would be considered a serious breach of that rule, bringing down a hefty fine on whoever initiated the program. "Monitor, who wrote the code for this camera?"

"Monitor Technology department."

Miles grunted. "Who placed the code on this camera?"

"The recognition program was applied to this camera."

"How many others?"

There was a pause. "Twenty-seven."

"Authorization for this."

"Monitor."

"Good to know it's someone who works here," said Miles. "Which employee of Monitor?"

"Monitor."

A shiver ran down Miles' spine. That couldn't be. Someone had made this connection. *Hollingsworth?* "Monitor, call Cyber Security office." Hollingsworth answered the phone. "Did you add the program to recognize Chong Bai to sites where there was construction hoarding?"

"No, but that is a good idea."

"Whose idea was it?"

"Monitor must know," said Hollingsworth.

"Monitor answers the question as itself."

Hollingsworth frowned. "That's impossible. But who would hide the fact that they scaled the program in this way?"

"If you can't give me a clue, I'm stumped."

"Sorry to leave the problem in your hands." Hollingsworth ended the call.

Miles rubbed the lines between his eyes. "Monitor, why was the program added to additional locations?"

"These sites match the ones where the program was installed."

"Show me the locations." Twenty-seven blue dots appeared on his screen. He scrolled through quickly. Most were construction sites at intersections. One showed a cube van parked on the sidewalk at a corner. The surface stood in the right place for the moment, but the van would be moved.

"Monitor, why is this site being watched?" Miles asked.

"Criteria matches the other sites."

"Who decided the criteria matched?"

"Monitor."

"The criteria in this location are not permanent. Remove the surveillance."

"Authorization?"

"Miles Franklin."

There was a pause. "Instruction cannot be completed."

Miles glared at the screen. "Then, I will remove it myself." His fingers flew over the keyboard, deleting the identification code. "James, add an encryption code to all the surveillance we put up and these sites as well, something that will ensure it can't be copied."

"Like what?"

"Just a minute." Miles stared at the keys, made himself focus. Once he had the code ready, he sent it to James. Then, he pushed back his chair. He felt like he was in a science fiction story with a computer that started acting on its own. Had Monitor decided to watch these locations? Random surveillance was the kind of thing Martha Hollingsworth's group accused Monitor of doing, the kind of thing his department ensured did not happen. How did this scaling of the surveillance program take place? Palms on his desk, he wondered how he would answer these questions.

# CHAPTER TWENTY-SIX

Turning onto Jenkinson Way, Giovanni looped his arm through Brindle's. "This street is so quiet. Do you ever wish we lived out here?"
"And leave your great-aunt's house?"
"I didn't say I want to, just wondered. There is more psychic space here."
Brindle gazed at the house across the road. "You can't hear the woman's worry that her teenage son is experimenting with the newest opioid? Or the anger that her husband denies the possibility? There is the fear that the neighbours might find out, might report him." Brindle shook their head. "Additional space does not eliminate the battery of problems that assail people."
"But the open spaces."
"And the closed in single family dwellings. Out here, in neighbourhoods like this one, the emphasis on nuclear family persists. It's why some people look with askance and distrust at our people in the Houses. Community living is not approved of here."
"The space for a garden is perfect for Rickie," said Giovanni, "and Angelique loves the fact that she can cycle for kilometres without worrying about traffic."
"Miles' new friend Jen seems to be able to get the same benefit and live in the core." Brindle ran their fingers

through their red hair. "I get what you mean. There is more space than the apartment towers or even a crowded street like ours provides. I am just not sure it is enough for Geoff."

"Which is why we are here. Did you tell him we were coming?"

Brindle nodded. "Surprising Geoff is never a good idea. He assured me he is fine, but I said it had been too long since I come out here to see everyone. He answered that Trinity is worried that she is not Gifted, that I should reassure her."

"Will you?"

"I asked Julie to talk with her, to tell her that Julie's hearing Gift did not develop until she was thirteen, and how important, helpful, that was."

Giovanni looked away, as if studying the house they were walking by. "You think Geoff is okay?"

"He deflected my question, which shows capacity. But he always claims that the children's worries are easy to push aside, and Trinity's got under his skin." Brindle looked down the street toward their destination. "That's him pacing from the porch to the sidewalk and back again."

"You can feel his worry?"

"It is like the tide of the Bay of Fundy pouring down the road at us. But it's also different. It's worry, but it's also just energy without any specific content."

"Which is what you were afraid of." Giovanni tilted his head as if listening. "One thing building on another."

"So, breathe deep, and think good thoughts."

"You're a fine one to talk." Giovanni moved his hand onto Brindle's neck, dug his fingers into the tense neck muscles, thought relaxation into his partner's shoulders.

Brindle let out a long, slow breath. "Thank you."

"Hello, Geoff," called Giovanni. "Waiting for us?"

"Wondering what on earth you came all the way out here for. A video call would have been just as good."

"Giovanni's ability to ease tension only works by touch," said Brindle. "It would be lovely to find someone who can send relaxation through a cell or computer connection, but until then, we need the subway and train to bring his Gift to you." Brindle smiled. "Besides, Trinity and Gillian asked me to come see them."

"Trinity needs your attention all right. She is desperate to be Gifted. Can you imagine what it is like to live with people, all of whom are special, and you are not. I don't think you understand what it is like."

Rubbing their hip, Brindle limped slightly. "Do you think we could sit on the step. Not sure if it is bursitis or the start of a bigger hip problem, but I've had enough time on my feet."

Geoff strode toward the steps. "You don't take care of yourself. When did you last see a doctor, or at least a good physiotherapist? No point seeing an ordinary one who just reads x-rays and instructions. You need a Gifted one who can see what is going on in that joint."

"If you knew one, I would go," said Brindle. "Sit beside me."

Geoff threw himself down on the second step, made room for Brindle. Giovanni put out his hand. "Can I touch your fingers, Geoff?"

Jerking his arm out, Geoff flinched when Giovanni took his hand. "Your pulse is racing, friend," said Giovanni, "though I am sure you already knew that."

"When has it not been. My heart knows its business. It's my head that takes in too much information. Do you know…"

"Shhhh," said Giovanni. "If you still think I need to know once I'm done, I'll let you tell me. Right now, your blood pressure is spiking."

"That's only one reason my head hurts. Rickie's been a tsunami of worry."

"Do you think I need to find Rickie when we are done here?" Giovanni gently rubbed the base of each finger on Geoff right hand. "He is home I presume."

"He's here. Not too bad this evening. Seems to think that

there won't be any more attacks on High Park. But there is something about the apple trees that he thinks he needs to deal with, was mixing soap and water and muttering about proportions when I escaped the house." Geoff pulled his right hand away, and sent out his left. "This one now."

Giovanni gave a slow, half nod, and took the proffered hand, started massaging the palm at the base of the little finger and worked toward Geoff's thumb. Carefully slowing his own breath, Giovanni watched Geoff's chest begin to stop heaving, move to a more relaxed rhythm. "May I massage your neck now?"

Geoff rolled his head from one shoulder to the other. "It always helps when you do. Though if you had started there today, I probably would have slugged you."

Giovanni smiled. "Thought that might be the case." Moving around, he sat on an upper step, knees by Geoff's shoulders and began to massage the base of his neck. Never had he felt this kind of knotting in the empath's body. Closing his eyes, he thought of the peace of a still lake under a full moon, visualized calm, black water with a white path lying on it.

"I should have called days ago." Geoff massaged his right palm with his left fingers. "Sorry, Brindle. You've told me before. I just need to reach out. It's just everybody's problems were real, and I was…" He shrugged. "Absorbed."

"What you absorb is real." Brindle sat still with folded hands. "You know that."

"I do. I usually do. Just these days have been so crazy. Work too."

"Have you thought about the offer to move north? Gilda would love to look after you."

"What about the people she lives with?" Geoff asked.

"The couple are empaths with good self control. Their youngest adult child got a job here in Metro, so it would just be the four of you. And you know how calm Gilda is these days."

"The job is for real?"

"Gilda says so, though you will have to pass an interview."

"What happens when Gilda gets sick? At eighty-two, that could happen at any time. Then, I would be the one responsible to keep everybody calm as we dealt with the failing health of our matriarch. And when she dies." A shake went through Geoff's body.

Giovanni moved his hands down Geoff's spine, massaged gently but firmly, thought peace into his fingers, into Geoff.

"No life is ever completely stress free," said Brindle. "But as soon as she got sick, you know Giovanni and I would be on the way to support you all. Gilda has a lot to still teach that you would benefit from, Geoff."

"I have to give two weeks notice at work."

"Call your doctor who, after listening to you for five minutes, would put you on medical leave. You can head north, spend a week or so recovering, check out the job there, and decide. Your place here would remain if you want to come back."

Geoff breathed out slowly. "I'm city born and bred. How will I know how to live in the country?"

"It isn't as if you have to run their farm," said Giovanni, "though I imagine they would invite you to lend a hand. Animal reactions don't reach you, do they?"

"I am deaf to them." Geoff looked down at his hands, clenched his fists, then spread one finger at a time. "I'll call my doctor. Will you two drive up with me tomorrow?"

"Giovanni has a meeting in the morning, but we can keep the afternoon free."

"And you'll tell everybody here?"

"We planned to stay," said Brindle. "We brought our computers to get some work done this afternoon, and we can stay in one of the guest rooms. Indeed, we need to stay. If the twins heard I had been here and not seen them, there would be a ruckus."

"Can't have a ruckus." Geoff shivered. "Enough, Giovanni. Calm me down too much, and the doctor won't believe I need a medical leave." Geoff stood slowly. "Thanks for coming, you two. Things have seen so tense here."

"And at our place," said Brindle. "Though some of the problems have been dealt with, I am not sure that the protests against AI-controlled machines are going to disappear right away."

"People were taking them too much for granted," said Giovanni. "We all knew there was a pilot in the car because the driver's seat was empty. But people ignored their presence monitoring all the rest of the city's systems. Remembering is good."

"People will forget again." Brindle stood, running fingers through their hair. "Accepting and fearing is a seesaw that will continue for a while I expect."

"Oh no," said Geoff. "Will I have to drive myself to work?"

Giovanni shook his head. "Bet you don't know how."

"Of course, I don't know how. I grew up in Metro."

Brindle smiled. "It is allowed in that part of the province, but the cars all have AIs. I expect the car will drive you to work, then go home so others can do errands."

Geoff let out a long slow breath. "There is going to be a lot to get used to. But if there is less noise, less psychic noise, what a relief. Fewer sirens would be good. Maybe I should have tried this sooner."

\*     \*     \*

"But Ms. Narayanan, I just need another hour."

"Come in tomorrow then," said Darshani.

"But today is the last day of class."

Darshani put her fists on her hips. "I will be here tomorrow. A full day will make a lot more difference in this project that an hour of rushed work now. "

"But Ms. Narayanan..."

Darshani raised one hand. "Enough. I am locking the door, and you need to leave. I'll be here at eight-thirty tomorrow morning." With one last swing through the room to make sure that nothing was more out of place than usual for this time of year, Darshani headed for the parking lot. She'd taken the car the Scarborough houses shared to work to make this trip easier. Sliding into the front passenger seat, she spoke the address of the bar in the Parkdale neighbourhood that John-Boy's graffiti club claimed as their hangout. The car pilot asked her to put her seat belt on, then pulled out of the parking lot.

Opening her tablet, Darshani reviewed the comments for her report cards. That part was almost done.

"Ten minutes from destination," said the car pilot.

"Thank you." Darshani rolled her eyes at her courtesy to the AI. The pilot would not change its behaviour whether she swore or expressed profuse gratitude. Looking out the window, she wondered how the woman whose taxi had gone rogue felt. *We take these pilots so for granted.* The car made a turn down a one-way street, and then a quick turn back.

"Passing location," said the car. "Parking available a three-minute walk straight ahead."

"Perfect." Darshani glanced out the window. A red and green striped awning shaded a crowded patio in front of an apartment building, the colours a nod back to the Portuguese heritage of this part of Metro. Before these high-rises were built, this had been a neighbourhood of three-storey houses with Mediterranean style gardens crowded between the houses and the road. She'd done a project in art school based on photos taken before the area was bulldozed, suggesting ways of incorporating the older landscape into newer constructions. She closed her eyes. The designers of these squared off, grey buildings had not asked her advice or that of any other designer, but there were hints of the older heritage. A few ground floor restaurants had herb gardens out front. Buildings displayed potted plants. A few Portuguese flags flew from balconies.

The car parked in front of a tall building called Little Tibet. Signs indicated that a Buddhist temple could be found through an entrance at the back of the building, and the restaurant out front advertised the best momos in the city. Two old women dressed in traditional Tibetan clothing strolled up the walk and into the restaurant. Darshani told the car to lock and walked back to the bar.

A quick scan of the outside tables did not show John-Boy or any of the other artists she knew. On the sidewalk leading from the road was an elaborate chalk picture of a snake entwined on itself and eating its tail. Interesting to depict an image that suggested eternity in a medium as impermanent as chalk.

Stepping inside, she hesitated in the dim light. From the walls, bright spots of colour jumped out at her. As her eyes adjusted, she saw that some of the particularly bright spots were in the faces of mystical animals, a few in the tail of a peacock, others in faces of people twisting in some form of dance or painted onto their swirling clothes. She also realized that every human eye in the bar had turned to her, looked her up and down, then looked away.

Clearing her throat, she spoke quietly. "I'm looking for John-Boy."

At the back of the restaurant, a lanky figure stood. "Not to worry, folks. I know her. She's a moderately good artist but way out of her territory." John-Boy approached, arms folded. "Why are you here?"

"You're in trouble."

"How do you know anything about me?" Though his arms remained folded, his hands became fists.

"People I live with, they work for Monitor."

"Monitor." John-boy spat at her feet.

"I've been hearing about the graffiti that confused the AIs, graffiti you painted." Darshani took a deep breath. "There's a project that I think you might be interested in, one that could use your help. I have funding for a summer program working with young street artists not associated with a club. A couple who've applied are interested in how AIs respond to graffiti. I'd like you to spend some time with these youth." Darshani tried to shrug casually. "You want to prove we can deceive the pilots; this is a chance to show

how."

John-boy shook his head and laughed. "Show how it works so that the folks in charge can teach the stupid cars to avoid the mistake. What fun is that?"

"What fun is jail going to be? You'd make a difference."

"I won't be going to jail. I know how not to get caught."

"The people who want to stop you are pretty smart."

John-boy laughed. "Saying I am not is a great way to convince me."

"What about the mentoring idea?"

"We do our own recruiting."

Darshani looked him straight in the eye. "From what I hear, you are headed for trouble. Make sure your club's head knows about your outside activities, because you may find that all your friends here get caught up in what you started."

A woman at a nearby table stood. "That sounds like a threat, girl."

Darshani didn't take her eyes off John-boy's face. "If you know what he is up to and are okay with it, fine." She reached into her shirt pocket, handed the woman a small cube. "But maybe you don't know the extent of his actions. This has my contact info stored in it as well as details of my proposal. If you or any of the artists in your group are interested, use it to call me."

"This is new tech. Where'd you get it?"

"A friend. This last couple weeks, stuff has been going on that makes the folks who maintain Monitor strung tighter than a snare drum. I'd hate to see any street artists caught if they tighten enforcement, even if those artists have pushed the limits."

"What club are you part of?" the woman asked.

"I'm independent," said Darshani.

"Independent with friends."

"I live with people who share certain interests," Darshani said. "I thought you meant art club."

"Guess I did. Now, I suggest you leave. John-boy doesn't

seem to like you."

Darshani met John-boy's eyes again. *I could tell her you threatened me the other day. You know that don't you?* "I'm going. You know how to find me. The potential for trouble is real, and so is the way out. It's up to you."

Turning away, she took three steps toward the door. Then, she turned back. "The picture out front. That kind of snake points to eternity, but also to cycles of change. When change comes, we have to adapt."

"We have to hold on to what we know," said John-boy.

"And adapt," said the club leader. "But the direction we shift toward is an open question."

Darshani sighed. "That is the purpose of working in chalk, isn't it? To remind us what will be swept away, and what we must hold on to." With that she left, determined to breathe the air of the Tibetan restaurant, taste their food, absorb this attempt to hold on to history.

\*     \*     \*

Climbing the stairs from the subway, Miles felt his hand shaking on the railing. He rubbed his palm with his thumb. *I have to get my head settled before I meet up with Amanda.* At Rickie's request, the two were going to take a walk to the place Amanda first saw the insects and the potential destruction of trees. Rickie wanted to be sure that the actions taken by Monitor's administration would hold.

*And what about Monitor itself?* Miles' thoughts circled back to the moment he found the surveillance code on more cameras. The nagging worry surfaced again. Had Monitor actually set the alarm itself as the AI seemed to claim? And if so, what did that mean? A move toward sentience? That thought sent a shiver down his back.

When he got to the Houses, Amanda sat on the front porch waiting for him. He pushed aside his worry and studied her to see if she was anxious about the visit to High Park. When she glanced his way and smiled, he relaxed.

She looked calm and unconcerned.

"You're ready?" he asked, stopping at the end of their walkway.

"I think so." Amanda stood. "I hope you are right that the problems have been dealt with. I am tired of taking the long way around."

"I'm hopeful," Miles said as they walked south together. "But it will be good to know what you see. Or don't see."

"And because the situation might not have changed is why you are coming too."

"To lend a strong arm, yes."

Amanda punched the arm closest to her. "Don't start thinking I need looking after."

Miles rubbed his arm. "I know how distraught the first vision made you. I cannot imagine how disorienting it is not to know which thing you see is real."

"They're all equally real, for a moment at least."

"Poor choice of words."

Amanda pulled Miles to a stop, looked up into his eyes with a steady gaze. "You keep thinking of sending a text and then deciding not to. It's like there are two of you walking with me."

"Two arms. One of me. It's just..."

"There's a problem with Monitor. Another?"

Miles closed his eyes, rubbed his temples with his fingertips. "Monitor may have learned something that we did not program."

"Isn't that what AIs are supposed to do?"

They crossed Bloor Street and wound their way between apartment towers. "AIs learn within the parameters of the information we give. They act within the limits we program. What happened earlier this afternoon felt uncomfortably different."

"Unless you decide to text your coworkers right now, can you leave it?"

"I am considering setting up a meeting to discuss my concern. It will wait until I get home."

"Just decide to do it, and I'll stop seeing options." Amanda dropped his arm. "Now you're calling and not calling that woman I met. Jen."

"That one is simpler. I will call her after I send the text."

"Good. Now stop worrying." Amanda took his arm again and picked up the pace.

Miles shook his head. The challenge of placing limits to ensure Monitor did not learn to scale instructions beyond what was intended turned his mind upside down.

"If you can't stop on your own, let me distract you." Amanda started to recount each of the piano students she had taught this day and whom she would be teaching after the visit to the park and a quick supper.

Listening, Miles focused on the stories, laughed at the moments expected, asked the questions Amanda set up. Before long they left the street and took the path that wound through the trees toward the pond.

"Now, give me a bit of space," said Amanda. "You are still radiating options. Good thing Geoff isn't anywhere near us, but too bad Giovanni isn't home this evening. I think you could use his calming influence." With careful steps, Amanda walked forward.

Watching the way she tilted her head, the way she leaned one way then the other, Miles worried that he was too far back to catch her if the visions made her dizzy. She flicked her fingers at him, and he realized he was doing it again, creating interference. He tried instead to listen for birds, to study each tree he walked by. She gave an okay sign. When she slowed more, he knew they were near the place where she first saw destruction.

Amanda turned slowly, making a full circle. Then she spread her arms and twirled. With a grin, she motioned for Miles to come closer. "You did it. You plural I mean. All of you. The park is healthy, alive and vibrant. It is even growing I think, so that some new wild birds will make this home. Well done."

"You should take some of the credit. What you saw here

got us ahead of the person who wanted this land."

Amanda shook her head. "You're not going to include me in the public thank you."

"Given the circumstances, not much of what happened is going public. But I'm glad to know that the cage the administrator built for the developer will hold."

Amanda folded her hands together. "There will be another. The pressure for development in Metro is huge."

Miles smiled. "My gramma used to say 'Don't borrow trouble from tomorrow.' Today, we kept this green space whole. And stopped the hacks into Monitor."

"And most of the city will never know the Gifted helped. Don't you ever wish people knew what your Gift can do?"

Miles imagined how non-Gifted people would treat Amanda if they knew, how she would be pestered by folks who wanted to know what decision to make, used by someone who wanted an advantage playing the stock market. In the late nineteenth century, someone like Rickie might have ended up in a circus sideshow featuring wild and wonderful plants. *And me? Who would believe I can follow electrical pulses the way I do?* Likely, those burned as witches in earlier centuries had been Gifted people using their special skills. Miles shook his head. "We know. That has to be enough."

Cathy Hird lives in a forest on the shore of Georgian Bay. Cathy weaves tapestries and scarves, and she tells stories that pull together the threads of ancient myth and modern questions.

Cathy has published novels, stories, poems, and creative non-fiction pieces. She writes a weekly column for an online news magazine, owensoundhub.org. She is an avid reader who loves to discover new authors and the worlds they build.

Along with her first two novels set in ancient Greece, Cathy has also written a contemporary fantasy trilogy that draws on Celtic mythology and Arthurian legends. *Unseen*, her near future Sci/Fi fantasy novel set in Toronto, is her first crossover novel with Sci/Fi and fantasy elements.

CPSIA information can be obtained
at www.ICGtesting.com
Printed in the USA
LVHW041414270123
738018LV00004B/174

9 781928 011903